Lilith

Ambika Devi

Lilith

Ambika Devi

Mythologem Press
Publishing Literary Brilliance

ISBN: 978-0-9978678-0-0

Library of Congress Control Number: 2013909707

Published by Mythologem Press
www.MythologemPress
VOX 772-223-8229
MythologemPress@gmail.com
www.LilithNovel.com

Printed in the United States of America

A Divine Blessing

॥ शूरी गणेश शलोकः ॥

गजाननम् भूत गणादि सेवतिम्

GajAnanaM BhUta GaNAdhi sevitaM

कपत्थि जम्बू फल सार भक्षतिम्

kapittha jambU phala sAra Baxitam

उमा सुतम् शोक वनिश कारकम्

umA sutaM shoka vinAsha kArakam

नमामि विघ्निश्ववर पाद पङ्कजम्

namAmi vighneshvara pAda pa1Ñkajam

Lord with the elephant face, served by all the Ganas, who takes as his food,

The essence of kapitta and jambuphala (two favorite fruits of Ganesha),

Son of Uma (Parvati) he who is destroyer of sorrow and remover of obstacles,

We worship at your divine Lotus Feet.

In deep gratitude I honor Lord Ganesha, guardian of the gate that leads to Mother.

Dedication

I dedicate this to you, Great Mother Goddess. You are mother of all mothers. I see you in the smile of my own mother and the glowing memory of her mother. I hear you in all voices and listen to you in the rhythm of my own breath and heartbeat. I am supported by you under my feet. I taste you in the sweet air I breathe and the food you provide. I soak and relax in your calming water. May we all come to cherish your unconditional love and divine gifts.

Acknowledgement

I thank all of the people who gave me encouragement while this story took form and wrote itself. Special thanks go out to my mother Roz Schaeffer and her mother, my beloved Nanny Fannie, who inspired many of the stories within these pages. I am forever in deep gratitude to Nick Ligidakis, my publisher, for believing in me and always being here for me with his love and support. I also thank Michele McAfee for being the first one to say, "You should write a book!" and to Don for giving his blessing when I told him I used bits of our past as inspiration. I thank Debbi Lis and Shri Manabawa for being the first readers to offer their loving feedback, and to my editor Jessica Lyn Roberts for giving such great advice. A very special thanks to MaryEllen Smith who conducted the final editing process with me and to Ron Birchnough who brought the pages to life with lettering and my artwork. It is amazing to have someone love something as much as I do, and I am very grateful to you. Thank you to each and every one at Inkwell Productions for all of the input and creativity that goes into realizing a final project. I thank all of my friends who listened as I read bits to them and to my guardian spirits whose mystic teachings I am sharing. I offer deep gratitude to my Guru, Yogi Amrit Desai, and to the many wise swamis and great teachers who have patiently taught me and illuminated my path. Your brilliance sparkles in this story. And finally to you, dear reader, I thank you for picking up this book and turning the pages to drink in the feelings of my heart.

May you all feel my love, my profound gratitude, and my appreciation.

Foreword

Writing this foreword in the fringes between velvet dark and not quite brilliant dawn on a midsummer morning. Listening to an ancient Sanskrit chant emanating from the speakers of my laptop. Primal and progressive, all in one here-and-now moment. Such is the feeling that comes when one reads Lilith; a journey through time and space, the earthy and the ethereal. A literary masala with the commingled aromas of Nag Champa incense, redolent with Indian spices, blended with the mouthwatering gastronomical scents of the Italian Market in iconic South Philadelphia, the reader is conveyed, nearly at the speed of thought, with the heroine and her motley crew of companions. Some are visible; others exist in the recesses of her mind. All have some basis in reality. What is that, anyway? Is it only what we can touch with our five senses, or does it move beyond into dreamscape and vision? Modern day mythologist Ambika Devi takes the reader on a journey that in "real time" spans a day in the life, but could just as easily take a lifetime to experience and glean meaning.

Herself a fusion of grounded and mystical, astrologer and yogini, Ambika Devi has an impressive background as yogic scholar and teacher both on and off the mat. She has immersed herself in the worlds of chanting and drumming; heart chakra and throat chakra rhythm in motion that feeds her soul. My first encounter with her—more than two decades ago, although we have not met physically in this lifetime—was through the sounds of her drumming, back when she was known as Amy Ford. Influenced by various cultural traditions, her voice, which is also an instrument of healing that transports the listener, just as her words gather the reader up on their ample backs to be ferried from shore to shore across boundaries of the physical and spiritual.

She bases the story of Lilith on three classic tales: the myth of the Divine Feminine, the myth of the Divine Masculine, and the myth of creation interwoven with her master's thesis. Lest you think this is a crackly-dry scholarly cerebral exercise, you are in for a delicious surprise. As I read, I found myself laughing with delight as I imagined one of my favorite authors, Tom Robbins, ticklingly whispering in Ambika Devi's receptive ear. Shades of *Jitterbug Perfume* meet *Still Life with Woodpecker* with its sacredly profane and sometimes profanely sacred verbiage scattered throughout. Although, in parts, it may feel like a hallucinogenic trip into psychedelia, it arrives by more natural means. Autobiographical and symbolic, the book was inspired by events in her life, which are woven into metaphorical meanderings. This is the mark of a talented storyteller. Ambika Devi is indeed that.

By chance encounter or divine appointment, Lilith meets Don in the Italian Market of South Philadelphia, which feels like a portal into other dimensions. Together they embody the Sacred Feminine and Masculine, and are explorers in the desire to comprehend the mysteries of gender and relationship.

"I know," Lilith said after she caught her breath. "I get it—we humans can search and crave and devour, but unless we desire to merge with the great ocean of the divine bliss, we stay hungry. So, therefore, if we build up the ideas of relationships and tear them down when they appear to be not what we want, we are left with the rubble of destruction. The demolition leaves the ground more conceptual and, like insects, we humans yearn to reestablish and rebuild."

"When two people come together, the relationship they form becomes a separate entity. It has a life and breath all its own. Unfortunately, no one is ever taught this. Most people figure it

out the hard way, living the archetypical roles necessary for the evolution of the individual soul. The sooner we understand this, the quicker we cease making mistakes. Couples experience a quantum shift when they wake up to the fact that their union is a third being."

The Sanskrit name Ambika Devi reflects the Divine Mother Goddess, and she embodies that essence in her daily life. It is that nectar which she sweetly pours into this book which you will find yourself wanting to alternately sip and savor and drink down in great gulps, licking your lips with a satisfying sigh.

Namaste, Om Shanti, Jai Ma~
Edie Weinstein

Edie Weinstein, a.k.a. Bliss Mistress, is an Opti-mystic who sees the world through the eyes of possibility, a colorfully creative journalist, dynamic transformational speaker, licensed social worker, interfaith minister, and radio host, as well as the author of *The Bliss Mistress Guide To Transforming The Ordinary Into The Extraordinary*. www.liveinjoy.org

Part I

Receptivity

The Divine Feminine.

She is earthy and mysterious and often funky.

We must love her, for our being is truly a gift of her body!

Chapter 1

Acceptance

The sacred mirror.

The oversized wooden rocking chair creaked against the gritty ground. Sounds peaked rhythmically like the squeals of a cat trapped in a dryer set on fluff. A tiny dark-haired figure of a woman stared out into the vastness of space, dwarfed by the enormity of the rocker. Above her head, mammoth leaves the size of Cuban getaway rafts created cooling shade, relieving the heated thoughts steaming her mind. Slender fingers tapped a systematic Morse code on the oversized book she held in her lap. Tinks and clicks rang eerily from the binding, rattling the book's ornate metal embossed design. The steady, ominous beat marched like tribal feet moving in, closer to the kill.

Misty eyes scanned the watery horizon as gentle rain fogged the windows of her tear-streaked heart. She sat alone on the tiny little island, staring out at the horizon. In spite of the great emptiness she felt inside, she realized she had indeed made the right decision. Now the only thing left to do was to make peace with this seclusion, for she believed she had traded earthly love for Goddess wisdom—or so it had seemed in the negotiation.

The outline of a tall, dark lover materialized in the screen of her third eye as the rocking chair creaked. Tap-tap-tapping her fingers, the corners of her mouth curled and her tongue recalled the taste of oregano and heirloom tomatoes. The smell became real as a male apparition gently placed a bowl of spaghetti alla vodka sprinkled with fresh herbs before his dark feminine *honcha*. Once in her grasp, the dark angel took two very cautious steps back, awaiting her approval.

The shadow feline took the bowl and placed it on top of her book. A question mark formed on her brow, and she asked the Gandharva, "Why on earth have you chosen to bring me this? Semolina pasta is the last thing I long for. You know what it does to my digestive tract!"

"What, then, wilt thou have, my she-line," growled the sable cherub as he snatched the bowl back, causing a bit of the sauce to splash onto the thick, dark cover of the book. He quickly whipped out a crisp handkerchief from an invisible breast pocket and, with eyes turned downward, wiped the red slurry away.

"You are kidding, right?" she snapped in bitter admonishment, her mouth flicking ashes of disdain. She continued, "If we are to converse on these mystery visits of yours, at least use a street version of your Anglospeak. I know you have many more styles to choose from."

"Right on," replied the creature. He appeared to be leaning on an invisible wall. His face projected the taste of lemons and stink at which the tiny woman rolled her eyes and sighed dramatically.

"Got it," he retorted in a much more businesslike manner. "Perhaps a visual, then?" With that, he waved his arm like a game show hostess. A giant screen the size of a ballpark formed in the distance out over the water. The cosmic monitor blipped a series of colored sparks and then fizzed into dynamic view. There, glowing in RGB and LED, a male shape took form. There he was in 64-bits of color—there was Donny.

Chapter 2

Now

A smell or a sound brings us right back to the present moment.

Her eyes closed slowly, shutting out the immediate surroundings. The chair rocked and squeaked an incantation of her memories into a tangible experience of the first time she had seen him. The scene of the old neighborhood oozed into her awareness, swamping her emotions. Small pools of reminiscence filled the petite reservoirs of her psyche.

It was the Italian Market of South Philadelphia on a late summer morning, which felt much cooler than the sticky, sweltering night which had preceded it. She awoke with the bed sheet bundled around her shimmering body. The nip in the air had awakened her much earlier than she had planned to be up on a Saturday morning. Her quilted blanket lay flung in a rumpled heap across the room, a testament to the night's heat. If she had been able to reach it, she never would have left her cozy little morning nest.

Cool air streaming into her nostrils beckoned with aromatic promises of tea and cheese and bread, so she rose and dressed herself, exiting the house wearing her favorite green sweater and indigo jeans. This South Philly morning felt "deliciously crisp," one of her favorite ways to describe the sensation. "It was like biting into the perfect apple," she would explain to new acquaintances—"cool, refreshing, and a little bit tart."

The streets were quieter than they would be in a few short weeks when the college kids returned and visitors, along with locals, would flock to her neighborhood in search of holiday fare for their tables. But not today, as the heat of the previous night had everyone fooled. The coolness was a gift for her and the select few braving the dog days of summer. It would be a week or two before the Jersey Shore would shut down and, for now, the South Philadelphians had the Market all to themselves.

Down on the pavement she stopped on her way to Ninth Street to admire the turn-of-the-century brickwork on the façade of the huge, square city block she called home. She pressed her delicate cheek against the bricks and stared down the massive wall of the building. The glissade of a sitar caught her attention, and she backed up a few steps to gaze up to her fourth floor walkup. She had left the window open for the first time in months, and mused at the wispy purple paisley silk curtains dancing on a breeze. She held her breath to listen for the music she had left playing. The melodic strains of sitar and fluttering riffs of tabla came rolling down the bricks. They swirled in psychedelic patterns at her feet, honoring her inspiration, the great master Ravi Shankar, with offerings of yellow roses, smoking ghee lamps, and fragrant incense. Ravi's music played the lilting soundtrack of her breath, and his beloved drummer Alla Rakha beat the pulsating rhythmic ride she danced through existence upon.

Chapter 3

Parents

How is it that we landed here?
We are made of DNA from two complete strangers.

A few months before, on a much warmer morning, she awoke with the desire to listen to meditative music. She scanned her music collection to find the perfect track and realized she had more recordings created by Ravi Shankar than any other artist. Confused by this, she decided to call her mom to see if she had any insight.

"Mama," she said when she heard the phone click.

"Yes, darling girl?" responded her mom, causing her to giggle. "Why do I have more CDs by Ravi Shankar than any other artist?"

"Well," her mom said, "I will tell you." She then proceeded to enlighten her beloved child as to why. The story spun from her lips like a smooth silk sari.

"The year was 1957. Your dad and your brother and I were living in Queens, New York. Dad was working in the lighting business and, having grown up with an electrician for a father, this had been an easy choice for a career. You know your dad's gift is sales?"

"Yes, Mama."

"During that time, your father was offered the esteemed position of managing East Coast sales for a company in Philadelphia. So he quickly

packed up his family and moved us to Rydal, Pennsylvania."

"To Lindsey Lane, where I was born?"

"Are you going to let me finish? Do you want to hear this story?"

"Yes, Mama, I do."

"Dad bought a brand new split-level house on a hill and established us in our new surroundings. Your older brother was just finishing elementary school, and everyone was enjoying our new suburban life.

"Soon after the move, Dad's company went through a downsizing. Your father, along with four other executives, were let go. Dad wanted to stay in the same type of job and was unable to find anything in Pennsylvania. In an effort to support the family and survive, he accepted a job in Brooklyn, New York. After all we had been through with moving, he didn't want to uproot his brood again. So he opted to travel by train each day, back and forth, from the nearby station.

"The daily commute was long and hard and lasted two hours each way, five days a week. Your dad stuck to it with great determination. The daily journey had him traveling by train from our suburban neighborhood to New York City. Each day he would then catch a ferry to Brooklyn and finally a cab to the factory. Every evening he would reverse the trip."

"Wow! I had no idea. That is a lot of traveling back and forth."

"Your dad was grateful for his new job and for being in charge of East Coast sales for this new company. He was willing to take on anything in order to stay in the business and find success. In addition to his vending tasks, he had the added chore of chaperoning Alfred, his new boss's—I.R. Rosenblatt's—whimpering, unstable, bipolar son. Dad was a trouper and took Alfred on all of his calls and business trips. He worked his butt off as to please his superior.

"And as if that wasn't enough of a test of your dad's tolerance, one day I.R. got the brainy idea to have his daughter design a line of lighting. The Far Eastern influence in music and design was just beginning to find its way into the psyche of Americans, and this was to be the inspiration for the new fixtures. The contemporary lighting manifested as a wildly colorful line of merchandise. It reflected the East and the Orient with a rainbow of brilliant glass insets and twisted brass details.

"To launch the collection to his list of buyers, Dad planned a big party in the grand ballroom of a well-known New York City hotel. He chose an East Indian theme and called on antique dealers to rent him their wares. These were used to decorate the space and set the mood—an oasis fantasy with rich woolen oriental rugs and mysterious artifacts magically transformed the neutral tones of the space. To top it off, Dad hired the great Ravi Shankar to play his sitar, backed by his orchestra. Floating from the ceilings on the celestial strains of Ravi's music, the lanterns and lighting were displayed like sparkling jewels.

"The menu consisted of Indian fare with fragrant pakoras, samosas, curries, and papadams. I was ecstatic to be a part of such an event! I had never experienced anything like it before. Being an adventurous eater, I tried all the different delicacies and grooved on the rhythms of Shankar's sublime sounds. I was in bliss with pride for my husband. Dad wrote many sales that night. I.R. was euphoric—the entire event was a huge success!

"Together we floated back to our hotel room filled with peaceful happiness. We awoke the next morning thinking life was good. Then, after checking out of the cushy room, we traveled back to our Pennsylvania home where your grandmother had been watching your brother.

"The next morning I awoke in misery. I was sure I had been poisoned or was experiencing a powerful allergic reaction to the Indian food. This was odd, considering the one-day delay. Later in the afternoon, not having a clue what to do to make myself feel better, Dad encouraged me to visit our physician.

"My doctor recommended that I see a gynecologist due to the puffy, bilious state of my belly. I thought this was quite strange."

"Why is that?"

"Dad had married me when your brother, my son from another marriage, was a baby. We had tried and tried to conceive a child together and gave up in desperation. After six years, we figured it just wasn't in the cards for us.

"Five years later, I was thirty-seven, Dad was forty, and your brother Marc was twelve years old. None of us ever imagined what we were about to learn. We never thought it was even a possibility. It turned out that the state of my belly wasn't food poisoning or an aversion to the Far Eastern flavors, but rather a huge surprise. That weekend, aroused by the inspired intonations of the master, my hormones had kicked in and I was having my first bout of morning sickness!

"That weekend, awakened by the richness of Ravi Shankar's music, you made your debut—physiologically—to our family."

"So Ravi Shankar was the first live concert I ever attended?"

"That's right! Ravi Shankar's music was the first music you ever heard, amplified through the warm ocean of my womb."

Ravi Shankar's music vibrated through the bones and fluid of my mama's being, thought the little goddess. "And in that moment I awoke!" she proclaimed.

"And that," explained her mama, "Is why you like Ravi Shankar so much."

Chapter 4

Home

Wherever you are, there you are.

This enclave, the place she'd called home for the last year, was the paradise of bohemian artists in the City of Brotherly Love. It was owned by a famous artist who had systematically purchased the entire square city block over the course of two decades. This baffled the locals of "the neighborhood." They justified it by chattering in their newsy manner, sitting on front stoops with electric fans squealing through hot summer afternoons, sipping icy sodas from sweating glass bottles. She knew the conversations were about him when sentences were punctuated with "San Valentino," his namesake, even though her Spanish was better than her Italian.

The consensus in the art community was that he must have inherited family money from his renowned mother, the opera star. Valentine was a painter, and by no stretch of the imagination could he be considered an ordinary artist. He was brilliant and perceived as famous by students from the Philadelphia Museum School as well as the Philadelphia College of Art, where she had studied. This man was golden, born on the sainted day of Valentine. Recently he proved himself a legitimate contender in the field of modern art and painting. He had gotten himself an agent and was in the process of hanging his first major New York show at the Metropolitan Museum of Modern Art. This caused the local gossip to dive into underground whispers.

King Valentine ruled over his bohemian fortress in dictatorial fashion. He could choose you or spit you out on the pavement like stale gum. The apartments in his sanctuary were coveted by all local art schools' students, particularly painters and sculptors. This was due to the carte blanche entry to two open-studio times a week, with live nudes modeling in the giant courtyard salon which stood in the center of the fortress. It was seemingly impossible to get an apartment at Valentine's. No one who lived there seemed to know the formula, and no one ever seemed to move out.

Down on the pavement, she pressed a cheek against the cool bricks and mortar of the Tenth Street wall. The sensation transported her back to her freshmen year of art school, on a crisp autumn evening when she had begun modeling for night-school drawing classes at her university.

Students were only allowed to work opposite their school schedules, and she was a day student. The work was ridiculously easy and the money was really great. She loved the life-drawing classes in her own course load, and figured she would pick up ideas watching the night school crowd paint. She loved the completely different feel of the nocturnal students, and her understanding of the teachers' needs made her a favorite choice for live modeling. Within a month's time, she was the buzz of the night school faculty and turning work down. It was like being a celebrity.

On a Tuesday night during the second semester, while on break from an advanced painting class of upperclassmen, she was approached by the portrait painter she had named "Hat Guy." He had a seemingly endless collection of caps and fedoras which she believed had to contain the personal magic of his artistry. Hat Guy offered to buy her a tea as she was pulling on her indigo-and-white block-printed Japanese kimono robe just after the professor called, "That's break, people!" Amused that he knew she was a tea girl, she accepted his offer and followed him out to the elevator bank in the center of the high-rise. A vacant car dinged open and they stepped in. The large elevator glided swiftly and silently down the eighteen stories to the cafeteria level on the mezzanine. Contented to be treated as the queen she was, she sauntered over to a café table, sat down, and watched Hat Guy purchase her a tea.

He strode to the table, placed the tea in front of her, and introduced himself as Gareth. She mused at the flawlessness of the name, allowing a smile to crinkle onto her lips. To her, his name went perfectly with tonight's earthy green outback style sombrero.

"Why do you only paint my face in this class?" she asked. "It seems a waste of a perfectly good nude!"

"It's your eyes—they blow me away!" responded Gareth.

Over the previous month, Hat Guy had created endless portraits of her in pastels and oils, often producing two or three in an evening. It seemed slightly obsessive, yet flattering at the same time.

During the break, the two chatted about the other artists' work in the group, the genius of the teacher, and where they lived. When the subject of neighborhoods came up, she described the brownstone at Eighteenth and Spruce that she shared with two environmental engineers. Gareth was familiar with the Smedley Deli on the corner and the prestigious gay neighborhood just off Rittenhouse Square.

"There are great buildings in that neighborhood," Gareth said.

"I know," she said. "I love my brownstone. I have a fireplace in my bedroom and access to the roof. The only downside is that my two roommates are graduating and my lease is up in June. So it's time for me to find a new place to live."

Gareth nodded, seemingly fixated on her lips as she spoke. She liked the feeling of his attentive admiration. His obsession with her mouth burned with the blazing heat of an out-of-control brush fire.

"I've been working down in South Philly for a pizzeria, as a delivery girl on roller skates. So I'm thinking it would be great to be on the east side of Broad Street. Plus, I figure being near the Market is an excuse to never keep anything in the fridge!"

Gareth was making notes on a tiny piece of paper, which caused her to clam up on the personal information and turn things around to question him.

"Where do you live?" she asked.

"If you are familiar with Ninth Street and you are a skater, have you been by the playground on Tenth where the—"

"Local boys play street hockey!" she chimed in.

"Yes, exactly!" Gareth exclaimed.

"I have indeed, sir!" She loved to be formal for added punctuation.

"Well then," continued Gareth, "you must have noticed the brick-fronts across the street. Behind them stands the bohemian mecca of South Philadelphia. Inside those walls are many of the great graduates of the Museum School and your university."

"Really?" she questioned.

"Yes, and it is ruled by a genius painter," he added.

She had heard of this infamous city block and was deeply curious about the reality of it. Her ex-boyfriend supposedly went to the mysterious courtyard studio to paint and be critiqued by the presiding virtuoso, but she had never believed that was what he was really doing. She looked up at the clock on the wall and jumped at the thought of being back late from her break.

"We have to get back, Gareth. I'm on the clock, you know."

"Yes, I realize that. I look forward to picking this conversation up later," he said.

"Thanks for the tea." With that she rose and strutted off for the elevator, leaving Gareth at the table alone.

An elevator chimed open as a group of spiky, leather-clad photography students piled out to find munchies for their fifteen minute break. Slithering past them, she jumped in just as the doors were closing and zoomed straight back up to the eighteenth floor. This gave her a little time to look at the evening's work.

During the painting classes, when the students were on break, she loved to stroll around the classroom and admire her two-dimensional form on the easels. Different interpretive styles joyously honored her still beauty and patience. Gazing at the art in progress was her favorite part of the job, aside from the easy pay. This semester's class had a lot of passionate painters, and she loved to feel the weight of the brush strokes and listen to the music of the colors on the canvases.

The following week, before the start of class, Gareth invited her to join him for tea in between her sittings. She accepted and leaped up on the platform for a quick round of three-minute croakies, which allowed her and the artists to warm up, before the first long pose. When the professor called break, Gareth swooped in as she was pulling on her robe. She kindly shook her head in a no-thank-you gesture when he tried to help her on with it. The azure satin knee-length wrap slid out of his grasp, and she held it across her chest and belly for a moment before continuing put it on herself. An embroidered Chinese fighting dragon flashed a wide smile from the back of the short kimono and danced in the soft studio light.

There was a moment of hesitation and mistrust. She had no desire to date this guy. He seemed a little overly friendly and his actions were turning her off. Gareth sensed the energy as they walked to the elevator bank. He decided to keep a polite distance and then cleared his throat. "I've been attending a Saturday open studio with my landlord, Valentine."

Her curiosity overrode her turnoff as Valentine became a reality and was no longer an urban myth. *Apparently he exists*, she contemplated silently.

"I recommended your modeling skills to Valentine," said Gareth with a proud smile. "He asked all of us to find him a decent model, saying that the last few were crap! He wants to try you out for open studio this Saturday, on my recommendation. I showed him one of the portraits I painted of you. He says that if he likes you, he will hire you for private sittings."

"Really?" she purred. A private sitting with a famous artist! Ebony-outlined, tanned bodies on the canvases of Gauguin flashed through her mind.

"Yes!" he exclaimed and then continued, "He wants your number."

In that moment she must have looked frightened and reluctant. Gareth assured her that he would be there on Saturday, painting during the session, and added that Valentine was strictly professional. She watched as if in a dream as her hand wrote her number on a page in his sketch book. She figured nothing would come of this.

Chapter 5

One Man's Kingdom

Perception opens the door to an empire.

The next morning, as she was opening her apartment door to drop off her huge drawing portfolio and backpack full of ruling pens, paints, and brushes after her two-dimensional design class, the phone rang. Her first feeling was that it was Gareth looking for a date. She was shocked to hear a velvety, deep Italian accent coming through the handset. The artist spoke so directly and self-assuredly that she was instantly charmed. He got right to the point.

"I hear you are able to hold challenging poses for longer than most models?" the thick Italian accent questioned.

"Yes, I am indeed!" she replied, adding, "And I am able to find my marks impeccably when returning from breaks."

"I am told you are a dancer and can roller skate as well. Is this true?"

"Indeed it is, Mister…" she trailed off as the artist continued.

"Valentine. You may call me Valentine."

"Yes, Valentine," she responded. All of this is true."

"*Ciò è perfetto!*" said the maestro. He gave her the address and added, "I will see you this Saturday at noon. Ring the bell and I will send my assistant out to meet you. He will lead you back to the studio."

A loud click was followed by the dial tone. She couldn't believe he had hung up.

"Amazing!" she exclaimed aloud.

That Saturday morning, she had laced her white skates with fluorescent orange wheels onto her rainbow-knee-socked calves. Two thick, long braids tied at the bottom draped like thick skeins of silk down the back of her embroidered jean jacket. The skate to the South Philly address was a flash, and she chuckled at the thought of the word *flash* because she was wearing her orange baseball cap bedecked with yellow lightning bolts. She stopped in the street and pulled a little piece of paper with the address on it from her pocket. In the middle of the block she spotted the matching numbers, rolled over, found the bell, and rang it. A middle-aged, balding man answered the door and motioned for her to follow him down a dark hallway to a mysterious garden. She glided through, feeling the slight bumps of ancient wooden floor boards beneath her wheels.

In the center of the four square street fronts, behind brick and marble façades, lay the original courtyard. It was a paradise unlike anything she had ever seen in center city. Within it the artist had preserved the original architecture of a carriage house, trees, and an array of flowers and greenery tucked into stone lined beds. This truly was utopia, with rose bushes and a marble fountain.

Valentine had claimed the premium ground floor as studio space. His living quarters were high above on the top floor in the north wing of the building. Perched in the clouds in his block-long penthouse, he was able to overlook this entire kingdom. Almost all of his tenants were graduates of the city's top art schools, many well-established and gallery-backed. Every year, many applicants seeking apartments were turned away, and those who were accepted stayed on for what seemed like eternity. She again remembered hearing that it was almost impossible to get a place here.

***

The memory faded as she turned her gaze back to the brick wall. *It's surreal that I'm living here now*, she thought as she moved a step closer and tilted her head, allowing her eyes to travel down the creamy-colored converging lines of mortar. She felt the coolness of the bricks and could hear the echo of her freshman year drawing teacher's voice describing the sutra of perspective.

"Everything you need to know about seeing is described by simply laying your cheek against a brick wall," declared her freshman drawing professor.

For some reason, the Divine always saw fit to place the most cryptic teachers in her path. During her freshman year she would walk around, looking into the other foundation drawing classes, wondering what they were doing. In one class it seemed they spent an inordinate amount of time building boxes out of grids painstakingly drawn on thick vellum, eventually placing tiny three-dimensional cardboard pieces of furniture into them. Only after two months had they begun to draw what was inside the boxes. One crisp afternoon, a classmate came back from a break whining about not understanding perspective.

"Why aren't we using grid boxes?" demanded the grouchy freshman of their drawing teacher, Doreen Stanford. The rest of the class gasped in fear, and a lesson in bricks resulted. Doreen grabbed the girl by the arm and dragged her out to the elevator lobby. Looking back over her shoulder, she barked to the rest of the class to follow and bring a pencil. Down to the sidewalk on Broad Street the serpentine formation of students marched, continuing around the corner to Fifteenth and Pine. The class stood shivering in the shadow of the Frank Furness building, wondering why no one had thought to bring a jacket or sweater.

Doreen ordered each student to find a place against the brick wall, demanded that they place their pencil in the mortar line at each individual eye level, and then guided them to press their right cheeks against the cold surface.

"Follow the line of your pencil into the distance with your right eye. Look at how it converges with the mortar lines above and below."

"I see it!" exclaimed Randy Love.

Of course he did, thought the majority of students. Randy was the only one of the group destined to be an actual painter. Right from the first assignment, he was Doreen's favorite. Unfortunately, he failed horribly at three dimensions. The whole class banded together and did his last few projects for him. They believed in his ability to paint and draw so much that they put their own well-being on the line. The 3-D teacher had no choice but to go with it and accept the class's backing of Randy. The entire section had threatened a mutiny and demanded that their submission of homework on his behalf be accepted.

"This is it!" exclaimed Doreen, adjourning the brick lesson. "This is all you need to know about perspective. This is all you need to see in order to draw! Drawing is the art of seeing the spaces between the objects."

Chuckling in amazement, the little artist actually got what Doreen was saying. Later she would come to know this same concept as it applied to meditation and eventually to the understanding of God. It was in this moment that she learned to create in two dimensions in spite of her aptitude being in the three-dimensional world. It was here, at the Philadelphia College of Art, where a major leap in spirit took place. Prior to this experience, the idea of having to learn anything about pens and papers made her skin tighten. It scared her so much that she would lose sleep and often her appetite.

Heaving a big sigh, she floated through the required two semesters of Doreen's cryptic lair of riddles and witty thought. She recalled her dread at the idea of taking this life-drawing class in the first place, and the comedy of having to study the subject with an abstract painter. The paintings and drawings she made during the proximal two years of a Chinese watercolor class and a chalk pastel class flashed before her mind's eye. She was always surprised by the compliments from the professors in spite of the doubts she had about her drafting skills and became forever grateful for the necessary irritation of her freshman drawing experience. The critique during her final meeting with Doreen produced the lowest grade she ever received in college. When she asked why, the response was, "You have had it too easy. You must suffer for your art!"

The morning sounds of South Philadelphia snapped her back to the present moment. A garbage truck thundered past, shaking the concrete of the sidewalk, and her cheek pulled away from the wall. She watched as her boots began to stroll down the sidewalk, guiding her toward the heart of the Italian Market. She let her vision soften, and her awareness noted how every movement was an integral note in a tapestry of sound. Her ears tuned into the hissing-whir of imported ball bearings as skaters thunked against the blacktop in rapid progression on the ball court across the street. Her eyes closed, and she imagined a symphony of yellow and green colored lights dancing to the music of the street hockey players. The thwacking and growling grinds of wooden sticks against the blacktop kept time.

She rode her next breath around the corner of Christian Street and continued down toward the belly of the Market. The eerie calm was odd, as it was close to ten o'clock. This morning the sounds were sweet and subtle. No yelling, no delivery trucks, no screaming mothers, no crashing cans. When she had gotten up that morning, her refrigerator was almost empty—just the way she liked to keep it. Living in the Market, there was no point in hoarding. Five or six days a week, depending on the shop, everything a person could possibly crave was a block and a half away, often for free.

On toward the Spice Sisters shop she floated. When she got near Lorenzo's Pizzeria, she took extra care to sneak past by crossing over Ninth Street and then ducked into the corner doughnut shop. Once safely inside, she wove through and out the back door and onto the pavement. Seeing no one was in the wooden armchair outside the pizzeria pickup window, she sighed deeply, relieved. Continuing the weave, she crossed back over to the west side of Ninth. Her feet touched the safety zone, creating familiar creaking sounds from the raised porch. Heady aromas of cinnamon, anise, chiles, and coffee flooded her nostrils. A board squeaked under her boot.

"Hey, sweetie," called Maria, the eldest of the spice sisters. "I just brewed some chai tea. Want some?"

"Do I need to—" she smirked as Maria cut her off by placing a warm mug of spicy Indian tea topped off with creamy milk and a sprinkle of chocolate in her hands.

"You're better than a sister and a mother, Maria! You're like a mama with no guilt or strings."

"I'm your big sister, little one. I'm always looking out for my girl," Maria said, giving the tiny woman a squeeze with one arm.

The two sat in big wooden chairs and chatted over a second cup of tea, giggling and bagging little bundles of garam masala spice blend they scooped from a large steel bucket. It was completely natural to show up, have a treat or a cup of tea, and help out with whatever was needed in the moment.

"Here," said Maria, "take one of these for later, just in case you want some tea tomorrow or Monday when we're closed." Maria wrapped the little nymph in a cozy hug and handed her a small paper bag filled with her favorite tea.

"You overwhelm me with love," purred the dark-haired feline as she curtsied and continued, "I could stay here all day, but I have places to go and people to meet!"

"I get it! Off you go, sweet one! See you next week," said Maria, smacking her on the bum as she headed out the door.

With a proper cup of tea in her belly and a heightened awareness, it was time to saunter back to the corner pizzeria to have a slice and a schmooze. Upon arriving, she leaned in the window to flash her million dollar smile to Sylvester, the owner's son.

***

The creak of the giant rocking chair and the island surroundings snapped into focus for a moment, returning her to the stark surroundings. Her eyes slit open for a millisecond, allowing the moist blue hues of water, clouds, and sky to leak in. With the next creak of the chair, her nostrils filled with the aroma of a dark-crusted slice of Margherita pizza steaming through a generous shake of oregano. The skin of her chest warmed as if she were leaning in the order window, feeling the glow of the brick oven. It was really the sun heating a silver chain with a gold and crystal pendant that she wore around her neck.

***

Then she was right back in that early September day, standing on the corner of Ninth and Christian by the pizzeria. Her velvet boots hugged the pavement, and the left shoulder of her sweater slid down, exposing her tawny, silken skin. Out of the corner of her eye she caught the gaze of a floppy-haired guy in the doughnut shop across the street. Was he checking her out? It felt like what she had always called a "destiny moment." Shrugging it off with a long exhalation, she returned to consuming her free slice of pie while dishing out countering jabs at Sylvester's questions.

"Were you at the Banana last night, bella?" asked Sylvester. "I didn't see you there."

"Nah," she replied coolly, chomping away on the chewy crust, ignoring his use of the pet name.

"What-choo-do?" he probed in South Philly-ese.

"I stayed in and wrote for a while, read a little, and fell asleep. I knew you would be wondering where I was, my darling, and pining for me," she quipped , "so when I got hungry this morning, I came here first to see you!" She winked and flashed her impish smile.

"Dat's cool, pizella. Maybe next weekend we can meet, right, amorina?" snorted Sylvester.

She was not at all fond of pet names; her likes and dislikes were strong regarding what men used other than her given name. Foreign language was more acceptable than the common English choices. Fruit was out of the question, but squash and baked goods could pass as acceptable.

"We'll see, Sylvester, my friend. But now I have a craving for more cheese. Thanks for the slice. I'm outta here!"

Sylvester leaned out the window and craned to watch her as she whipped around the corner and strutted back into the Market, down the sidewalk, and disappeared into a palace of imported creamy delights.

The House of Cheese was run by a band of round brothers whose physiques resonated in the rotund waxy curves of the giant ripened wheels of dairy the family imported from Europe. This fortress sat on Ninth Street, on the north side of Hall. On the southwest corner stood the competition—The King of Cheese. The teams were eternally divided as to which was better; you either shopped in one or the other. Perhaps it was chance which store you were first drawn to. For most visitors to the Market, it was random.

Bells jingled as the thick wooden door opened and the tiny goddess stepped into the calcium castle.

"What can I get you today, baby?" called Anthony Junior, who was buried inside the large white cheese case in the front of the store.

"My favorite, of course," said the imp in a buttery tone.

"You've got it, doll face!" Anthony Junior exclaimed, his hands deftly slicing a delicate taste from a huge beige and red wheel. In one smooth motion he handed it to her, hunched down into the giant enameled case, and snatched the enormous round. Without disturbing the slumbering cheese, he laid it gently on his carving table and cut a generous wedge. A.J. deftly ripped crisp white paper from a roll, then wrapped and folded with the perfection of an origami master folding a crane.

"Five'll do it, doll!" he said, smiling, without thinking of weighing it. He placed it in a bag, and handed it to the dream girl. In turn, she handed over a fiver.

Normally being called "doll" or "hon" made her skin crawl. But for some reason, coming from Sylvester or A.J. or any of the family boys in the Market, these pet names somehow created a cosmic balance and a sense that everything was right in the universe.

There was a honey-dripping moment of silent smiles and eyes glinting with a slight pull of magnetic energy. She knew it was safe to flirt, as this young father had just welcomed the birth of his second child—a son—which, in Italian, translated as a deal-clinching lifetime commitment. There was no danger here, just an innocent moment. She had very strict rules about playing with the fire of taken men, and always honored her sisters in the world first and foremost.

A shuffling commotion broke the twinkling when the two caught a glimpse of rumpled hair and breadcrumbs flying in the air across the store. There was the guy from the doughnut shop, teetering and almost falling into a very large oak barrel. She hadn't even seen him come in.

"Donny!" bellowed Vinnie as he stood up from rearranging the display in the front of the store. Salvatore came running out of nowhere and tore across the floor, deftly negotiating the obstacles of colossal barrels and stacks of cakes and crackers like a figure skater.

"What the heck are you doing?" he barked causing Don to leap a foot in the air.

"Oh, crap!" exclaimed Don. "Sorry."

The tiny woman hovered near the front cheese case and cracked up silently, trying to catch her breath. Her belly heaved against her sweater.

She recognized him; it was the floppy haired guy from the doughnut shop window. *The destiny moment.*

She stared in fascination, calculating the possibility of the two of them being here, in this space, at the same time. Don looked down into the giant olive barrel and batted like a hungry bear at a jumping salmon.

Salvatore grabbed a handful of Don's sweatshirt and steered him away from the barrel.

"I got this. It's okay, man," said Sal, whacking Don's hand. "I got it!"

"Geeezu," jabbed Vinnie from the front case.

"That's what I get for feeding you, Donny!" laughed Sal.

Everyone in the store cracked up. The dark goddess turned dramatically to face the scene, pretending to not know who the clown was. That was the moment they made eye contact for the first time; that was the first picture he thought she saw of him. She remembered the feeling of trying to keep her cool as quaking laughter rose inside her and visibly shook her body like a geyser getting ready to blow.

"Nice one, Donny," she chortled.

***

A shattering creak from the rocking chair flashed to the forefront of her awareness as she let the scene drift into the mist over the water. The weight of the humongous book pressed into her lap. She felt the imprints of the oversized metal binding in the skin of her thighs as her eyes melted open, allowing the surroundings of being in the middle of a watery sea flood into sight.

"More?" questioned the Gandharva, causing the little pixie to jump a few inches up off her seat, ringing the metal of the book's binding.

"I forgot where I was. I forgot you were here." A tear trickled down her cheek. With a vehement move, she swiped it away and held both hands out for the bowl.

"Ha!" said the winged one, hovering above the lower branches of the tree. He swooped down with the food.

"Eat your pasta," he said, handing her a transformed dish with buckwheat noodles and bitter melon in black bean sauce as he stroked her long bangs to one side.

"We are all a part of the great web of energy that is Divine. Like the crying of human beings, the elements cleanse the atmosphere and the land. The wind in turn clears the mind. Sometimes the weather we experience is gentle and at other times it is strong. All things that happen are for the greater good. It is a difficult task to remember this and to wrap the ego-mind around it when we suffer the archetype of the victim during a strong onset of feelings. This opportunity is a reminder that we are connected."

"Of course, my kind one, I know this. If I have been cruel today, forgive me…" Her voice trailed off as her eyes lowered. She drew in a slow, definitive breath and continued, "I know this is a reminder that we have the ability to reach out and ask for help and support. This is how we remember that the body is an illusion and we are all indeed one."

She looked deeply into the guardian's eyes. All particles of frustration and disdain quickly melted into gratitude for the companionship and, even more so, a deep thankfulness for the warm bowl of noodles.

"Indeed, little one!" he said, sliding the bowl a little closer to her. "I have always been here with you and always will be. We are timeless!"

Part II

Potency

The Divine Masculine

He is the frame of existence, the empty container of infinity.

Chapter 6

Dreams Within Dreams

A crack in the dark silence of the night.

Donatello lay alone in his single bed, the sweat of a South Philadelphia summer night beading up on his forehead. The vast darkness shook as distant thunder rolled toward him in the endless nothingness, but there was no hope of a rainstorm to quench the thirsting city streets. He squirmed as images of his family and their summer house in South Jersey flashed through his head, playing along in rhythm with the lightning outside his window.

Salty memories of ocean breezes fanned the blazing heat of Donny's melting consciousness. He craved the beach, the taste of the briny air, and the feelings—lost feelings—of youthful happiness. Longing desire welled in him to feel his mother's hand brush the dark floppy curls from his forehead, to feel her arms wrap around him tightly like the wool scarf she tied snugly around his neck on cold winter mornings. He had always wanted her all to himself; he'd never wanted to feel the frustration of having to share her with his sisters, their spouses, or nephews and nieces. From the moment he lost her, he wanted her back.

When he was a boy, Don fought for "alone time" with his mother during the blazing heat of summer when the entire Lombardi clan packed into their tiny green clapboard bungalow "down the shore." He

always felt smothered there.

In spite of this, each year when the choking heat of July became unbearable, he would give up and hop on a Greyhound to escape the smoldering city. Riding in the back of the bus, he watched out the rear window as the Philadelphia skyline melted into the distance. When it disappeared into a wiggly line of heat, he turned forward to look down the Atlantic City Expressway, preparing for the guilt his sisters would pile on as a side dish to a large, welcome plate of pasta. They never let him forget that he was the only one of his siblings unmarried, childless, and obviously alone. Their respective men would sit outside, slugging down canned beer, cackling about his artsy-fartsy existence in South Philly. Gianna's husband Orsino would chase him with lopping shears from the shed and threaten to give him a haircut.

Struggling against his feeling of shame, Don gulped at his aloneness and fell fitfully into deeper sleep. He rolled over on the moist sheets and slid through the misty veil into an unexpected vision. Uncanny awareness overhauled his psyche and his dream-body glided into an intoxicating garden. In every direction, lush landscape tiptoed, like a cat on hot bricks, into vibrant focus.

Chapter 7

Delusion

Misty feelings and tasty recollections.

Don's dream body knelt down to feel the grass. He watched his right hand touch odd little plants. They looked strangely like his favorite microgreens from the salad bar he frequented uptown, on Sansom Street. The apparition body lifted a handful to his mouth, paused, and then dipped it into a nearby puddle. The tan, soupy goo tasted like a hippie version of the Russian dressing his youngest sister Angie made with soy sauce and sesame paste. There was a time when she was on a health food kick. Back then he would stop by her place often to scarf free dinners. He loved the flavors and textures of her culinary creations.

Don continued to explore the dense green dreamscape. He hesitantly reached out to touch a bizarre-looking tree with cracked bark and spiky little thorns protruding through the crevices. The stinging sensation of a wound caused him to jerk back his dream hand and spontaneously lick what looked like a bead of blood. But the color was darker than that of blood, and his dream body wasn't fazed at all to find it tasted of bitter chocolate, saturnine and not at all sweet.

Inside his sleeping physical brain, synapses launched like a fireworks finale. Consciousness struggled to reason with Unconsciousness. A summit meeting was held in the Boardroom of grey matter; a debate ensued. Consciousness pleaded the need to change Donny's workout and eating schedules. Grids and spreadsheets flashed on the projector screen of his frontal lobe, and he flipped Reason the bird. A gritty representative from Unconscious Mind countered that perhaps he needed more time to socialize outside his family network. The argument thawed into a display of reorganizing and redecorating the third floor of his tiny trinity house to make it a more efficient space for painting and sculpting. A messenger from the depths of his spinal column plopped a calculator on the table and fueled the argument.

"Why keep space in the uptown group studio? Your buddies don't give a rat's ass about your work. All they do is eat up your supplies and suck down your ideas!"

Reason bellowed, "It is better to spend less time in the art studio up near Broad Street! Stay here, close to the Italian Market. Eat a regular and more balanced diet at home."

The astral stomach painted a door on the eastern wall, and the dream body walked over the threshold. The assembly felt slightly more at ease.

Don continued to explore his dreamscape. He proceeded with caution, like a little old lady crossing the street. The dream body ate plants and rocks, all deliciously pleasing in their flavors. Childlike happiness welled up inside his many layers. The sleeping mind watched as the dream body danced and laughed and sang. A smile appeared in the sweat-soaked humidity as his corporeal eyelids fluttered rapidly within the vision.

He was much different than the others. Don was an oddball even within the art community, where he stood out as a renegade and nonconformist. His college professors found him a little spooky. Former girlfriends never let him completely into their hearts, and their fathers did everything they could to keep him out of their daughters' jeans.

A feeling from childhood unfolded around Don like a page from a popup book. He saw the nine-year-old version of himself with a group of neighborhood kids as they made their way through the urban streets of his youth. Ronnie, his slightly older best friend who was destined to lead a street gang, had organized the outing. Ronnie steered the clutch as they coasted to the Stanley movie house on Nineteenth and Market Streets. He believed it was the only movie theater in the city. It had been Ronnie who ordered rather than asked Donny's mom to let him join the group of kids for a Saturday afternoon matinee.

Ronnie had an even greater obsession about Al Capone than the Stanley Theater. He had a riff about how Capone had been arrested at the Stanley for concealing weapons in 1929, and told it over and over to any willing audience. The account never changed in tone, gesture, or tambour, no matter how many times Ronnie repeated it. The story kept the beat in Donny's brain as he imagined flickering scenes from the movie *Camelot* blazing on the forty-foot screen of the antique theater.

The dream body took a fistful of dust from the path and stuffed it into its mouth. A flavor identical to the taste of his very first malt ball filled his senses.

The large white movie palace had been torn down in the early seventies. Don remembered the glistening travertine in the Stanley's lobby, and the tempting smell of popcorn that hung in the air. He had an unusual attraction to the milky sheen of marble and, when he encountered it, he felt compelled to kneel down and feel it with his hands.

Unfortunately, the love affair was jilted five years later when he was moving and stacking similar slabs of raw rock in a holding yard behind the Lombardi family's business. Don's grandfather Fabrizio was an expert with stone, tile, and brick. He had come to the New World with a dream and a trowel. When he landed in America and did not find streets lined with gold, he decided to carpet them with cobblestones.

Fabrizio carefully trained many cousins and nephews of the Lombardi clan in the art of stone masonry. Early on, he began teaching his seven-year-old grandson Donny to recognize the craftsmanship of Philadelphia's streets and buildings.

Fabrizio had a divine love for industrial artistic expression. His creations were a declaration of his heart to Fiorella, the love of his life and matriarchal goddess of the family. The expression of his feelings fanned in undulating rose petal designs decorating the stony streets of West Philadelphia.

During his teen years, Don worked in the family stone yard. He thought the blistering heat of summer had to be worse than any sweat shop in history. It was sheer torture. As soon as the phone rang in the shop, he begged the heavens that it was one of his sisters calling to tease him from the family's Jersey Shore bungalow. He prayed under his breath to be challenged by them so he could leap at the opportunity to bug out from his horrid job and head down the shore. He never felt regret for having left the rock yard and the men of the family behind.

Vegetables and salads melted into Don's attention as his dream-self stuffed its mouth with what looked like a handful of grass clippings. They tasted a lot like collard greens, cooked Brazilian style. He had first sampled this odd vegetable when he visited an old girlfriend, Cherry, at her college in Bethlehem, PA. Pennsylvania Steel was still in business back then, and the college town was booming with shops and restaurants.

Cherry was a vegetarian and frequented a little hippy establishment on Fourth Street called Nature. The owner, Nancy, took an instant liking to Don and turned him on to his first taste of the dark green vegetable. Nancy told him about her discovery of the leathery leaves in the tropics. Her family had been missionaries, and the only part of that experience she saw worth keeping were the local veggies and fruit. Don wanted to learn how to cook them, and so one evening Nancy invited him to join her at the stove and create his own.

Don eagerly hopped off his stool and swooped behind the diner-style counter. He reached for the chef's blade with one hand and the top leaf of a clean stack of collards with the other.

"First, you must remove the stems. It's easier to roll them if you leave the tips of each leaf connected like this," said Nancy as she demonstrated how to take the spines out of the thick leaves.

Don did exactly as she guided him and quickly had about ten leaves prepped. Nancy was impressed that the floppy-haired boy was so eager to learn, and even more skilled with a blade than her own children. She took the stack of prepped leaves and rolled them into a tight cylinder enviable of a Cuban *tabaquero*. Then, using a sharp blade, she deftly cut them into a chiffonade of perfectly even, skinny little matchstick-sized slices.

Don was amazed at how easy she made it look.

"Now what do we do?" he asked.

"Just watch how simple this is," she replied, lighting the gas burner under an iron pan. Into it she put a splash of golden olive oil, and then the entire pile of green slivers. In a matter of seconds, the volume was reduced to a small handful.

"Amazing!" exclaimed Don. "Is that it?"

"No," responded Nancy. She continued, "This is the trick—you add just a splash of water and a tiny bit of salt." She covered the pan with a lid as the greens sizzled in steam, then whipped it off as she announced, "Voila! Here they are, the perfect side dish!"

"Who would have suspected that I would like collards?" said Don, taking a mouthful. "I thought they were overcooked, greasy greens from the South. These are amazing!"

The ethnic birthright of indigenous food defines us early in life. Nourishment which is more than protein and vitamin enrichment infuses us as children. Nancy's cooking soothed him maternally. For years to come, he would teach many friends the wonder of this vegetable, and would try the same technique with almost every leafy plant that he came across.

As he watched the memory unfold, nurturing contentment wrapped around his psyche, giving him the feeling of warm motherly love. Deep in the center of his heart he felt pain for his mother's passing. He remembered what it felt like to lose her. She had died when he was a little boy. It had all happened so fast. The cancer took her quickly, and he really never had the proper time to digest the nightmare of her loss.

Don's fingers spread and contracted, squeezing the sheet to his chin. He wished he could feel his mother holding him in a never-ending embrace, rocking him and singing sweet and low. It was one of the only recollections he had of her.

Though Don had few memories of his mother's voice and her smell, he retained a clear remembrance of the flavors she placed on the dinner table. Whenever he tasted them, his dwindling reserve of motherly love was fed. After his mother's passing, he began to embrace and adore even more international fare. Eating the foods of a variety of nations was one of the only ways he allowed himself to be loved.

Like a beast, Don's astral body went on and on, eating his way through the cryptic dreamscape. When he felt almost satisfied, he paused and realized that he was standing at the foot of a large oak-like tree. *This seems like a good place to stop for a rest*, he thought. So, very cautiously, the dream body crawled into a comfortable position. Simultaneously, the physical body curled up and the dreamer then found himself deeper within the dream.

Part III

Creation

There is no beginning or ending, only magic.

Chapter 8

Shakti

The ten thousand eyes of the Great Mother.

Ripples of water rocked as if the entire world fit into a small bowl that was being shaken by a sumo wrestler. Dark liquid lapped at the tips of mountains which never gave up their intention to protrude through the choppy waves. A piercing golden hue thrown off by a great disk of light hovered high above the stratosphere. It threw a flood of brilliant, colorful shadows on the murky sea. Deep underneath the surface, the great planet slumbered in silence, blanketed by the darkness of her depths.

The golden disk yawned, spewing a green-and-purplish mist of tiny bubbles full of potential, which turned orange and blue as they swarmed like a hive of bees toward the water.

"Are we dead?" gurgled the she-being.

"There is no such thing!" belched the masculine counterpart, this time in rust and rich umbers.

"Uuutsssssssss…tah…kah uts uts uts," came a hissing from far in the distance, not unlike a serpent.

"What the heck was that?" blinked the female voice again in the inky darkness of the waters.

"Uts."

"What?"

"How should I know?" retorted the infinite emptiness.

"I thought you were the container of everything, the place of all knowingness!"

"Yes, but in order for this to occur, I need…" His voice gathered what seemed like endless air. "Brrrrraaaaap." This great belch released a third cloud of bubbles, this time in earthy reds and golden yellows.

"I just thought…whoa!" exclaimed the maiden voice as her attention was drawn into a marmoreal white corridor. The enameled, smooth chamber stretched from a great distance and disappeared into the infinite vastness. It glimmered unreal, bright, in its shiny brilliance. After an eerie stillness for what seemed like an eternity, she noticed there was no sound. It was as if every sound had been swallowed up.

The "she" sound wondered in silence what would happen next— if there ever was a next. The "he" sound held his invisible arms open, cradling the event, giving it a place to exist in the vast container of his beingness. All at once, in the spark of a moment, a dark shape appeared in the depths of the distant passageway. It seemed to grow in size and momentum as it slithered and wound its way forward into the instantaneous present.

The vision of the endless corridor slowly became clearer. Vibrant colors in fantastic hues flashed reflective on the glistening, lacquered walls. The single point of darkness that had appeared in the center of the distant profundity steadily grew, slowly coming closer and closer to the present moment.

"Uts te kah tah mateya. Uts uts uts tah ka. Uts, uts, uuutsssssss," hissed the voice of the moving energy.

"This is freaking me out!" the she-voice managed to squeak.

"Just go with it," coaxed the masculine space, reaching his ever-growing embrace wider and wider, becoming the universe. "Follow the sound."

Then, on his commanding encouragement, with all of her energy balled up tightly, the she-voice transformed into a floating face in the glinting white of the passageway.

The dark point continued to grow closer and closer. It seemed to be swaying side to side as details began to emerge. Huge eyes the colors of a preternatural rainbow sat atop thick, moist, gleaming lips that appeared to be made out of a thousand glass beads. As the face came closer, countless colors of an unreal palette bounced, reflected by the white walls of the corridor.

The she-being, in the form of a floating face, gulped as she floated in the rectangle of space. The multicolored rainbow serpent gained velocity like a high-speed train. This caused the floating face to squint, imagining great pain upon the imminent impact. Stopping on a point tinier than a dime, the Eternal Serpent was now face-to-face with the she-being's floating face.

There were no words exchanged, but a deep, unblinking stare engaged the two sets of eyes. The Serpent began to speak in a booming telepathic tone without moving her lips.

"Open your mouth!" commanded the Serpent.

"Open my mouth? What on earth for?" questioned the she-voice.

"Open your mouth!" instructed the telepathic voice.

"Open my mouth? What the heck is this all about?" pleaded the she-voice, sounding a lot more frightened than before.

"Open your mouth!" demanded the great snake.

"Just do it!" a male voice yelled from nowhere in particular.

The female form imagined opening her mouth and what would happen. Without any control, compelled by an unseen force, her jaw opened, flipping the top of the face back. The Serpent flooded into the gaping mouth and, in an instant, the two were once again face-to-face. The gleaming lips of the Serpent yawned open as the telepathic voice commanded, "Enter me!"

Any drops of fear vaporized as the floating face dove into the Serpent's throat. "This isn't so bad," thought the she-being, who was opening her mouth in a spontaneous gesture without thought or control. Again, the giant snake lunged into the female's mouth. Once again, the two floated facing one another in the gleaming corridor.

The weaving back-and-forth of mouth-diving continued and, after an eon, there was only one being. She was the complete union of the previous two beings. She was marvelous, a combination of the pure consciousness of the Divine Feminine and the powerful energy of Prana, combined with the Goddess power of creation. The completed celestial she-form combines with the universal receptive masculine energy in a state of jiva. They are drawn together by the magnetic force of universal energy known as Prana held together by the glue of desire.

After the formation of the Great Goddess, she went on to be known as Ma Shakti, the Divine Mother. She is now known by thousands of names in many different tongues in every corner of existence. She possesses the womb of creation. She is the fertile ground where all seeds of thought are planted, and then made manifest in nature by the vibration of sound.

Her voice is the celestial music which vibrates in every quark. It is her energy which combines with the vast nothingness to make everything we perceive real and full of substance. It is against her breast, cradled in her arms, that we desire to be rocked and nurtured. She is our true mother, the one who heals our wounds and paves our path of learning. She gave birth to all of nature as we know it, and in her enormous heart she understands our quirks and needs.

The newly congealed feminine being began to speak in the original tongue.

"Uts te kah tah mateya. Uts te kah tah. Uts te kah tah. Uts te kah tah mateya. Uts, uts, uuutssssss."

Chapter 9

Desire

Watch out what you wish for.

The sky somehow seemed different, and Don's artist's eye could not describe exactly how or what was causing this. There was an eerie hiss in the wind, which seemed to be picking up. This new layer of consciousness exhibited the same scenery as the previous, but with odd exceptions. The plants and trees possessed the same shapes, but the colors were somehow more aggressive.

In the center of his gut, he felt frustrated in spite of his stomach being thoroughly packed with tasty shrubs and succulent stones. This malcontent transmuted into the earthbound body as it kicked the covers off the bed angrily while the Mind experienced feelings of deep-set unhappiness.

Reason stood up and addressed the cellular assembly rather loudly. From a distant corner, the other emotions chimed in. A great debate ensued about how Don had become bored and a bit lonely in his life. In the dream within the dream, the body sat up grumpily, its back against the same oak-like tree where the previous level of the self had fallen asleep. The deeper-level dream body began to speak aloud. Complaining whines of aloneness fired down like freezing rain upon the soul. It was like just like walking into the wind on a frigid Philly night with no bar or restaurant open to offer a much-needed cup of coffee. Loneliness cloaked Don in damp darkness.

Suffocating cries squeaked from his physical throat, sounding vaguely like "Ma, ma, ma!"

The discourse continued with scenes of alienation and sibling rivalry. Don was always the oddball, the black sheep. His girlfriends had kept him safely outside of their social circles, yet gladly took him into their beds. The sacred key to his heart had been hidden, but not hopelessly tossed over a cliff into the abyss.

Realization pounded its fist on the Boardroom table and gestured savagely in the air. The Acolyte Teen lit a candle, incanting that there indeed exists a more perfect path in life. The deepest dream version of Don begged pathetically for a playmate. He screamed to the reddish-grey sky for a partner. The sound came through the lips of all three layers of the body simultaneously.

"I need a mate, someone who understands me. I want to share my heart with her," he fizzed from a deep layer of unconsciousness.

"Someone to understand me," the physical body croaked.

"To see my inner light shining," added the astral body.

"Ssshakti," the wind hissed.

"What the heck is Shakti?" the Astral asked, as clouds pushed the brain into a sparkling white studio.

Spontaneously, the Artist in Don's psyche got to work. Paint, brushes, and easel, followed by clay, sticks, and wire, materialized in the vision. The inner gaze watched as a thousand arms sprung from the core of his being and began to create while a thousand eyes discerned and assessed the constructions. A lynx-like goddess with dark, flowing hair and piercing metallic eyes began to take form. The Poet described her out loud in a dream voice while the Artist sculpted the shape and size of her breasts and bottom. The whiteness of her teeth was forged with titanium. The feel of her tan skin tingled on the assembly of left hands as the collection of right hands painted canvases with thick bamboo and yak-hair brushes. One image glistened in rich dark marble, as the dream body carved the stone as easily as a hot knife moving through fondant.

Mysterious renderings of this Goddess flipped rapidly, like a deck of cards bursting from the hands of a happy child. First she appeared tall, about five feet, eight inches. With one of the left hands on his chin, Don stood back to study his creation. He twisted his mustache on the right side of his lip, thinking, *Too much.* Forty arms reached out to squeeze the wraith like a Slinky recoiling in the hands of a toddler to a more manageable five feet even.

The apparition sprung to life, exploding all but a primary set of arms off the dream artist. Excitedly, Don began to play with her within his vision. He caressed her face and held her hand. He fed her fruit-flavored rocks. A mile-wide smile stretched across his face. He picked up his Guild guitar and sang her poetry, which was composed from his core. He held her gently in an embrace, being mindful to keep his lower body from touching against hers. Deep inside the physical belly, something was freaking him out. He couldn't figure out why, but he was feeling a little more than scared.

The wind blew strongly through the astral body, shaking it into the original level of dreaming. The physical brain watched as the dream body sat up in the dawning light of an early morning. It stretched, yawned, and shivered while reaching for a fistful of salad-like grass and a stone that tasted like a pear. Gusts picked up outside the second-floor window, cooling down Don's still-sweating physical body which lay on the bed. He had thrown off the remains of the sheets as the predawn air rang with distant sounds coming from the Italian Market.

Inside the dream, the wind became forceful, slapping like heavy metal bass strings along with the groan of twenty tubas. Droning beneath the blaring clamor was a basement incantation. The sounds grew louder and even more intense. A delivery truck drove past the intersection at the top of the alley-like street. Its diesel engine echoed, vibrations ringing down the tiny block and in through the open bedroom window. Simultaneously, inside the dream, the growling wind formed a phrase, causing Don to jolt at the howling current of sound.

"As you wish," squealed a tenor pitch.

"A-a-a-s y-o-o-u wish." The sounds came again, stretched like black licorice about to snap. Confused and unsettled, Don tossed in his bed.

"As you wish!" the phantom sounded once again.

"Holy crap!" fired Logic. "I am losing it!"

"Behold!" the voice decreed. "Stand you over there!"

"Who is scripting this crap?" challenged a particle of Teenage Arrogance.

"Watch as I create the female you desire," the voice yowled. "Stay over there, out of my way. Prepare to receive that for which you beg so pathetically."

Shivering from fear and from cold, Don's dream body cowered to a space he thought was far enough out of the way. He wasn't quite sure if it was the right "over there," and prayed that it was.

Clouds clustered rapidly above his head and clung to the sturdy trees of this sinistral dream grove, enveloping Don in a cartoonlike manner. The vapor parted, and from its center a giant hand appeared.

"Observe as your wish is granted!" wailed the colossal voice, accompanied by an earsplitting crash of cymbals and the screech of fingernails on a blackboard.

Don's dream body fell to its knees. Every molecule felt the magnitude of the tremendous hand. The synapses in Don's brain began to register that this had all somehow turned real. Within the REM state, he accessed the teachings of Aleister Crowley, which he had devoured as a teen. Remembering the ways of lucid dreaming, he struggled to be in control.

The Warrior pulled out a cutlass and assumed a fighting stance as Don tried to pull all his energy to his core. Consciousness scanned the dreamscape for phantoms as the terrain began to feel and smell more alive and real. The physical flesh and bones in the South Philly bed jerked in fear as the dream body took refuge near a flaming reddish bush that seemed to give off some warmth.

Don's dream-vision self crouched and watched as the giant hand dove deep into the landscape and lifted up a fistful of earth and stone with a horrific cacophonous yawn. It then raised the monstrous cache up to the sky in a ceremonial presentation and flung it at a high velocity past Don's shuddering dream body into a clearing. He gasped in awe as he felt a riffling of mud and gravel stinging his right arm and the back of his head.

Again the mammoth mitt dug deep below the land's surface and hoisted up more humus. This time, Don thought he saw a bone sticking out from between the ring and pinky fingers, which brought on an uneasy sensation. Repeating the ritual, the giant hand showed fecundate fistfuls to the sky and proceeded to hurl them past Don. A heap began to grow where there had been empty space. Each load contained an assemblage of mud, sticks, and decomposed leaves. Each repetition left Don feeling queasier.

He cowered in the clearing as the hand continued to launch fistfuls of elemental matter toward the ever increasing heap. The mammoth hand raised up chunks of clay, decaying branches, and jagged rocks. Faint with fear, Don began to think he was seeing things that looked like veins and vessels. Giant clumps flew over his head and splattered bits of the mixture against his back. The smells and sights caused him to gag.

As the great hand flew past where he stood, a wake of air practically bowled him over. It disappeared into the distance, diving and grabbing at what looked like a beach. Sand, pebbles, parts of dead fish, and seaweed rifled past Don's shivering dream frame, increasing the menacing mass.

A salty spray of sea water filled his nose and mouth as the ocean's muck flew all around his head.

Out of the corner of his eye, the organic structure looked vaguely like a tree trunk, quivering and oozing shimmering goo. Don's dream body retched a couple of times beside the red bush, then heaved. Nothing came up. He proceeded to have repetitive dry heaves and fell to his knees as his physical body twisted into a knot. The inky black South Philly night eased a pitch toward the cool grey hues of morning.

"Breathe," he said from both sets of lips at once, tears streaming down his faces. "Stop, please stop," he begged.

There was no stopping. The hand continued its ritual of digging, presenting, and casting huge fistfuls toward the shaft-like mass. The central portion parted into an upside-down *Y*. Branches sprouted off the top, reaching up to the sky. The heap throbbed and pulsed and looked as if it were beginning to dance.

"Behold your consort, your equal," blared the voice, splitting Don's mind like a thousand trumpets. "She is everything you asked for. The Yin to your Yang."

Don unfolded, flipped a leg off the edge of his bed, and almost awoke at the sound of the words *Yin* and *Yang*. He had dabbled in Oriental philosophy only a bit more than reading the Chinese characters found written on white paper fortunes tucked inside lightly tanned, hollow, moon-shaped cookies. Don knew how to pronounce Yin and Yang, and had a peeve about people saying "ying-yang." He had a vague idea that his Yin meant his opposite. He was correct.

Stinking clumps of earth and sea continued to fly through the air. Rough lines refined into clear definition. The branches of the slimy mass pulsed rapidly, and a face began to emerge. Don could see the undeniable curves of a woman forming right before his eyes. He gasped in disbelief that beauty could be formed from such god-awful crap.

The muck moved and undulated as the wind played music like

the kind he had heard one night at The King of Falafel, a Lebanese joint down the street. Don frequented the restaurant as a devout takeout customer. He always ordered from the counter immediately inside the door and trotted home with the tasty sandwiches and tangy pickles, devouring them while reading or painting. On occasion, he would run around the corner to the doughnut shop for a coffee to wash them down.

Falafel sandwiches were the staple food for Don and his art school compadres. They had discovered them during their sophomore days. Don tasted his first pita bread stuffed with the crusty little burger-like falafels at Layla's, a restaurant across the street from his favorite dive bar, Dirty Frank's, which was near the uptown studio. It was a Saturday night when he stumbled into the bistro after downing too many pitchers of cheap beer. He had seen people bringing the odd-shaped sandwiches into the bar, but was not at all attracted to them or their oozing, pinkish sauce. But curiosity got to him, and one day he wandered across the street to see what all the fuss was about.

"Donny! Come sit down with me!" he heard his friend Andy call out.

Don staggered over and sat down in an empty seat opposite his buddy. Andy offered him a crunchy falafel on a little paper plate, pushing it in front of him. He handed Don a fork and said, "Don't knock it till you've tried it, man!"

Reluctantly Don stabbed at the little ball and twisted his face as it hopped away like a rabbit fleeing a farmer.

"Come on, Donny. Put some of this sauce on and go for it! Use your fingers if you want."

Don sighed deeply, and broke a piece of the crunchy falafel off with his fingers. The inside burst into fluorescent green as a hot cloud of aromatic spices wafted into his nostrils. He popped it in his mouth and savored the moment, chewed slowly, and was instantly hooked.

Andy smiled. "Now try the sauces," he said, squirting the elixirs onto the plate. First was some beige goo, a delightful concoction of aromatic sesame paste, and then some red—the hot, spicy version. The painter in Don saw instantly that the pinkish goo was the result of the two sauces blending together.

In that moment, Don realized that this was the start of a new and exciting relationship. He popped the remainder of the falafel into his mouth as he walked up to the counter—still chewing and licking the sauce from his right thumb and forefinger—and ordered his first sandwich. Andy told the counter kid to hit him with the works.

The sandwich was ready in a few minutes, with lettuce, pickles, feta cheese, tomatoes, and the two sauces packed into a perfectly toasted whole-wheat pita. Don ate one, and then ordered a second for dessert. Weeks later, he had become a connoisseur of the crunchy little balls and vowed to stick with only one sandwich at a time, as two in a row seemed to make him feel awful. He was sure this was how the falafel got its name.

When Don moved to his South Philly trinity house, he was pleasantly surprised to find a Lebanese restaurant just around the corner at the top of his block. The sign boasted being "The King of Falafel." It took only one visit to the tiny eatery to convince Don that it should be his regular stop for dinner and late afternoon takeout snacks.

Chapter 10

Provinces

Give in to the unusual and accept all invitations.

A few months prior, on a crisp spring evening, Don entered The King of Falafel for a dinner fix. Behind the counter stood a short, stocky man dressed in a deep maroon velvet vest with a matching fez. He introduced himself as Thami Habib and invited Don up to the restaurant's tiny second floor dining area. Don waved off the invitation and quickly ordered his food. The fez-bedecked man took the order with a knowing smirk and teetered off into the kitchen. The stranger's self-assurance frustrated Don and threw him off. Then he suddenly had an irresistible urge to visit the restroom.

When Thami Habib returned, Don asked if there was a men's room he could use. It felt so weird to ask. He realized that he had never needed to know more than the counter and cash register—he'd always carried out. After a quick transaction, he would scurry home with a takeout box of deliciousness. Thami chortled and motioned him up the stairs. He pitched hard and convinced Don to stay and eat. Don needed to pee, so he decided to go for it.

He climbed the twisting staircase typical of the trinity houses in his neighborhood and easily found the tiny men's room. When he came out, he saw a small table with his usual order on a china plate. A steaming cup of Turkish coffee sat next to it in an ornately painted cup on a saucer. He didn't remember asking for the thick dark liquid, but was happy to see it. He sat down and took a sip. Cinnamon, cardamom, and the tang of darkly roasted beans twirled on his taste buds like tiny ballerinas.

Don was crunching into his first bite when the background music suddenly shifted and cranked loudly through the small space, summoning a shimmering belly dancer into the dining area. Howls, whistles, and hairy hands waving one-and five-dollar bills filled the air. The dancer slowly undulated into the center of the room. Don was grateful to be on the edge, near a dark corner. He hated to be forced into this kind of situation. By nature, he was a creature of shadow and much preferred to be a hidden voyeur.

The dancer's movement etched an indelible pattern into his mind. She snaked and slithered through the crowd. Onlookers shoved money into her belt and bra. Don was sure he could never have a woman who was able to do that, yet he secretly wished for it.

Chapter 11

Crystallization

The sacred dance of formation.

In the clearing, the mound of smelly matter began to bend and flex. The wind whined an Arabic *çiftetelli* rhythm, accompanied by weird deep bass bellows from the trembling ground. It was almost identical to the first song Don heard the night he watched the belly dancer at The King of Falafel.

The she-glob rolled and spiraled, riding serpentine sounds. Don was getting the same feeling he would get when walking down an alley at night—the gripping sensation of not knowing whether you can see light at the end of a passageway when you begin to notice foreign smells as the creepy darkness overpowers and envelops you.

Sulfur, mud, sweat, and salt combined to out-stink low tide in the marshes that lay just before the shores of his family's south New Jersey getaway. Don knew that smell so distinctly. His brain thought of the swampy water and cattails, traversed by bridges leading to the sandy coast where his family and a big plate of lasagna awaited.

The recollection of the blue-green kitchen inside the beach bungalow in Wildwood caused his body to quiver. He missed his mother and realized that he had forgotten what she smelled like. All his mind was able to recall was an image of his sisters and their families. He watched a scene of them cramming into the tiny beach house kitchen, performing their August ritual of cleaning and preparing hot cherry peppers for pickling.

Fiery spice is a must in the southern region of Italy where his ancestors came from. The first time Don tried to help with the peppers when he was a boy ended in humiliation. No one told him to rub his hands with olive oil before handling them. His fingers began to sizzle and burn. When he wiped some sweat from his forehead, a drop of the peppers' oil snuck into his left eye like a mobster with a machine gun. He ran to the sink and splashed water wildly on his face, which exacerbated the pain. His oldest sister Rose wrestled him onto the living room sofa, poured olive oil on his face, and placed a frozen bag of peas on his head. His middle sister Gianna came with a clean cloth and dabbed up the unctuous mess. She instructed him to be still until the fire subsided and his focus returned. Four hours passed before Don felt relief. Sympathy never came from the laughing crew in the kitchen. Even Angie, the sister closest in age to him, danced around in hysterics, mocking his pain.

The murmured giggles continued in the background as Don's grey matter swirled into the dream once again. In the darkened grove, coagulated gunk was moving toward him. Out of the mouth of the sleeping physical body came a curdling shriek. The astral body echoed. The dreamscape became adhesive. He tried to run from the clearing, but something invisible had his feet glued to the ground.

A twiggy branch lurched at him, transforming into a hand. The upside-down Y sprouted a mossy mound of dark and tangled fur at its connection to the trunk. Globe-like protrusions peeled dry bark, which fell to the moist ground, revealing creamy hues and giving forth pinkish nipples.

Don screamed again. Molten eyes slit open in the brutish face of the tree creature. He felt them pierce right through his soul. More splinters and shards fell from cracking lips as the mouth kinked, forming sounds in an unrecognizable language. They were chanting, "Ehyeh-Asher-Ehyeh," which in Hebrew means, "I am that I am." Don had no recollection of this part of the dream after he awoke.

The desire to run ebbed, but his dream self was stuck in an invisible swamp of terror. He wanted to scream, but had lost most of his voice. He wanted to puke, but was empty and could only dry heave. Fear swept through him like a raging river. Sea water reared up and charged forth, swallowing him, sucking him out of the syrupy ground and off his feet. Sudden freedom brought a moment of exhilaration, like the feeling of catching a wave on a boogie board and riding it into shore for the first time. For a brief second, Don had the sensation of flight.

Then the water swelled and he lost control. Excitement and fear elevated as his physical heartbeat and breathing intensified. He felt like he was being eaten, savored, and digested. In the dream, his bladder let loose. In his bed, his sleeping body exploded in an orgasm. As he awoke to a sticky mess on his leg, he heard a woman's voice say,

"Dance with me, baby. I'll take the lead."

Don yelped as he shivered into the reality of his room. The feminine growl seemed to be coming from the corner, near his armoire.

"Mommy! There's a monster in my closet!" screamed Six-year-old Donny.

Completely freaked out, he sat up, wide awake in the clammy bed. Flipping off the top sheet, he hobbled off to the bathroom to clean up. Thirteen-year-old Donny took over, grabbing a washcloth and swiping at the gooey slime.

Damn, thought the present mind. *I haven't done that since I was a teenager.*

Images from the dream began to emerge, inundating his conscious mind. He stopped all movement, including breathing, and tried to put the pieces together. The startling wetness of his awakening confused his ability to make sense of it.

Don sat down on the toilet and held his head in his hands, wondering what the heck had just happened. He'd dreamed strongly before, but never like this. Sitting in his tiny bathroom, he counted the random black tiles on the floor that connected at their corners amid the large groupings of white ones. Doing this had calmed him down since childhood. The tessellating pattern was soothing during disturbing times like overeating or insomnia. Soon he felt relieved and slowly made his way back to his bed.

Staring into the obscurity, Don retched a bit, recalling the construction of the female he had just witnessed. It was horrific and more macabre than any visual epoch he had ever created. At the age of fifteen, he had become obsessed with horror flicks and loved to draw images of their monstrous stars. Back then, a collection of dark comic books and posters from B movies decorated his school books and room. Memory flipped through a Rolodex of drawings and paintings, posters, and movie scenes, looking for a match with no success. He scoured the recent past for a commercial or advertisement that he may have seen that could have conjured up this dream, but to no avail.

Chapter 12

Dawn

Wake up and smell the cheese.

Sleep would not return, although Don shifted from side to side for over an hour. His room went from charcoal grey to the softer shades of the city morning. After what seemed like an eternity, he heard the familiar crowing and cackling of roosters and hens from the Italian Market. He blinked at the ceiling and listened to the gentle mooing of the cows across the street that were awaiting slaughter later that day.

Don's gratitude for the light and sounds of daybreak inspired him to pull on a pair of jeans splattered with oil paint and a grey sweatshirt. He stumbled out of the house, down the street, and around the corner to the doughnut shop. Just like every morning, it was packed with cops. They had good taste; this was the home of the best coffee in town. Don was a supreme connoisseur of caffeine. He visited the doughnut shop most days, figuring that there was no point in making coffee and dealing with the messy grounds. The best morning brew was always ready and waiting, served up by surrogate sisters a half a block away. Seeing how many cops were squished into the tiny orange and white corner store, he wondered who was watching the streets of Brotherly Love.

Don smirked as he ordered a coffee with two creams and three sugars from a thick-boned woman with dark hair and a distinct mustache. Though he was a full-blooded Italian, he had never gotten used to the bristles on his ethnic sisters' faces. The woman behind the counter handed him a paper cup filled with the sweetened and creamed brown liquid, and he cradled it in his hands like a long lost lover. He made his way across to the west-side window and found a perfect place to lean on the tiny Formica counter, his favorite spot to stare out at the intersection of Ninth and Christian Streets. From here he loved to watch the mouth of the Market open wide, accepting tourists and locals into her belly. Traffic sounds steadily increased and filled the air as the morning progressed. A second cup of coffee was purchased as the city awakened.

The fishmonger down the street called out the catch of the day. The sexy babe who owned the spice store began to bring out her large barrels which showed off various crackers, cookies, and sweets. Her sister climbed on a stepladder to hang garlands of spices from the eaves of the shop's wooden porch, while a third wheeled out the coffee display.

The produce guy next door brought out crate after crate of citrus, pears, apples, and plump raw green olives. Soon it would turn cold; the hard, green fruits were a sign of harvest time, which would soon be followed by winter's icy bite.

So many cops swarmed into the doughnut shop that the windows steamed up with their moist buzzing. Don giggled to himself as he pulled a pen from his pocket and doodled on a small napkin. He chuckled at his own cleverness as he drew a picture of pigs dressed as policemen enjoying the morning delights of steaming brew and twisted crullers.

Blinking his attention back out across the intersection, his eyes focused on the pizza joint on the northwest corner. There he saw a girl, a lynx. She was dressed in a chunky, deep-earthy-green sweater and indigo jeans which gripped her curves firmly. A silver belt buckle flashed, but he could not make out its shape. On her feet were velvety lace-up boots with what looked like the bold strokes of Vincent van Gogh on them. Her hair was dark and textured, somewhere between dreadlocks and thick curls. A heavy silver chain with a glimmering amulet accentuated her firm breasts, flashing a searchlight of rainbows. Silver rings adorned almost every finger. She glided past his view and headed south on the west side of Ninth into the Market. Her undulating walk was mesmerizing. It caused Don to spill a little coffee on the brand new white sneaker on his right foot.

Damn, you can never keep anything clean and stain-free? his sister Rose's voice scolded mentally.

It's time to leave, he thought, as he tossed the last sip of his drink into a small trash can. He took off down the street, staying on the east side, trying desperately to track the sultry woman, bumping into crates and people, unable to maintain his concentration or to see where he was going. All the while, his eyes were transfixed on the dark vision which had come into focus through the steamy window of the doughnut shop.

He paused for a moment and realized that the corner trash can had never once—as long as he could remember—been overflowing. Nor had he ever once seen anyone empty it. A spooky shiver crawled up his spine. He shook it off and continued, driven like a hungry wolf keeping its prey in view.

He followed her to The House of Cheese on the northwest corner of Hall, and slipped in unnoticed. Once inside, he walked away from the door and pretended to look at the provolone and prosciutto hanging from the ceiling on beige strings. Continuing on, he walked the length of the back of the store and then watched the dark-haired beauty as she chatted with Anthony Junior. She smiled at the older Giovanni brother behind the counter, and held her hand out for a tiny treat.

"Donny!" a voice called to him. Shocked, he looked up to see Salvatore smiling and handing him a hunk of bread with his favorite Fontina slabbed on top. Don happily accepted the gift and watched as Sal disappeared across the store and into the walk-in refrigerator.

"We should come in here more often without a shopping mission," jabbed Reason from the Boardroom of his mind as Don savored a delicious bite.

"What can I get you today, baby?" the voice of Anthony Junior said from behind the large white cheese case in the front of the store.

"My favorite," the goddess of intrigue purred.

"You've got it, Lilith!" Anthony Junior exclaimed, his hands deftly slicing a delicate taste from a huge beige and red wheel. "Here you go, doll face," he said as he hunched down into the giant enameled case and hoisted out the enormous round of cheese.

"Lilith," Don said slowly and almost silently, taking care to feel the vibration of each letter inside of his mouth.

"Lilith." Lust and Desire sang like a chorus of suitors to a high wind from the base of a turret.

"Lilith," chanted Don, like a dark ballad from a movie about unrequited love.

Lilith, thought Don pensively.

"Lilith," he howled like Marlon Brando in *A Streetcar Named Desire*.

"Lilith," he inhaled deeply, savoring the flavor as splashes of deep blues, crunchy reds, and velvety purples colored the canvas of his mind.

"Lilith?" he questioned as he realized he had never known another soul with this name.

"Lilith," he whispered under his breath.

Just then Lilith flashed a glance in his direction, causing Don to teeter off balance and bang his hip on a huge barrel of salty, oily, jet-black olives.

"Lilith," he mumbled as he watched a mouthful of the sandwich roll in slow motion down into the barrel, leaving a trail of crumbs on his sweatshirt.

"Donny!" bellowed Vinnie, as he stood up from rearranging a display of biscotti near the door.

"What the heck are you doing?" barked Salvatore, who arrived out of thin air, causing the floppy-haired artist to leap a foot off the floor.

"Oh crap!" exclaimed Don. "Sorry."

Don looked down and saw a chunk of his white sandwich swimming among the black slippery fruits. He backed away to prevent more from marching off his chin and into the barrel.

"It's okay, man. I got it. I got it," said Sal, smacking Don's hand out of the way.

"Geeezu," jabbed Vinnie.

"That's what I get for feeding you!" added Sal, laughing.

Everyone in the store burst into laughter. Sal steadied Don by grabbing a fistful of the artist's sweatshirt.

Lilith whipped around to see who the clown was. That was the moment they made eye contact for the first time. That was the first clear picture she saw of him. There he was, crumbs and stains and drool. It was all she could do to keep from doubling over as she cracked up in delicious peals of laughter. Her belly heaved under the thick chenille of her sweater. She tried to hold it in, feeling the muscles jump, but it was too funny.

"Nice one, Donny," she cooed.

Inside his head, a tiny boy's voice danced and sang, *She said my name, she said my name.* His inner child leapt and rolled down the streets of his mind on a scooter, drifting into a full-blown daydream.

Don imagined he was thirteen and Lilith was twelve. They were on his scooter, flying down the sidewalks of Tenth Street toward South. She held onto him, her arms twined around his waist from behind, her grasp velvety and divine. In his blissful fantasy, a younger, sweeter version of this creature—smaller and more tameable—played the female role.

An image flashed into his mind in a breath. His home studio; Lilith lying on a pedestal, naked. Don had just finished powdering her body so she glistens like a marble statue. Thick dark locks of hair roll and curl to her waist. He walks to his easel and picks up his brush, dipping the soft bristles into a deep maroon wad of oily pigment, blending it with some violet, and painting the first undulating mark on a large, square canvas.

Just then, Don practically fell over into the barrel where Sal was fishing out the chunk of sandwich, now stuck to tainted olives. All Don could manage to do was wobble, smirk, and drool a bit. His left pocket tightened as his excitement grew, pressing against his wallet. He couldn't believe it was possible to humiliate himself further, yet his body was trying its best to prove him wrong. He tried to think of his sisters' body hair and their nagging to counterbalance the exhilaration he was experiencing.

"For God's sake!" shouted Reason. "This is neither the place nor the time for this kind of display!"

"Did you want something?" smirked Sal, fully aware of an almost tangible web of energy between Lilith and Don.

"No, I'm good. Not right now," Don called over a shoulder as he headed toward the door.

"Madonne!" barked Anthony, inspiring more laughter from the other people in the store.

Outside on the sidewalk, Don collected himself. He shifted the contents of his pocket and headed north on Hall Street, towards home, thinking it would be best to cool off in an icy shower.

"Yes," Reason affirmed, "a very icy shower!"

He turned the corner faster than a speed skater, muttering to himself as he walked in the direction of his tiny, three-story house. Mocking himself and shaking his curly black locks, he counted the cracks in the sidewalk and ignored all the sounds and smells drifting away as he left the Market behind.

Quietly, with the gentle padding of a stalking wildcat, Lilith followed him. She kept her distance and watched as he stopped to fish keys out of his jeans. She sized up his body and imagined what it would feel like to press against him. He was strong—she could see the lines of his biceps under the heathery sweatshirt. He was slightly disheveled but, as any woman would see, a good fixer-upper. A kaleidoscope of rich colors splattered designs on the legs of his jeans. *A painter*, she mused with an impish smile.

Don wrestled the key into the brass lock and opened the door. Turning to close it, he saw her standing directly across from his stoop in the middle of the tiny street, staring at him. He called out "Lilith!" just as he was about to shut the door.

She smiled and walked toward him.

"Oh my God, oh my God, oh my God!" screamed the Horny Teen inside Don's head. He couldn't believe this was happening.

"Would you like to come in?" he fumbled.

"No, no thanks. I think you should come out here and take a walk with me," she responded, holding out her cheese. "But first, would you put this in your fridge and keep it cool for me?"

Stupefied that this was possible, he reached for the white plastic bag.

"Sure, no problem," he said casually as his inner boy was springing on a brand new trampoline of bliss.

"Thanks. Let's go!" commanded Lilith as she handed him her shopping bag and reached for his free hand.

"Wait! Give me a second!" he smiled.

The siren stopped and stared at him from the threshold, tilting her head. Don took the bag from her perfectly formed hands bedecked with silver rings and walked to the kitchen. As he bent over to put it inside the refrigerator, he was shielded from her view behind the open door. He took advantage of the opportunity to peek inside her bag.

"Inconceivable," he whispered to himself. He couldn't believe that her favorite cheese was the same as his—Italian Fontina. Not the cheap stuff with the slimy tan coating, but the top-shelf brand with the thick,

chocolate-colored, waxy skin and a complex, nutty flavor.

Don was completely shocked and dismayed that this dark creature found him interesting enough to ask for a parking place for her cheese. He was elated that she was confident enough to leave her dairy products in his care. Now he was the guardian of her lactose, and he wore his pride like the breastplate of an ancient milk warrior, ready and willing to defend her creamy kingdom.

He swirled back into his boyhood fantasy world of knights and ladies in waiting. He recalled a story that he had loved about a wounded monarch and his journey of self-discovery. Then last night's dream rushed into his senses, causing him to teeter and bump his head on the refrigerator door.

"Are you all right in there?" questioned Lilith as she craned her neck to see what the floppy-haired painter was doing to cause such a clamor.

"Yeah. Just finding the perfect place for your cheese, milady— wouldn't want there to be any trouble in there while we're gone." Silently, he scolded himself. *What the heck am I saying? She's going to think I'm such a loser.*

"We are a loser," chimed the Nebbish. "It's obvious that she's way out of our league."

"There's no way we are getting any today," said the Playboy, pulling off his satin robe to reveal flannel pajamas adorned with monkey faces.

"Mine!" squealed the Toddler, reaching for the Playboy's leg.

"Can someone please get this off me!" demanded the Playboy.

"When are you going to get that we are all one!" shouted the Collective.

"I love living near the Market, don't you, Don?" called Lilith, giving up on a visual connection and choosing instead to take a few steps inside to look at the artwork on the living room wall. A ceramic nude caught her eye. It was somewhere between sculpture, bas-relief, and painting. The textures and colors were amazing. It was as if the piece drew her into its tiniest details.

Where has she been all my life? Don pondered, watching her.

The Boardroom table exploded in an overlapping uproar. "She lives here?" screamed Doubt.

"Oh my God! Why have I never seen her?" shrieked Low Self-esteem.

"How can this be? I've been here for three years!" calculated Reason and continued, "I shopped here before I moved here!'

Doubt chimed in, "I know everyone here. What the heck is the matter with me? Why have we never crossed paths?"

"Shut up! I need to talk with her!" interjected Consciousness.

Don peered around the dividing wall of the kitchen that created the entry to the original part of his little trinity house. He caught Lilith staring deeply, with wonder and admiration, at one of his older clay nudes.

She felt his stare and began to flip her head around, but somehow caught it in time to make it more of a melting slither.

"This is awesome!" she exclaimed, pointing to the clay bas-relief on the wall. "How did you get this texture on the skin and the detail of the fabric the model is reclining on?"

"I pressed a piece of lace into the clay" he answered. *Wow! She gets the art thing!* thought Don. Then, wondering where she had come from, he asked, "Where's your place?"

"I used to rent a room from my friend Katy, down on Eighth and Catherine. Two months ago, I got a third floor flat in an incredible building over on Tenth and Bainbridge. It's owned by an amazing artist named…"

"Valentine," punctuated Don.

"So you know him?"

"Any artist in the city worth his tube of aquamarine knows him!

Yes, I paint there sometimes in the open studio sessions—well, at least I used to."

"Dude, we have not been there for, like, years," said the Stoner, recalling some sweet Maui Wowie Don had smoked in the courtyard during a studio break.

"I haven't been there in a long time," Don resumed as his eyes searched her face and began to imprint her every pore into visual memory.

"Really? I've been doing pastels there lately," grinned Lilith.

Snapping out of it, Don first asked, "Which flat is yours?" and then continued in a knowing, more self-assured tone, "I know the building well and, now that I think about it, it's been more than a few months since I've been over there."

"Nice save, dude," jibed the Stoner.

"I guess we were destined to meet today!" said Lilith, recalling the eye contact when he was in the doughnut shop. *What the heck is he doing in there with my cheese?* she wondered. With a convincing smile, she stepped to the side of the armchair and leaned in to get a clearer view.

Don stood in a daze, his attention fixed on a Dunkin' Doughnuts coffee mug sitting precariously on top of the fridge.

What is that doing there? he wondered. The image of the brown and tan logo took him back to his junior year of art school and his girlfriend Amanda.

They'd met a few days before the first semester of her freshman year began. Amanda was weighing and mixing dry ingredients to make her first batch of clay in the dusty grey clay studio on Pine Street. Taking full advantage of his junior status, Donny snuck up on her to flaunt his knowledge and hopefully get lucky with the luscious, curvy freshman.

Amanda was no stranger to wolves, and her bullshit meter activated spontaneously upon encountering the edge of Don's energy field. She watched his quirky movement around the studio and assessed his advice regarding the collective equipment. He did know what he was talking about, and all of his technical advice became the foundation of her practices in the ceramic studio, the place that would become her sanctuary for the next two years. Don and Amanda became obsessed with the coffee mugs from Dunkin' Donuts and went on a mission to collect as many different versions as they could get their hands on. He reached up to touch the mug and remembered the sound of her laughter, quickly followed by the growl of her father's threats.

Don floated into her life and had parked in what Amanda's father had wished was a more clearly marked tow-away zone. The pair had a torrid affair, much to Amanda's parents' dismay. Between the arguments with her father and two years of hauling Don through a port of confusion, Amanda cut the lines and cruised off to find herself. Though hurt and frustrated at first by the way this had all played out, Amanda wasn't the type to harbor regrets. She let Don down as easily as she knew how, explaining that if they stayed together, she would be broke and that the relationship was doomed. Don dove into his art and renounced women for months. Amanda bounced back quickly, hoisted her sails, and landed in Barbados, where she sells paintings to tourists on the beach.

Lilith walked into the kitchen and stood staring at Don holding the coffee mug. He sensed her presence and broke the uncomfortable silence. "The Market is great," Don began, inspiring Lilith to heave a sigh of relief. "I love never having to…"

"Keep anything in the fridge!" Lilith said, finishing his sentence and displaying a supportive smile for Don. She thought about how it takes more muscles to smile than it does to frown, and likewise how more muscles are needed to wave hello than to flip the bird.

Chapter 13

Maya

Celestial tools are needed to negotiate illusion.

"Curiously enough, it takes more seconds to continue a positive thought than one that is negative," the Gandharva chimed in.

"Oh, for goodness sake!" squealed Lilith from her rocker. "Whose dreamscape is this, anyway?"

"It belongs to all of us, little one," soothed the spirit guide. He continued, "It is up to all of us to learn to dig way down beneath the surface. Things are usually not as they appear. We often react, which freezes thoughts into a one-dimensional point in time and space. Some have the ability to relax, breathe, and be guided through these moments. That is where all the next-craze, self-help, fad-routines come from. When we are able to expand our vision to see a greater vista than originally perceived, we find that all things are made up of essential energy. This is the heart of everything, from any initial idea or seemingly material object to what humans perceive themselves to be."

Lilith heaved a deep, knowing sigh in agreement and settled back into the steady rhythmic creaks of her rocking chair.

The creature continued, "Energy and thought travel in a helical pattern. A negative thought spirals and generates more negative thoughts within sixty seconds. A positive thought needs ninety-one seconds to regenerate. So there it is. It takes a lot more work to be happy and cause happiness. This is the great secret that everyone is trying to cash in on."

"And tell me again why I am so fortunate as to have you in my life, in this existence?" she questioned, one eyebrow arched and a slight smirk on her lips.

"Ah, my little one. My kind is trying to evolve, just as your kind is."

"My kind?"

"Yes. You know you are not like the other children!" Peals of laughter shook the winged guardian off his perch on the great tree from which his oration had come, ringing in her ears like a dissonant wind chime. His wings opened just before he hit the ground, causing him to loop-de-loop like a paper airplane with a properly pinch-folded nose.

"So," she began as her laughter subsided, "you believe our ability to cross the dimensional gateway, and our openness to discover that we can communicate in other realms, is a major puzzle piece in our dharmic evolution?"

"At least for the pair of us it is, my little cherub!" he said, tickling the tip of her nose with an unusually long wing feather. "Languages that we have no idea exist are at the tips of our tongues, and ideas we never perceived possible are within the grasp of our reach, right now."

"Makes me feel even smaller than I am, and how great the grand plan is!"

"This is most assuredly why we have been chosen!" And with that, he flew off toward a pinkish cloud in the distance.

Chapter 14

Embarking

Life is a great adventure and so is this very next step.

Lilith backed up a few steps in Don's living room, noticing a rosy-toned light flash across the back wall of the kitchen as Don stood up and placed the mug he had been holding on the counter.

"So, where shall we go?" he asked politely, bowing just a bit.

"Who are you, dude?" asked the Stoner, scrunching his face in dismay.

"Really?" asked Low Self-esteem. "Is this the best we have?"

"How about South Street?" suggested Lilith with a wide grin as she turned and headed for the front door. She hopped down the stoop and landed on the sidewalk like a ballerina. "The Market is so alive," she exclaimed, swinging around, her eyes catching a striking angle of Don's face gleaming in a sunbeam. It was one of several shafts of light shooting down through a fluffy cloud. Lilith called this type of light God rays, and one was glinting off the painter's face. She could see blues and purples on his cheek, and a flash of green in his hair. "It's so cool to be able to roll out of bed and get what you need for the day, right?" Lilith continued with an elfin gesture. "I never keep anything in my fridge for more than three days."

"Me either," responded Don, twisting his expression into agreement.

She really does live near here if she knows that secret, he thought.

Don watched as she skipped down the pavement and paused to observe her against the orangey brick wall across the alley. He wanted to grab her, carry her upstairs, and paint her. Instead, he locked the door and walked quickly to catch up. The two headed up the sidewalk toward Tenth Street.

"I thought you wanted to go to South Street," said Don. "Why are you walking toward Tenth?"

"I just want to go this way!" she insisted, continuing on. The real reason was that she didn't need all the newsy eyes watching her down at the Market, and then reporting to the Spice Sisters about this. *No*, she thought, *it's better to keep this a mystery for now.*

They turned the corner and headed north up Tenth toward South Street. As they crossed Christian, Lilith asked, "Do you ever buy ravioli over there?" pointing to the home of what had to be the best ravioli factory in the city.

"Of course! I think all the better restaurants in South Philly get it from there," said Don, trying not to sound too nerdy.

"So do the real Italian mamas!" Lilith teased. "Mmm, you should cook me some," she cooed.

"Me, cook? Nah. You should make me a big plate with gravy!" responded the Roman Warrior.

"It's so amazing to have someone cook for you, isn't it?" Lilith reminisced. "As a child, I loved to come home after spending time in the woods near where I grew up, in Bucks County, to a warm family meal. Have you been there?"

"To dinner with my family? Yes!"

"No! To Bucks County."

"No, I haven't. Usually when I leave the city, I go to New York or down the shore. My family has a house in Wildwood that's just a block from the beach."

"Ugh, Wildwood!" groaned Lilith. "The land of plastic and cheesy glitz! Or should I say "swamp"?"

"Hey! Be nice! Sounds like you've only been on the north end."

"No, I've spent time in Cape May, too."

"My family's house is all the way at the south end of the beach, almost in Cape May."

"Oh, that's better. The town is downright icky! I can tolerate the south end, though. The cute little clapboard houses are all different colors, and the beaches are really nice there. All the way at the end there's a funky little bar where an amazing guy plays the guitar and sings while he plays bass with his foot on organ peddles. Have you seen him? He looks like Robbie Robertson."

"Yeah, I have," he said, turning his eyes downward. Don was an aspiring guitar player, but that guy was the bomb, almost inhuman in his immense talent. Many afternoons, Don had gone there for a beer and stood just outside under the tiki overhang with his bare feet in the sand, studying the guitarist. He was a monster, seemingly an octopus. This guy never read a lyric from a sheet and could cover so many styles it seemed impossible. Don secretly wanted to be that guy.

Lilith detected a sensitive point and decided to wait until he spoke again, although she had no idea what the issue was. The two walked past the playground and stopped spontaneously by a tiny sapling growing through a crack in the concrete.

"So, you like the woods?" asked Don, grateful for the inspiration.

Relieved that the awkward silence had ended, Lilith took in a deep breath and responded, "I loved to play in the woods when I was a kid. My friends and I took thick, green moss and twigs and built houses for the fairies. If we had the luck of finding pinecones, we would use them as decorations for the roofs and doorways. Did you know that there are thirteen anti-clockwise spirals flowing from the center of a pinecone?"

"Who talks like that?" cowered Low Self-esteem.

"Anti-clockwise?" quizzed Reason.

"I thought she was an American!" jowled Judgment.

"No, I didn't know that," said Don. The members of the Boardroom chaotically buzzed, "Geez! This girl is talkative."

Lilith continued, "I was never the type of child who ran around, out of control. What I really loved—and still do—is creating things with my hands and putting my mind to good use. I guess that's how I got into art. How did it start for you?"

"My grandfather was a craftsman from Southern Italy. He was a master stonemason, brought here by the city of Philadelphia to build the cobblestone streets."

"Really? That's amazing!"

All members of the Board stood up and cheered in a flurry of ticker tape and confetti.

"I was always content to sit and draw or paint or make something. Even "Incredible Edibles" could keep me busy for a long time," Lilith offered.

"I remember those!" Don exclaimed, smiling. "My sisters used to make those and try to get me to eat them. I still can't stand the look of gummy candies!"

"Are you hungry?" asked Lilith.

"Are you kidding me?" Don retorted.

"Well, kind of," grinned the goddess, reaching over and poking him in the ribs. She took off running down the street, prancing like a pony, weaving around trees and ending in a spiral, laughing like a hyena.

"No, not right now," called a quickly shrinking Don, "but maybe in a while, if you switch the subject."

"We're doomed!" screeched Low Self-esteem.

"Should we run or not?" Lethargy apathetically whined to the Board.

"Run!" the conglomerate shrieked back, standing and fisting the table so that it shook the edges of Don's mind.

He tried not to puff as he caught up to her, and continued as if there had not been an embarrassing interruption.

"I started drawing when I was about eight. Monsters and cartoons were my thing back then. Also music—I play guitar."

Good one! jabbed the voice of his older sister. *Every chick loves a guitar player.*

"Oh, my mama warned me," said Lilith. "Never date a guitar player!" She turned her back to him and took off once again.

"What is with this chick?" questioned Casanova, twisting the end of his moustache between his middle finger and thumb.

"Oh, give it up, dude," chided the Stoner.

Don chased after her, laughing out loud, giddy as a homecoming queen who had just accepted an invitation to the prom. He couldn't remember the last time he felt so free. Even the air tasted different in his mouth. It seemed surreal to experience this much joy. Under a large maple tree up ahead, he could see that she had stopped to gaze up into the thick foliage. Her head tilted back as her eyes closed. Her chest moved gracefully as she absorbed the subtle music played by the gleaming leaves in the late summer breeze.

"Listen to the rhythm of this tree," Lilith sang.

"The rhythm of the tree?" asked Don.

"Yes. All things vibrate. They produce light and color. Light is sound and its frequency is measurable. Everything has a number. All things have beats and melodies, and this tree is playing a symphony!" Lilith's hand moved in a graceful gesture as if conducting the orchestra of sound she perceived.

Don shifted his weight, creating a more centered stance. He took his hands out of his pockets, closed his eyes, and tilted his head back as he had seen her do. The light skipped on his cheeks, and he found himself listening with his entire body to the shimmering sounds. The amount of variation and texture he began to notice was incredible.

Sensations shot through him at warp speed. This took him back to the first time he had stood in front of a van Gogh painting at the Metropolitan Museum of Art. The great master's huge canvases were paying a visit to the northeast. Don came around the corner to find himself face-to-face with *Starry Night* and spontaneously burst out crying. The intensity of the strokes and the thickness of the paint moved him to tears. He had seen it for years in books, but had no idea what it would feel like. It was passion and music captured in texture and color. Standing next to Lilith, listening to the leaves, gave him the same feeling. He felt a welling in his eyes and squeezed them shut before opening them very slowly. The light gently flooded in and Lilith came into focus. She took a tiny bell out of her pocket and held it out, awaiting his hand.

"Put this in your left pocket," she instructed. "Make it an offering to your own inner music. When you walk, you'll hear the sound of your receptive side."

He complied and placed the tiny silver chime in his jeans pocket. They continued on and, as they did, Don became aware of a humble song played out by the motion and stillness of his stride. This new cognizance opened him up to even more movement and sound. He noticed the rolling of a plastic bag blowing down the sidewalk and its punctuating slap as it hit a chain-link fence. Children laughed in the distance in squeaks and pops, and lilting melodies floated in the air. A group of boys came out to play basketball at the Palumbo playground. The sounds of their sneakers squeaking, along with the bounce of the ball, created an African rhythm as they took to the court.

Don and Lilith began to walk again and, though their lips were silent, the mysterious music of breath and the tiny bell in Don's pocket joined in resonance with the sounds of South Philadelphia. The vibrations entrained and became an honoring song and a prayer of love and hope, splashing the rhythm of life into the air.

These sounds reminded Don of the importance music played in his world. It always set the mood in any space while he worked or relaxed. He thought about how a baby learns to crawl in a hand-knee, hand-knee pattern, and how that is the driving rhythm of forward movement, like the merengue.

Don had played guitar for most of his life. His biggest dream was to have a rock band and paint the covers of his albums, just like Joni Mitchell had done. Though he grasped the concepts of chords and harmony and his poetry was strong, he just didn't have the intensity of a front man or solo act. It was obvious that his true calling lay in his grasp of "the art of seeing." His talent was to translate the feelings his eyes generated through the golden gate of his third chakra into drawing, painting, and sculpture.

Wanting to impress the enchantress, Don paused after crossing Fitzwater as they came upon a chocolate-brown brick building. It was an almost perfect cube. The architecture was much different than the deep red bricks of the row houses punctuated with staunch white marble stoops that lined the entire block across the street. The bricks of this building were burnt sienna, and mahogany sills graced noticeably smaller openings for its windows and doors.

"Do you know this building?" Don asked, and then continued before she could answer. "It was believed to have been a part of the Underground Railroad."

"Yes! I know it well, as a matter of fact."

"Of course she does!" cringed Low Self-esteem.

Lilith went on to say, "A friend of mine tried to sell me this house a couple of years ago. He said that Harriet Tubman had owned it. He told me that when his boys gutted the place to begin the renovation, they found all sorts of artifacts buried in the walls and in the dirt floor of the basement."

"A friend of yours?" challenged Don. "I heard a mobster owned this place—the one who thinks he's Frank Sinatra, always riding around in a baby-blue Caddy with a cup of espresso in his hand."

"Yeah, that's the one. He does own it! He owns a lot of properties in Bella Vista. He was planning to give it to his son, but the family is already too big for it."

"Why didn't you buy it?"

"I love it and the location—and believe me, I tried to—but it's too expensive for my budget. I rent instead."

Don couldn't believe their connection. It was as if they had crossed paths over and over without seeing one another—or maybe he had been invisible the whole time.

"Cloaked like a starship!" chirped the Adolescent Geek.

Lilith continued, "I decided I wanted to be higher up in a building," she shrugged, shaking off the fact that her dear old dad did not think buying property for her was a good investment. "Besides, I prefer being on top," the Devi continued as her left eyebrow rose and her nose scrunched, "and I was offered a top floor loft, looking out over the most beautiful courtyard. So I took that instead."

"A courtyard here, in the Market?" quizzed Don. He knew of only one such place, and to get an apartment there was impossible.

"Slightly off the Market. Right here, actually."

"You live in Valentine's palace?" he questioned.

She nodded. "Yes, right up there!" She pointed to an open window on the top floor, where a paisley curtain had blown out and was draped along the brick facade. The silence signaled that the Shankar album had long since ended.

"Unbelievable!" exclaimed Don. "Why didn't you say so earlier?"

"I started to. Actually, I thought I did. I guess you just weren't hearing me! Are we really relating?"

Chapter 15

Hologram

The continuum keeps on keepin' on.

The Great Mother Goddess rolled over and from her luscious, curvy body sprung massive mountains reaching upward to the sky, covered with thick blankets of green. A rainbow of bubbles floated down from the Divine Father and mixed with her murky, deep waters. These cast colored waves upon the shores of Mother's abundant body. As they met, swirling patterns formed in her sands. A grouping of purplish-blue bubbles sunk to the bottom of the thick waters and spontaneously began to morph. Within them, new life beat in a rhythmic pulse.

A flap of wings caused a shudder to run up Lilith's spine. High in the branches of the humongous tree, the angelic creature crouched like a crow, observing the sunrise.

"What is it about relationships?" Lilith quipped as she opened her eyes and focused on the muscular curves of the great creature. She thought, *He really is quite buff. Must be all that flying around.*

"It is just how we roll," jibed the winged one, cocking his head to the side.

"How you glide is more like it, don't you think?" giggled Lilith, smiling. "Continue, please."

"What do you mean, dear one? Which question would you like me to address first?"

"Just the one about relationships. Please, my devoted guardian, tell me your feelings about them. They seem to be like towers that we build, only to knock them down. Then we build another on the rubble of the aftermath."

"Yes, you human beings often opt to scramble from one relationship to the next. It is as if you are moving holes."

"Moving holes?"

"Yes, moving holes. If you dig a hole, you have a pile of dirt. So you dig another hole to put the dirt into, but then you have another pile of dirt."

Lilith's face screwed into her classic question-mark expression, inspiring her companion to continue.

"The funny thing is—at least to my kind, as we watch you humans—that you only see the holes." The Gandharva began to laugh so hard that his feathers trembled and took on a rosy hue that quickly turned to violet and green. Lilith loved to watch the snowy white of this being change colors like an aluminum Christmas tree in the beam of a creaking rotary light. She laughed as he went on.

"You all feel so empty that you try to fill the space with food and drink and the attention of another. You take and take and take. You eat and drink until your bodies are so filled with putrefaction that you can't think and feel, so you continue to pile it in. The sad thing is that you never empty completely. It would be in the emptying that you would find what you are looking for—the sensation that you are never alone or separate in the first place."

"But you have taught me exactly this, haven't you?"

"Yes, it has been my mission and assignment to teach you and guide you and somehow, without my doing, you got it."

"I did, huh?"

"Yes, you did! At a very early age, you realized there was so much more to life than playing house and shacking up. Most importantly, you realized that completion was more important than beginning new projects. I have to hand it to you," he said, plucking a feather from his right wing and placing it on top of the book in her lap. "You know how to finish what you start."

"And where has it gotten me? I am alone on this island with only you, your consort, and my memories."

"No, sweetheart. You must look at the positives. You know there is so much more to be grateful for. I have shown you your infinity, and you are already connected. You are the greater and, at the same time, you are a drop of water in the Ocean of Cosmic Consciousness."

"Yes, you are right; I know better."

"Word."

"Hey! What did I tell you about that silly teen lingo?"

"I like it!"

"Word!" they said in unison, inspiring fits of laughter.

"I know," Lilith said after she caught her breath. "I get it—we humans can search and crave and devour, but unless we desire to merge with the great Ocean of the Divine Bliss, we stay hungry. So, therefore, if we build up the ideas of relationships and tear them down when they appear not to be what we want, we are left with the rubble of destruction. The demolition leaves the ground more conceptual and, like insects, we humans yearn to reestablish and rebuild."

"It is the animal mind that drives you to try again. Nothing can be built on a sketchy foundation."

"Ah, yet another trick of the limbic brain."

"Yes. And speaking of tricks, do you remember when you gave up on men altogether? You had a series of bad relationships and then renounced the whole idea!"

"Saruk AUM! Did you have to bring this up? Today of all days!" The Gandharva started at the sound of his name. His ward had so rarely

uttered it lately.

"Yes," the angel said as he plucked a small feather from his left wing and proceeded to use the quill end to clean between his teeth. "Yes, apparently, I did. There seems to be…" he began, waving his hand around Lilith's head, "some residuals in here. My darling one, some days the energy is high, and on others it is challenged. It is in the stillness and quiet space that you are able to dive deep into the soul to have a look. This is a great opportunity for evolution, for growth. Tell the story. Maybe this time you can clear it out," he said, letting the feather drop to the ground. As it gently touched down, a mist of blue-green bubbles sprayed up like a geyser. In the clearing vapor, a striking female version of the guardian appeared.

"Yes. You decided to go out on a girls' night out with Yvonne," said the female Apsara, Ambo Shanti, dusting off a spray of shimmering bubbles. She turned to Saruk AUM and asked, "You called for me, my darling?"

"Yes, I must have," he replied, raising an eyebrow and smirking. His wings fanned the last of the bubbles away from his complement's face, allowing him to stare deep into the liquid pools of her eyes.

"As I recall," continued the seraphim, "your friend Yvonne was tired of her man not wanting to tie the knot, right? His argument was that they were common-law bound, so what was the point?"

"He was so paranoid about rocking boats or shifting even a single hair," continued Saruk AUM.

"Yes, and we all know the Divine has a great sense of humor!" chirped the celestial nymph. This caused the two winged beings to glow like luminescent rainbows of light.

"So Yvonne came to meet you at work when you were done for the day. Remember?"

"Of course I remember! You go over this story all the time, like a tape loop!"

"Ah, that is the precursor to getting it! Identification! Good. We all have carts filled with this sort of baggage that we drag down the same paths over and over. This causes very deep ruts, and the more we trudge through them, the deeper we sink." Saruk AUM paused to see if Lilith was getting his point. "So would you like to tell it this time?" he asked.

"Sure," she responded, knowing exactly what he meant for her to do. "I was working at that cute little boutique in New Hope, selling satin and silk couture. At the time, Yvonne and I were on a roll, going out for drinks and dinner, and then dancing every Friday night. Our intention was to completely ignore men."

"Do you remember meeting Matt?"

"You had to go there right now?" Lilith's head sunk forward, and a single tear crept down her cheek and came to rest on her chin. She wanted to frown and flip the bird at the winged beasts who were prodding her with life lessons. Matt had been the ten-year education about marriage that she was in no mood to relive again.

"Don't bother with the rude hand gestures!" scolded the Apsara, reading her mind like an open book. "You know it takes more muscles to smile than it does to frown and, likewise, more muscles are needed to wave than to flip the bird."

Lilith knew these curious algorithms regarding positivity. Likewise she knew the clock was ticking and that this must be turned around in the next fifty-nine seconds with the addition of another thirty-two to create a positive spiral. If she failed, the winged sentries would be on her like white on rice.

To make it happen, she opted to press her fingers into the corners of her mouth and force a grin upon her face while repeating, "happy, happy, happy," for the required minute and a half. This sent the Gandharva and Apsara into peals of laughter that caused Lilith to join in and really feel a shift in her feelings. After a few minutes the three were in hysterics, tears streaming down their collective cheeks.

When the hilarity settled, Saruk AUM commended Lilith on her ability to break the swirl of negative thought that would potentially have been damaging.

"It is true," belched the Sun Disk. "Thoughts travel in a helical pattern. A negative thought spirals and generates more negative thoughts in sixty seconds. A positive thought needs ninety-one seconds to regenerate."

"Who said that?" blinked the Serpent, flashing one eye open.

"It takes a lot more work to be joyful and generate happiness," fluttered a newly hatched purple trilobite, which had been resting on the enormous sandy-bottomed lake near the freshly forming shoreline.

"Yes, little being," the Sun Disk replied. "This is one of the great secrets that everyone is trying to cash in on." He then exhaled a magnetic wave and hurled it toward the glassy surface of the great water. The force of energy caused the sea to stir. This in turn inspired an endless army of trilobites to sprout linguini-like fins, which allowed them to lift off the silty bottom and swim toward the developing beach. Soon the pasta-like appendages became stable, and some of the creatures began to move like centipedes. Others inched like caterpillars. Once on land, they found grass to eat and rocks to burrow under.

"What the heck is cashsss?" hissed the Serpent.

The night Lilith had met Matt, her best friend Yvonne had called her at the boutique a few hours before closing. Yvonne announced that she was coming by to pick Lilith up after work, and that the two had reservations for dinner at their favorite bistro on the corner.

Lilith was always ready for an adventure, especially on the weekends, and had a change of clothes stashed in her backpack. When Yvonne showed up, Lilith was already changed and locking up the front door.

"Are you ready?" asked Yvonne.

"Of course I am! Can't you see me locking the door, girl?"

"Of course I can!" snapped Yvonne, trying to stay serious as she held back her laughter.

"Let's go then!" Lilith smirked.

"Okay then!" Yvonne smiled, opening her arms wide.

"Allrighty, then!" Lilith exclaimed, falling into her friend's sisterly embrace as the two cracked up.

"I'm hungry!" said Lilith, offering her elbow to Yvonne.

"Me too!" Yvonne replied, weaving her arm into Lilith's as the pair strutted off toward the restaurant.

After the entrees were cleared and a second round of red wine had been sipped, the two headed to Zadars, a local club where they proceeded to cut loose on the dance floor. They had enforced their sacred pact to not give males any attention and just immerse themselves in the joys of sisterhood. Yvonne told Lilith that she had simply had it with her longtime boyfriend, Panos, on the walk to the club. To celebrate this, she declared this night devoted to girls only!

For some reason, the plan completely backfired. The more they thought about it being "just us girls," the more men wanted to be with them. Yvonne had grown so weary of trying to get her live-in boyfriend to fully commit. The two had been together longer than any other couple Lilith knew. After that night of dancing, Yvonne would return home extremely late, have amazing make-up sex with Panos, and—with the magical blending of DNA—create Sadie, the most adorable baby girl Lilith had ever known. The pregnancy, in turn, would seal the deal, and finally Panos popped the question.

In an overwhelming display of love and gratitude, Yvonne's parents finally had the opportunity to give their daughter the wedding of their dreams. Yvonne chose a tasteful Pocono resort for the occasion. Her dad was so overjoyed that he flew in the best mariachi band he could afford from Mexico. The band was such an important part of the event that the wedding date was planned around the musician's schedule.

"What is it that makes us more attracted and attractive when we focus on the opposite of our perceived desire?" asked Lilith.

"Opposites attract!" Saruk AUM exclaimed, hovering just above Lilith.

"Oh, for goodness sake!"

"Somehow you knew I would say that," he said, landing gently on the arm of the chair.

"Right," groaned Lilith as her eyes rolled up toward the grey sky.

"There is an odd paradoxical energy that works with us regarding the laws of attraction," Saruk AUM said. The statement caused him to flush a pinkish hue.

"I know," Lilith empathized. "We have either known someone who desperately wants to be in a relationship, or have been that person. They try and try—and fail. They want and wish, but no matter what they do, they can't seem to manifest a mate. Then, when the same person gives up and lets it all go, they seem to call in exactly what they had been asking for previously."

"Precisely!"

"What about being able to maintain a relationship without causing a mess? What is the best way to keep one going and growing?"

"Ah, good question, little one. Relationships are like gardens that need to be nurtured and cared for. Just like a garden, a relationship is conceptualized, planted, and grounded. It needs sustenance, cleaning, and clearing, but most importantly it needs love. Relationships must be fed with inspiration and passion. They need to be watered regularly with emotional clearing. The negative thoughts and unprocessed pain in a relationship are like weeds that choke and eventually kill it.

"When two people come together, the relationship they form becomes a separate entity. It has a life and breath all its own. Unfortunately, no one is ever taught this. Most people figure it out the hard way—living the archetypical roles necessary for the evolution of the individual soul.

The sooner we understand this, the quicker we cease making mistakes. Couples experience a quantum shift when they wake up to the fact that their union is a third being."

Saruk AUM watched as Lilith's eyes blurred into the distant waters. She drifted off into a meditative space, absorbing the lesson the Gandharva had given.

The silence was broken when Saruk AUM began to sing a little melody. "You are an image of the Goddess, my little one."

"You are right!" agreed Lilith, returning abruptly from her trance.

Saruk AUM raised a feathery eyebrow and continued, "You possess the power of attraction; you are Venus, you are Aphrodite."

"I am the Goddess of attraction," sang Lilith. "I am Aphrodite, I am the Goddess, I am the Goddess," her voice harmonized.

"Yes. This magnetism is what draws others to you and you to them. Venus induces a flowing river of enchantment. Some days we gently coast on her currents and, on others, we are swept uncontrollably downstream by her intense force."

"Really? So please explain to me why I am here on this floating mud pie, alone, with you."

"Alone is a figment. You know we are never alone, and I am but a wisp of energy that is and always has been a part of you. True, I am a guardian, not an equal. I am but a humble servant and can never be your match. But we are not together."

"I have known that all along!"

"You tried so hard for so long to find a connection, like so many who spend their entire lives searching."

"But all of you seem to have partners!" responded Lilith.

"True, we have counterparts, but we are all on separate assignments, each completely driven to fulfill our duties to the Divine first and foremost before any personal satisfaction."

"That sounds intense."

"It is funny to me how you humans turn to religion in the hope that being a part of a group will fill the gap between you and the Immortal. The humor is that you are immortal, and there is no such thing as separation. There never has been. I have watched you, Lilith dear, go through many relationships and friendships, straining to fill the gaping hole at your core. It has tortured me beyond belief to watch you struggle and take on people, places, and things to ease your feeling of loneliness."

"Well, now I am here," said Lilith, "and I guess that I have finally gotten the message that I never need to settle for less than that which I truly desire."

"True. So many people find that in the situations they manifest, there is no happiness."

"What is it about our need to connect? When does that begin?" Lilith asked.

"The primary attraction on the physical plane occurs when the sperm and egg that create the physical body are uncontrollably attracted to one another. It is the power of two, of duality, and—if grace is upon you—polarity."

"Saruk AUM, can you please give me a little more to work with?"

"On a spiritual level, two is the symbol of souls attracting to the Divine. The magic of the number two is the initial feeling of spirituality. It is the first time the senses perceive that there is no such thing as complete aloneness and, at the same time, a deep knowing that there is a greater force outside of what is perceived as self. Self is just a projection of scattered electric pulses coming from the ego mind."

"So how does this occur with another human being?"

"The key to understanding this is held in the concept of being. Religions name it God. People build empty houses with a variety of uncomfortable chairs or hard benches, and force themselves to sit there in groups on days when their time would be better spent in nature and honoring each other. They devote themselves and tithe their money, thinking it will bring them closer to a connection with the Universal Great Spirit. But even thinking of it this way is not completely clear. The all is the one-self. It is within the restricted mind that projections of self as an object skew belief and trust. This in turn creates pathetic limitation."

"You watched me renounce that at an early age!" Lilith rejoiced.

"Yes, I did, dear one! Look at the power you possessed at age nine, confronting a rabbi and telling him what you knew to be right, from the center of your being. The truth pulses within you at a cellular level. It always has. You were a deep kid!"

"I still am," she added, inspiring them both to laugh. Then she continued, "So why did I struggle so hard to find a soul mate?"

"Realize that when I speak of numbers, dear one, that this encompasses much more than mathematical equivalencies. It is the magic and the vibrational power I am sharing. In the case of the idea of soul mates, you must understand the essence of Two. This number creates a perceived duality. The mind gets warped into craving and believing that it needs a profound connection to another being. The funny thing is that the only true soul mate any of us have is the greater power. The truth is that we are already a part of the great Cosmic Ocean of oneness. We are the Divine."

"And this goes for the Gandharvas and the Apsaras?"

"Of course it does! This is the yearning of every spark, every molecule, every cell, and every organism. From the moment when the Two vibration, in the form of the biological forces of sperm and egg, join in the vast emptiness of the womb, organic-based beings spend their entire lifespan trying to find connection. The problem is that most keep looking to other people, expecting them to give a sense of oneness. When others don't give what is believed to satisfy this craving, many humans turn to food or possessions when what is really desired is a deeper bonding. It is as if all of you are individual pieces of a puzzle and just want to feel locked in with an energy that complements your curves. The sensation of belonging is a combination of feeling and being."

Lilith closed her eyes and rocked gently, pondering all of this. With her eyes still closed she whispered, "Be-longing…this is a transformation to the state of being created by the sensation of longing."

"Exactly! You really are getting this!" exclaimed Saruk AUM.

"What about the idea of a soul mate? Does it exist?"

"For me to answer this, you must understand my view of what a soul is."

"Well, please explain."

"It is like a giant crystal with a set number of facets—like a three-dimensional cut gemstone."

"Really?"

"Yes, really!"

"Wow, I like this so far! It sounds beautiful."

"It is! Shall I continue?"

"Yes, of course! Please."

"Okay. Think of a soul as a three-dimensional egg. The ovoid is faceted, like a cut gemstone crystal. Though it appears as a solid object, it is made up of just over six hundred five-faced planes. Each surface is important and holds a particular sound. The edge of each facet of each of the faces has a purpose and possesses a unique vibration."

"Like a tone?"

"Yes, a distinct tone, and a word to go with it."

"What are they?"

"One of the words is your soul name; another is your given name. A third holds one of the many thousand names of the Divine, and a fourth embraces the particular name that is unique for you to call the Great Spirit. The fifth is your word of power. This is Vak."

"What is Vak?"

"It is the language of the Divine. It is the power of manifestation, the way you are heard by the Infinite Energy as well as the way you receive the word."

"Like prayer?"

"Beyond prayer."

"But what does this have to do with soul mates?"

"In order for your light to be recognized by another person from the soul's perspective, the vibrations must add up. It is all quite mathematical."

"I see."

"That is good, but can you hear it? Can you feel it? Can you feel me?"

Part IV

Metamorphosis

Profound changes are always out of our hands.

Chapter 16

Relationship

True connection is in the math.

"Do you think we add up?" Don asked, smiling.

The sound of "we" felt awkward for a second but, in spite of it, Lilith decided to answer. "If I didn't think so, I would have left you back at the cheese store."

The Troubadour picked up his lute and began to strum a little ditty, inspiring Don with the courage to continue. "If we were a song, would there be harmony?"

"Definitely," Lilith responded.

"Would we be instrumental, or is there to be a story in the lyric?"

"Oh! There's a story, for sure!" she replied, her smile casting a glowing light through the eye windows and onto the Boardroom's table.

***

"The sounds of manifestation and healing are unique to you," whispered the Gandharva from another dimension. Lilith did not hear the words, but rather a high pitched whirring sound in her right ear. She felt the hairs on the back of her neck stand up. Little bumps rose on her arms. She took all of this as a collective positive sign.

"You wanted so much to connect with him that the winds of your heart caused swells as they blew across the formerly smooth lake of the unconscious mind."

"Yes, I can see this now, but while I was in the moment, I only felt the burning of passion," Lilith said with a look of confusion as she fizzled into a cloud of tiny violet bubbles.

"When others possess harmonically similar vibrations," continued Saruk AUM, "we see them as soul connections. It is what draws me to you, my little one," smirked the angel. He rose up and hovered over the purple haze which had been a physical form of Lilith just a moment ago.

"As a matter of fact," she said, materializing into flesh once again without skipping a beat, "where is your partner?"

"She is right here," he responded, patting his chest. He then waved his arms and wings in large circles as far as they would reach. "She is always with me."

"Is she your perfect mate?" asked Lilith.

"There is no such thing as a perfect mate. We are all the same thing. When we wake up to this, we will join as the family we truly are. We are already connected. We are all sparkles of light and a part of the one light, reflecting the Creator."

"It is as if we are all asleep, right?"

"At some level, yes. But, then…"

"What's the point?" Lilith overlapped.

"There is indeed a point," responded Saruk AUM.

"Well, what is the point?"

"The point, the point, the point," Saruk AUM chanted as he floated above her. "The point is light, or at least it is like light. You are able to see its reflection and sparkle, but you can never quite grasp it. We are all a replication and a refraction of this light."

"Like a rainbow?"

"Yes! Just like a rainbow. You can see all the colors if you are in the right place in the right moment. But then, at the same time, we are all just like water."

"Water, light…I am getting more than a little confused," puzzled Lilith.

"Stay with this for a moment," Saruk AUM encouraged as he hovered, speaking with his wings and hands at the same time. "It will start to make sense, I promise." He paused to think for a moment and then added, "We are water moving at lightning speed."

"Now you are losing me for sure!" exclaimed Lilith.

"Do you remember what I taught you about the Cosmic Ocean?"

"Yes! Yes I do, that we are all like drops of water in an Ocean of Oneness."

"And is it possible to separate drops of water and identify them in such a huge body of water?"

"No, of course not!"

"If we were drops in a river, would we pass the same shores twice?"

"No, of course not!"

"So you agree, just as the ancient ones taught, that we can never step into the same water of a river twice!"

"Yes, of course I agree. But is what you are telling me is that I am a drop in a river? I am getting this, right?"

"Yes, a drop. But the river is more like an ocean with no distinct boundaries. This is why it is so easy to be your guardian! You get it, and you get it quickly!" he complimented her, smiling.

"Just like the first time you were able to see me. Do you remember?" winked Saruk AUM.

"Of course, I do! It was a highlight!"

"Aha! Light!" Saruk AUM cheered as a brilliant flash connected his smile with Lilith's.

"You were on an island," continued Saruk AUM, "different from this one, but still an island."

"It was my Robinson Crusoe year, a time to get away from reality. I had the opportunity to shake off many years of confusion and escape to an unreal, lush, green, seemingly non-reality. There I was, floating in the middle of paradise. I had found a way to empty my head and pull all of the pieces of myself back together…" reminisced Lilith.

"The moisture of the jungle bathed you in long, lush moments of deep teal contemplation. The earth braced the infrastructure of who you are to become. It was your dharma to live at the edge of a tropical forest, near a tranquil white beach, where you could climb coconut trees and swim in sparkling crystal water. You were always meant to have the opportunity to chase fish and learn to snorkel and free-dive for shells."

"I remember seeing you in the water one day. You hovered in front of my mask and smiled. That night, you spoke to me in a dream."

"Yes! Following that, the island symbolically became the center of your universe. It was so then and it will always be what you need to feel whole. Every day a day off, a day of freedom so that you have time to sit under a palm tree and watch soldier bugs stack upon one another."

"I remember how they would pile up. Their red, white, and black bodies looked like British soldiers having an unreal orgy of love."

"In the shade of wild lime trees, you stalked hermit crabs and adopted them as pets. The dilapidated ruins of Great Mother's house gave you solace. Just as you sensed it then, feeling her presence here keeps you calm. Knowing that she lives here gives you a feeling, albeit slight, of not being alone. Being on an island, feeling peaceful and secluded, becomes your reason to be.

"Intensely rich colors reflected in the dancing light of the midday sun become all that matters. The smell of the ocean and the aquamarine sacred blue of the sky and water are all that you need to nourish the body, mind, and spirit. The realizations that the earth is magical and her resources are precious infuse your every breath."

"I get it. I am supposed to be here, comfortable in my solitude. There is no contact from the world. I am completely unplugged and disconnected. All I need is the sun coming up in the morning and the stars and moon at night. I have left everything that I had perceived to be the reality of life behind. It doesn't matter if my parents and friends understand where I am or why. What is important is that this is my chance to break away and truly get away into what I really am."

"This is because first moments and heightened experiences are impossible to duplicate."

"Just like drops of water."

"Yes, just like water. This is a theme that we have watched repeat over and over throughout history. Indeed, it is the primary step that led to one of the original stories, and to your story, my liege."

"My story? Isn't this moment a part of my story?"

"This moment is the only moment—the infinite moment. Your story is one and the same as the Vedanta writings which describe Prakriti, Purusha, and Prana Shakti. All of these stories and interpretations are the layers of the interrelationship of the Three."

"I thought we were talking about Two. What are the Three?"

"The Three encompasses the relationship of the perceived duality that is in reality the polarity of Two. Three is the joining of what appears to be these two opposites along with the wildcard of irresistible energy. When this third elemental vibration is added into the mix of Two, we experience that which is Three. This shows up in many famous tales. Take, for instance, the story of Adam and Eve. Notice that the snake in the garden is the third and crucial element. In the case of the Puma and the Condor, the Serpent is the necessary force that brings it all together. Study this in your mystic book. You will see the theme unfolding in all of the great stories. The vibration of Three unravels the web of all great mysteries."

Lilith had forgotten the enormous book was in her lap. It had seemingly become weightless.

"But what was it about the attraction I felt in moments when I thought what I wanted was a man? Why did I believe this to be true? It

was as if the sensation itself pulled me like a magnetic force."

"That is the third element about which I am speaking. It is the perception caused by intense feelings of believing that what you wanted in that particular moment was a man. Realize that you have encountered this responsiveness many times. It has happened when you strolled through a store touching the fabric of colorful clothing, or read descriptions of tasty delights on a menu in a restaurant. It has happened, too, when you caught the penetrating gaze of a man from across a room."

"Sometimes it feels like I'm not even here on an island."

"If not on an island, where are you?"

Lilith looked around. All she could see in every direction was water.

"I know in this moment that I am here," she said, listening to the crunch of the sandy ground beneath the rocker and noticing the vibration of the tree behind her, which reached high into the sky.

"How does it feel to be right where you need to be?" asked Saruk AUM.

"It feels oddly expansive."

"Now imagine feeling something you know as a wrong relationship. Where are you now?"

She felt as if she were looking down out of a tiny window that stood hundreds of feet in the air. "I am in a tower! Oh, I get it. It was as if I had locked myself in a tower and I could not get out."

"Exactly!" the Gandharva said, blushing a proud shade of orangey-gold. "A relationship is a tower built between two—together. If built too high without a substantial foundation, the tower must crumble and be destroyed, just like the image of card numbered XVI."

"Card XVI? The Tower? As in the Tower card in the Major Arcana?" asked Lilith, imagining the smooth feel of her deck as she shuffled.

"Yes, the card of the Tarot," said Saruk AUM. "It is the epitome of construction and destruction. The construction is a result of mind-stuff.

The deconstruction of these projections is out of our hands, as shown in the Tower's imagery."

"There are many layers to the meaning of each and every card in the deck, kind teacher. Can you illuminate the meaning of the Tower for me?" asked Lilith.

"My pleasure, little one," Saruk AUM replied, smiling. "The Tower sits on a craggy bit of land. It seems to be in the middle of nowhere. This is often how humans perceive their aloneness." He paused to observe how Lilith was absorbing the information. "Remember who you are when reading the cards, Lilith."

"Yes, I remember," she answered. "I am the Fool."

"Correct! And what is your purpose?"

"I am on a journey," she responded.

"Correct again! And to whom or to what does this journey really belong?"

"It is the journey of the soul!" exclaimed Lilith. "The Zero, the Fool card, represents every being. I am the Fool."

"Exactly!" praised Saruk AUM as he floated slightly above the rocker. The Gandharva continued, "So, now for the meaning of the Tower card. The Fool recalls being a part of the construction of this tower. The event took place in his past, when his main concern was the material world. He was joined by other like-minded individuals in the project, whether he was aware of this or not. When the Tower card shows up, it reminds the Fool that there are still bits of his old mindset remaining. What represents the mind in the image?"

"There is no clear representation of the mind, Saruk AUM, but rather the ego-mind," answered Lilith.

"Correct! Where do we find this?"

"It is signified by the symbol of the crown. I love how in some of the decks, the image of the crown is made out of tiny towers. This shows the holographic continuum of existence."

"Indeed! The Fool realizes he is the Tower, and that everything is a projection of his mind. Comprehending this, he experiences a moment of profound knowing. This is symbolized by the lightning bolt. When he encounters the other people in the Tower, he realizes his human mistake of believing he is separate."

"Is the Fool one of the people flying through the air?" Lilith asked.

"Not exactly," answered Saruk AUM, settling down once again on the arm of the chair.

"Who are they?"

"They are all people, and they are aspects of the person who is looking at the image of the card at the same time. This is a reminder to embrace everyone as a holographic chip off the Great Divine. Are you getting this?"

"Yes, I trust I am!" Lilith said. Her face flushed a warmer hue as she continued. "The bolt of lightning flashes an instant of knowing on all who are brave enough to look at it. The people flying through the air are ripped away from their preprogrammed ego-minds and are chaotically flung out into the cosmos. The only signposts leading the way are the Yods."

"Stupendous, little one! And…?"

"The Yods represent the finger of God. To take the leap of faith is to trust that everything is going to be all right, even in the terrifying chaos of what seems like mass destruction. Following the direction of the yods is the act of trusting and letting go. It truly is surrender."

"And…?"

"And this is a great illusion! We are meant to trust only God!"

"You've got it! Well done! After the air clears and the rubble settles, the ground is left fertile and more conceptive, offering itself to a new foundation. The creation of fresh earth is irresistible and inspires rebuilding."

"So this is why we are driven like ants, to try again and again,"

Lilith said with an expression of knowing on her face.

"I know that you know and understand the laws of energy and attraction. Indeed, this is all a bit odd and can be quite paradoxical. When one wants desperately to be in a relationship, they try and try and fail. This is because they are acting as the doer, rather than just letting the cosmic forces take over and resting in a state of being. It is like getting swept up in a wave. We have to learn to let go and allow ourselves to be carried to the shore of new possibilities. It is like your guru used to teach you. Do you remember? Recite it for me now!"

"Recite for you? As if I am in elementary school?"

"Yes, little one! You are in school and moving forward. You have been cut out of the herd and you are most certainly moving on! After all, you are the number VII, the card of the Chariot! Feel victorious in this new beginning. This lesson is a most integral cornerstone in your foundation. Now, kindly say it!"

"Okay, I understand! You know that I know this and that I practice it…daily."

"This is a test of the Divine Broadcast System," the Gandharva announced in his best FM voice, which caused a few leaves to shiver from a nearby limb and float to the ground.

"You are so crazy sometimes!" Lilith laughed. "I can't believe how you can instantly make me feel like I am six again."

"Where do you see God?" he asked, moving her mind in a new direction.

"I see God in what I perceive as myself first. I see God inside the spark of the flame that sits inside the jewel, which rests upon the lotus flower of this heart. I see God in the light of all sentient beings and every construct in this perceived reality."

"And how do you surrender? Say it as if I am not materialized here. Say it to the grace that is."

"By knowing—"

"No, no, no! Don't explain it to me! I know you have the meaning. Say it! Say it with true feeling!" Saruk AUM coached. "Proclaim it! Sing the song of the Divine!"

She understood and began with a long-practiced centering. First she took several deep inhalations through her nostrils, each followed by a slow, steady exhalation through a tiny straw-like opening in her lips. Her eyes closed as she wrapped her words with all the good intentions and love inside her heart.

"I am at peace with myself as I am, and the world as it is."

"Excellent, my darling. Continue, please."

"I release, allowing you, Great Divine Essence, to steer this vessel. I am in your hands, guided by your love. I am this present moment. I am completely in a state of feeling and being. I am that I am."

She gathered in another long deep breath followed by a smooth exhalation, and drifted into a state of bliss. This caused her to disappear into the vapor of nothingness, where she merged with the great Ocean of Harmony and Divine Love. Even the Gandharva could not see her as what she had been just a moment before—a tiny female body.

A paisley cloud of tiny purplish-green bubbles floated above the Gandharva's head. A sparkling smile glowed on his face as he fizzled into smoky foam, joining his ward in the Ocean of Oneness. They drifted, peacefully submerged in a divine expression of sacred reflection, as the vibration of ten thousand AUMs echoed through existence.

Chapter 17

Spark

When we fully participate, the embers of knowing begin to glow.

Don was falling in love with the way Lilith was able to pick up on every detail of her surroundings. He mused at her skill in hanging on to every sound and noticing every color. When she stared into his eyes, he felt her in the center of his abdomen. Though he had said very little, he noticed that when he did speak, she listened and was fully engaged. She seemed to use her entire body, her heart, and not just her ears.

He wasn't sure if he had ever felt so acknowledged. Perhaps when he was a tiny child and his mother looked deeply into his eyes as he explained an event on the playground, a painting he had created in kindergarten, or the taste of a cupcake from a birthday celebration. None of that mattered because, in this moment, he found himself completely mesmerized.

When Lilith spoke, every movement and every pulse had meaning. The way she formed her words and the intensity of her stare captivated him. He fell in love with the shape of her mouth and the timbre of her voice. The dance of her mind was an acrobatic ballet that kept him hanging from the clouds. She was sharp as a tack and swift as a dragonfly.

The concrete squares of the sidewalk glided under their feet as they swam in the vibrations of their new togetherness. They both sensed

a third force joining them. Though Don was unable to identify it, he knew it existed.

"What is that extra being?" demanded Reason.

"It is the force of nature herself," consoled the Guru, waving his hand in the air.

Don noticed that he was forming his sentences with single-mindedness and polite intention. He felt the way his gestures were soft and meaningful. To the side of the Boardroom, the Artist flipped a new canvas on an easel and demanded that they get her to model for a painting session.

"Not now, fool!" scolded Casanova. "We are nowhere near getting her out of those jeans!"

"He's right, dude" the Horny Teen said.

"We should get her high first," suggested the Stoner.

"Yes, yes, we all want to paint her," Reason agreed, attempting to calm the Boardroom.

Don wanted to sculpt her so that he could have his own unique access to her sensual curves. He imagined his hands sliding along the landscape of her body, molding it in moist clay.

Infinite space sprouted a thousand arms and began to carve patterns and textures into the growing landscape of the Great Mother. Cosmic music rang in the light of the stars, playing a song of creation. A spark ignited in the belly of Mother, quickly forming a zygote that flamed into the fire of existence.

Lilith noticed the way Don watched her mouth when she spoke. She felt the weight of his eyes on her lips and that, in turn, created the taste of appreciation on her tongue.

She was so grateful for the ability to reveal her thoughts through sound and the power center of her throat chakra in that moment. She loved the feel of her own voice. When she was twelve, she picked up a guitar and began to express herself through songs she created. It was a small miracle because she had been born with an infection in her eyes that had crept to her ears and throat. Her doctors never quite figured out what it was. In the beginning they named it staph and strep, and considered her to be damaged goods.

The doctors treated the newborn Lilith with synthetics and sent her home with more medicines. She began life filled with antibiotics, high fevers, and ear, nose, and throat sicknesses. Her mama did the best she could, following the protocols of the era as she struggled with guilt for her sick child.

Lilith was on fire most of the time, and learned to ride the visions of her fever-driven hallucinations as she peered out between the spokes of her crib. Fortunately, in those early years, she shared a room with her maternal grandmother, who gave her nurturing love and round–the-clock attention.

After two and a half years of burning introspection, her parents became concerned that she couldn't or wouldn't ever speak. Perhaps they had never heard the sounds she uttered to her grandmother in the inky darkness of night.

When the physical manifestation of her grandmother was long gone, the spirit of this woman continued to watch over the tiny goddess. Lilith was grateful to have such a strong connection with her. She often asked her questions, appreciatively receiving her Nanny Fannie's loving guidance. Lilith gave up trying to explain it to her mama, who felt more comfortable denying the ethereal presence.

When Lilith was a little girl and had just begun to walk on her own, the three generations of females went shopping. They loved John Wanamaker's, a swanky, free-standing department store in the Philadelphia suburb near their split-level home. Lilith was dressed up like a little Jackie Kennedy. This had always been a favorite look of her mother's, reflecting the fashion of the time.

Lilith walked along with Don listening to the sound of her boots against the concrete sidewalks of South Philadelphia. Their pitch noticeably shifted when they came to a section paved with broad slate stones. The cool, crisp resonance took her back to the memory of the marble stairs that lead out the back of the Wanamaker's store to a round white fountain near the parking area.

Lilith remembered how it felt to climb down the thin slab steps. They were manageable for her tiny little legs. As her boots clonked on the slate underfoot, she could hear the crisp click of her black patent leather Mary Janes with pearl buttons tapping against the travertine.

She smiled and closed her eyes, imagining the shiny ebony shoes and the white steps streaked with grey lines that swirled like currents in a river. In her mind's eye, the tiny Lilith looked down at the shoes, past the hem of her little grey wool skirt and thickly ribbed white tights.

The tiny Lilith paused at the top of the steps and felt her mama and grandma let go of her hands. She watched as they walked down and away, their backs growing smaller and smaller as they descended. This offered the little child a challenge to join them at the bottom. Instead, she stood atop the threshold shaking her head, refusing to comply.

The women stopped at the bottom, chided her, and threatened to go home without her.

"Bye-bye, Lilith! Bye-bye, baby! We are leaving and going home! Let's go!"

"No!" argued Lilith, screwing up her face with the strength of a Mongolian horseman.

The women waved and giggled under their breath as she continued to hold her territory, shaking her head in refusal.

A curling smile crept onto her grandmother's lips. It leapt across to Lilith's mother's face as all three realized the insincerity of leaving their precious doll baby behind.

Lilith continued to stand her ground.

Finally the pair of women pleaded, "What are you going to do?

Are you coming with us, baby? Shall we leave you behind? Do you want to stay here?"

Lilith had them; they were a captive audience. She figured she would show them how she really felt, and exploded into a full song and dance. There atop the smooth, terraced stage, she boogied back and forth, breaking into a full production number, her own rendition of the Peppermint Twist. It was just as she had seen Chubby Checker do on television. The performance was word for word, note for note, with every bump and grind.

The women laughed hysterically as their faces turned crimson, like those of the autumn leaves falling from the dogwood and oak trees.

Lilith's mother always said that from that day forward, they were never able to shut her up. Instead of justifying a miracle, she would add, "I guess you just didn't have anything to say before that!"

Chapter 18

Twinkling

Every glimmer is the same; it is the now.

In all dimensions, simultaneously, there was a lull in the sounds of speech as intuition took over. Consciousness became a continuum. Cosmic intelligence took the helm as instinct placed the entirety on auto-pilot. Everything became responsive. The cosmic central nervous system, spontaneous and animal-like, melted into perceptive awareness.

"They are using intuition through a place of inner quiet—I can feel them," piped the Feminine-voice in a lilting tone.

"Indeed," responded the Masculine in a slow drawl. "They shifted through the gears of the limbic into quiet clairvoyance."

"Isn't it amusing to watch them access their awareness? I can feel the hush of the collective mind!"

"Now they are emptying," hummed the Divine Masculine.

"You must know a great deal about empty, being that you are nothing but vast endlessness!" quipped the Great Goddess. She hiccupped an ocean of shimmering iridescent bubbles which shook in her waves of gurgling laughter.

"Let's teach them conscious intention! I could activate their root and third eye chakras. We could do it together. Just hum a little louder."

"It is out of our hands."

"What hands? We don't have any hands! You are infinite and I am a serpent wrapped around a rock!"

***

Lilith realized she was standing on the street. Her eyes were closed. A multicolored sunbeam washed over her forehead with warming light. The couple had stopped just after turning the corner onto South Street, and neither had realized it. Lilith began humming a Tantric mantra she had learned in her youth. At first, the sounds were faint, with no definition of syllables, just a trickle of soft sound, like gentle water flowing over countless pebbles. Don became mesmerized as he watched. Slowly the sound began to build in volume and intensity.

"She's doing it," whispered the Serpent.

"Yesss..." hissed her divine counterpart in a loving gesture of acknowledgement to his consort.

The Serpent goddess dove to the bottom of the lake, stirring an endless river of effervescence in her tumultuous passion. The waters swirled deep within the profundity of her enormous body as waves broke into frothy whitecaps on her surface.

The Gandharva landed in the great tree, high above Lilith's head. She rocked in her oversized chair, drifting inside infinite space. In the blissful gap between alpha and theta waves, she rested. There were no thoughts. Saruk AUM began to sing a lyrical Ram Chalisa about the divine devotion of Sri Rama to his consort, Sita. In that moment, as the story was woven through the lilting melody, all moments became the same moment; all breath synchronized and became the same breath in oneness.

Lilith floated back into her mama's womb. She could hear the steady drumming of a heartbeat, amplified by the mystic waters. Inside the rhythm, she heard her grandmother's heartbeat, and inside that tempo was the cadence of her great-grandmother's heartbeat. The pulse of this engaging cycle of sound took her into a spiraling journey to the origin, the beginning. She was transported to the center of the earth, to the heartbeat of the Great Mother of us all.

Saruk AUM nudged his gorgeous little goddess, and she slit one eye open, raising its respective eyebrow. The greens and blues of the great waters glinted off her iridescent irises. A waft of pungent cinnamon swirled into her nostrils, enticing neurons to respond.

The Great Serpent stirred in the depths of the abundant waters of Pachacuti, causing them to bubble up like a foamy chai latte. The Sun Disk responded and sneezed a flourish of mahogany dust over the frothy waves

Deep inside the Great Mother's heart, a tribe of drummers began to beat the steady rhythm of life. Trilobites fluttered their angel-like wings, causing them to split into ribbons which flapped like prayer flags in the high Himalayan winds. At the ends of the tape-like fins, limbs, feet, and tiny hands formed. The little creatures started to shake and dance to the rhythmic sound of Mother.

"Can you hear the rhythm, little one?" asked Saruk AUM, stirring Lilith like the tiny spoon in the cup of tea he was handing her.

"I do. I hear the sound of life pulsing beneath the surface of this water. It is like a multilayered heartbeat."

"This mysterious music is the original honoring song. It is a prayer of love and hope. This sound is the rhythm of life. It contains the steady rhythm that gets us going and keeps us motivated. This music sets the mood while we work and play. It is the pulse of existence."

"Can I become this rhythm?"

"You can allow it to shape your journey. Feel the vibration and witness as it crafts the contours and edges of the great circle of life. In its powerful pulsation rings a promise with no beginning and no ending. This is the round path that is the shape of the Zero."

"How can I identify with it?"

"Become the continuous curve of Zero. It is a circle within a circle within a circle. It is a lemon, a nut, a seed, and a stone. Zero

is filled with great potential, encompassing all—and at the same time, nothingness—all the while being a great vessel of magic. Indeed, Zero is the everything."

"How did it become known as zilch?"

"People are afraid of great depths. They like to know where the end-point is. But Zero goes beyond that. It is an amazing abyss where all the knowledge of the universe exists, and yet there is zilch."

The Mother Divine's cosmic chakras actuated, bringing everything into momentary balance through the sounds and vibrations of joy, love, and devotion. Though each mind initially thought a different thought in the Ocean of Oneness and, in that flicker of a second, all questions had answers; indeed, all beingness had connection. Though each seeming individual had different ways to calm the inner chatter of their respective minds, in this brief flash they were one; they were Atman. They broke the pots—the restrictive containers of existence—and shed the robes of bodies. For a brief nanosecond, they came together and realized the primordial unity of the individual soul with the plentitude of oneness.

The Serpent swirled to the surface of the great water, tossing multicolored froth onto a newly forming, craggy shoreline. Small bumps of mud, clay, and stone began to protrude through the roiling surface, creating landmasses. In a spontaneous reaction of intuition and combined energies and functions, the endless sky turned dark as the Sun Disk took rest in the curling body of the Divine Mother. Glimmering points of light blinked in the inky darkness as a canopy of stars twinkled in the heavens. They reflected in an array of colors on the surface of the infinite water.

The root chakra of the Great Mother and the sixth chakra of the Divine Father vibrated harmoniously in pure bliss. This moment of meditation efficiently accomplished a deep inner quiet, reaching everywhere, as the entirety of the universe relaxed in peace.

"It seems like a paradox," said Lilith, a look of confusion

scrunching her brow.

"It is, for this analysis and any attempt to rationalize it or explain it by means of interpretation, is an invasive interference with the concept of Zero. Instead we must imagine ourselves in a witness state, watching as if outsiders. We are an integral part of everything, and at the same time we are nothing. Let the two hemispheres of the brain unite. Allow this scene, in this present moment, to just be. Choose to follow the guidance of intuition and that which is of the right brain. This way, the derivative, linear, left brain loses power. There is no need for language."

The Gandharva began to hum and Lilith joined in. The cacophonous sound swarmed like bees in search of sweet nectar.

***

Lilith blinked her eyes open to find Don staring into her forehead. His steady gaze melted into her third eye.

"Do you meditate?" she asked.

He stayed steady, without blinking, as the two took in a series of deep breaths in unison. Don thought he was seeing an actual sapphire that was cut in smooth facets, blazing blue light, glimmering in the center of her forehead.

"I do now! What was that?"

"I'm never sure. I just go with what I'm feeling," she responded.

"You were vibrating," said Don.

"Dude, this is getting freaky!" croaked the Stoner as a puff of smoke twirled out of his mouth.

"I don't trust this at all!" said the Teen, heading for the door.

"Let's get out of here!" begged Low Self-esteem.

"Yeah, I guess I was," Lilith acknowledged.

"It sounded like you were singing tones. They sounded like intervals of fifths," said Don.

Part V

Alchemy

Fire rises up from water where it dwells, resting in potential, to transform everything it touches.

Chapter 19

Wizard

A soupy kingdom.

The morning mist clung like glue to the damp hillside where an ancient stone castle grew out of a craggy cliff. In a vaulted laboratory, Deagadh had completed an all-night experiment and was thinking about morning tea and a biscuit. It had been hours since he had seen his absentminded assistant, Alwyn, and he wondered if the boy had forgotten he was still working.

"Never mind," he grumbled to himself as he stirred a murky liquid in a giant iron cauldron. He squinted as he tried to make sense of the strange edifices and odd clothing on the people within the scrying vision.

The first beam of light crept through a slit between heavy purple curtains covering the two-story windows which faced out over a grassy knoll to the east of the massive stone structure. The sudden flood of color pouring in through multicolored glass caused Zahra, his African grey parrot, to stir on her perch.

"What's for breakfast?" croaked the plump little bird.

"If you continue to disturb me, I shall—" barked the scientist.

"Like that's going to happen!" groused his feathered companion.

"I need some tea!" they exclaimed in unison. This tipped them into peals of laughter that clattered like wind chimes in a sudden gust.

"Go and find that boy!" commanded the master, inspiring a spectacular takeoff by Zahra. She flew across the vast laboratory and out through the door in search of proper breakfast fare for herself and her master. Deagadh could hear the sound of her mighty wings beating as she flew down the great hall that led toward their quarters. As she soared around the corner at the end of the corridor, she mimicked the horns of the hunt. The haunting intervals of fifths echoed off the glass instruments in the laboratory in sympathetic vibration.

Deagadh's body curved over the great iron vessel. The giant paddle he held in his hands looked more like an oar than a spoon. His repetitive stirring strokes drew the shape of a Merkabah over and over in the murky, bubbling liquid. From his lips buzzed an incantation in a very ancient tongue. Each time he drew the downward pointing triangle, his voice was soft, as if he were stroking hair from the eyes of a maiden. In contrast, each time the paddle drew the upward-pointing triangle, his pitch dipped into a bass bellow reverberating like a blast of dynamite deep within a mine.

On his thirteenth repetition of the symbol, he added smaller horizontal lines just inside the vertical points of each triangle. Suddenly, he jumped back as the liquid turned an eerie lime green. Stiff peaks protruded through the surface of the glowing fluid. The rock-like summits seemed to move as greyish foam oozed down their sides. When the froth mingled with the surface of the iridescent soup, an opaque fog enveloped the chamber, causing every detail to disappear.

Deagadh heard a rustling and could make out the sound of Zahra's wings in the distant passageways, coming closer and growing louder as she returned to her master's workspace.

"I'm over here!" called Deagadh. The wind of his breath caused colors to appear in the cloud-like moisture hanging in the atmosphere.

"I see you," called the African grey as she swooped down to rest on the alchemist's shoulder, deftly shifting a Tarot card from her talon to her mouth.

"What have we here? Silly bird!" said Deagadh, taking the card from the bird's beak and inspecting it.

"Lovers!" squawked Zahra, sounding more like a macaw than the sophisticated bird she was.

"Six, like sticks!" she sang as she tap-danced side-to-side on his shoulder.

"And why have you taken this from Alwyn, my darling?" he asked, tickling her cheek and then placing the card back in her outstretched claw. This caused all the feathers of her neck and head to fluff in appreciation.

"Just a joke," replied the bird. "The boy was practicing his reading and did not see me remove it from the deck."

"Oh, a ruse!"

"Yes, a ruse," she retorted in her knowing voice. "A ruse," she whistled, hopping off and hanging sideways from the nearby curtain. She twisted her head and looked curiously at the cauldron. Then she swooped down to hover for a moment before returning to her master's shoulder.

"So, what are we looking for today?" queried the bird.

"Nothing in particular. Watching instead, rather."

"Ah…and witnessing," tweeted the bird. The two turned their collective attention to the great pot of liquid. Peering into it through the fog, they watched as a fortress emerged in the dense vapor.

"Where is this? Is it a castle?" the parrot whispered in Deagadh's ear.

"It is the kingdom of Jaulan, Zahra," the master said, cocking his head in an almost identical posture to that of the bird's. "Shhh! Can you hear that?" asked the alchemist.

"It sounds dreadful!" croaked the parrot.

Through the mist and bubbles of the cauldron and the shivering cold that froze the kingdom of Jaulan came a wail. The sound shattered the misty silence in the laboratory. The blistering cry seemingly emanated from the image of a castle that floated in the oily liquid. It echoed all the way into the great stone space where the alchemist and his bird looked on.

Deagadh expanded the vision using his paddle in one hand and a staff that materialized from thin air in his other. The power of his mind allowed Zahra to see into the great hall of the castle along with him. The vision came more clearly into focus, and Deagadh and the bird could see a warrior king lying in a pool of sweat and fear. Pain shot through his body. His cries curdled the morning air like lemon juice in fresh cream.

Once upon a time, this great king had been a mighty ruler, a knight most feared in battle. His ability had brought him great honor. Now he was pathetic and afflicted, having received the ultimate wound. He could neither heal and live, nor die.

The armor he had once worn in battle hung, tarnished, on a wall of the great hall. There, in the empty center, his body lay on a humble cot. He was unable to climb to his silky chamber in the upper level of his castle. Frustrated, he winced in agony and begged for salvation.

The people of Jaulan were distressed; no one in the kingdom knew what to do. They loved their leader and feared the hours and days to come as he struggled. Ever since their beloved warrior king had returned in this condition, the sky had turned dark and thick with sorrowful clouds that wept icy tears. The flowers' colors dulled, the crops produced less and less, and the herds of animals had become thinner.

King Heron lay on his bed, trembling in the cold drafty castle, swirling in misty memories. The sky grew even darker, coated by sticky clouds. Shattering thunder shook the heavy walls of the fortress. Each time there was a loud crack, Heron shuddered, thinking the booming of the roaring sky was his father's voice. The sounds jolted him into believing that the dead man's breath was steaming the tiny rosy cheeks of his eight-year-old face.

Fever had taken over; Heron forgot where he was. He drifted back to the day he had made a sacred vow in the center of his heart. He remembered the moment and the choice—which was to always be a winner.

He thought he heard the whining cries of hounds on the hunt coming closer and closer across the distant hillside. Then they seemed to pass under a nearby window.

Deagadh felt a shock of current which caused him to drop his enormous paddle and staff. They rattled as they hit the stones of the laboratory floor, and the sound echoed down throughout the laboratory.

***

"Where are you, Lilith?" asked Don.

It took her a moment to return to the sidewalk. "In my mind, I see myself on a horse in the dew and mist of an early morning in autumn. I can hear hounds barking and panting. I feel chilled by the morning dampness. The smell of moist, rotting leaves on the rich, muddy earth is filling my nostrils. I see all the animals scurrying deep into the brush, driven by the heartbeats and howls of the hounds. I hear the whips on their bugles blowing fifths."

"Whips?"

"Yes, whippers-in."

"Whippers-in? What the heck is that?"

"The guys with the whips who ride with the hounds on a fox hunt."

"A fox hunt? Are you kidding me?"

"Yes. I mean no, I'm not kidding and yes, a fox hunt. When I was growing up, my father thought he was a gentleman farmer. It began as an obsession with horses. As a young boy, he had a pony, even though his family lived in suburbia. My dad always wanted to have horses at home. Our family moved out of the city to Bucks County, where they bought a small farm. In an effort to fit in, my father got into fox hunting. We hunted."

"Fox hunting?"

"Let's get out of here man! She's a killer!" quivered Fear under the Boardroom table.

"Shut it, wimp!" barked the Horny Teen as he kicked the wretched cohort who had curled up near his feet.

"Yes, fox hunting. It's one of the reasons why I'm a vegetarian," Lilith said. "It's not in my DNA to chase down animals with a pack of hounds, nor is it in me to tear into the loin of a cow."

"Oof!" gasped Casanova. "I can see her in that little outfit with the tight britches and leather boots. I wonder what color satin lined her jacket?

"So you dressed up with the canary-colored pants and high boots?" Don asked as he imagined a Pytchley painting with a pack of hounds and a stately red-coated, statuesque gentleman. Oddly, the whole thing was a turn on.

"I did, but I never really felt like it was me. I do, however, love to ride horses. My dad put me on a pony before I could walk. He used to take me through the woods on a trail every week. I loved it! I could sense Mother Nature everywhere. I remember laughing and singing and feeling so much love. But later, the whole horse-show-and-hunt thing soured it for me. As a kid, I was competitive and able to get into it, but by the time I was teenager, I just wanted out. So when I was sixteen, I quit."

"Quit what?"

"I quit the competing and the hunting. Are you listening to me?"

"Yes, I am hearing you."

"But are you really listening to me?"

Attention woke from a nap and lifted his head off the Boardroom table to the smell of a fresh cappuccino being slid under his nose by Compassion. "Thanks, man. I needed that," Attention said gratefully, taking the last sip and tuning his awareness to the goddess in front of the eyes. "Where have I been?" he asked the stirring members of the

Boardroom. "Will you look at this vision?"

"I still rode," continued Lilith, "and I still love to whenever I get the chance. It's a great way to sightsee in nature. I love horses. I can hear them thinking and communicating with me."

"Okay, she is just plain nuts," said Reason, tossing a stack of papers in the air as he pushed back from the Boardroom table. "I'm outta here! He is just plain hopeless. This is over and I am done with trying to stop it!"

Don's face melted in appreciation for the tiny woman who had done so much. It didn't matter that she was from such a different world; he had to have her. He had to discover what she would accept from him, and then find a way to give it all to her.

Chapter 20

Books and Decks

A mystical game of seventy-eight-card pick up.

The flap of wings knocked Lilith out of a deep flood of orange and blue foam. It was the brush of Ambo Shanti's wing on her face that snapped her back to the present moment. The great winged angel was floating in the air, holding out her hands for the book in Lilith's lap. The binding and ornamentation had left impressions of Vedantic mantras, Greek goddesses, and intricate wheels of power in the skin of her bare legs and belly. She had no idea how long she had been traveling, but was sure she was in the here and now, in this present moment.

"Let me have that, sweetheart," said Ambo Shanti. "No sense in holding onto it. I will bring it back when the time is right."

Lilith released her clutch on the huge book reluctantly and watched as the celestial being flew off over the water. A sunbeam glinted off the brass and gold of the binding just as she vanished into the fluffy white cotton of a cloud.

As swiftly as she had taken off, Ambo Shanti returned and perched on the arm of the great chair. "When do you think you understood creativity, little one?" she questioned her student.

Lilith crossed her legs and leaned her face into her hands, thinking. She then rocked the chair forward, unfolded, and stood up.

This was followed by rolling to the ground and then a series of cat-like movements—her personal yoga. She loved to ride the energy of her spine and just move with no rhyme or reason, just being. Lilith paused for a moment and then began vigorously rubbing her hands together. This created so much friction that faint sparks sprayed out. Closing her eyes, she placed her warm palms against her cheeks with her fingertips gently touching her eyelids. This was a technique that had been taught to her by a great guru many years prior. After a series of odd breaths and belly pumping, she hopped back into the chair to answer Ambo Shanti's question.

"It was at a party. I was reading the Tarot for a man who owned a very large Fortune 500 corporation. He was miserable, and I was giving him the session at his wife's request. She came to me crying, saying that though everything in the man's life appeared perfect, he was miserably depressed.

"She explained that her husband had houses, boats, and cars. The list went on. He had all the things people crave and dream of, including financial freedom, a successful career, and perfect children who had graduated from Ivy League colleges. He had more money than his family would ever spend or need. Yet he was so unhappy. His wife was miserable, choking and sobbing as she explained all of this to me."

"I remember," nodded the Apsara.

"Thank goodness for the cards!" exclaimed Lilith.

"The cards have been very good to you," agreed Ambo Shanti. "They are a great tool given to you by the Divine."

***

Lilith stopped and opened her purse in search of some lip balm just before she and Don crossed South Street.

"It has to be in here," she said, fiddling around in the woven courier-style shoulder bag. "Hold this, will you?" she said, handing Don a small maroon velvet pouch that felt oddly stiff in his hand.

"What is this?" he asked, examining the tiny rectangular pouch.

"My Tarot cards," Lilith responded matter-of-factly, smoothing salve on her lips.

"Witch!" screamed Fear and Paranoia, grabbing pitchforks and torches.

"Oh, shut up!" Casanova said, drenching them with a bucket of water.

"You believe in that stuff?" Don questioned, handing the cards back to her.

"It's not a matter of believing," she retorted. "They just are, and I just am with them."

"Oh, good God! She is a witch!" screamed a dusty old version of an Altar Boy, flailing his arms about. This caused a cloud of confusion to haze the Boardroom.

"A succubus!" hissed the priestly Hierophant.

"Shut it!" snapped the Artist as he held his hands up, forming a frame to size her up for a portrait.

"We want her!" yelled the Playboy in unison with the entire right hemisphere.

"How long have you been doing that?" asked Don.

"Since I was seven," Lilith answered knowingly.

"Seven?" screeched the Hierophant, shaking his staff. "Look for a mark. There has to be a mark!"

"Back down, lunatic!" yelled Casanova as he assisted the Hierophant back into a chair.

"This is way beyond your control!" added the Horny Teen.

"How did you get into that?" Don questioned. "Isn't that a little young for a kid to pick those up?" He received a pat on the back from Reason, who had returned and joined the rest of the Board at the table.

"No, not really," responded Lilith.

"Who gave them to you?"

"No one. They came to me!"

"Explain!" shouted Reason so loudly that it came out of Don's mouth.

"Umm…" was the sound he made as he cleared his throat in an attempt at a save. "So, how is it that a little kid gets into reading cards? How does it come to her?"

"Nice save!" shouted the Stoner, grinning as he flicked a lighter and took a long draw from a bong. The Board members looked in his direction and applauded. Not shaken at all by Don's faux pas, Lilith launched into the tale.

"Well, my mom used to take me on a creative date and to story time at the local bookstore every week. Once a month, I was allowed to pick something out. I would usually choose a Dr. Seuss book or something about ponies. But on this one particular day, I wandered out of the children's book section into the main part of the store."

Don remembered how much he loved his mother's voice when she would read to him. The memory of the sound spun into the whining of his older sisters, destroying the sensation.

Lilith continued, "My mama gently steered me back to the kids' section and said, 'No, sweetie, the kids' books are here, you know that.' I proceeded to wander out again as if drawn magnetically to the back of the store. The titles of the books were a blur. Everything seemed so much bigger than in the kids' area, and there were so many books." Her mind reconstructed the maple shelves, feeling her tiny fingers run along the wood coping that were leading her to self-discovery.

She felt her feet walking through the aisles. She saw the colors decorating the spines of the books. She watched her body move to a shelf in the corner at the very back of the store. There she stood staring at a glimmering black package.

"No, darlin' girl," chimed her mother, who had followed her. "Let's go find a Dr. Seuss you don't have. How about a story about horses?"

She put her hands on the child's shoulders and gently turned her around, coaxing her through the arched doorway into the green carpeted children's alcove.

"No," said Lilith, spinning on her heels and trotting back to the rear shelf of the adult section. Her mother watched her and kept at a distance so as to not interfere.

The tiny Lilith walked straight over to the same bookcase and this time took the black cellophane-wrapped box off the shelf. She caressed the yellowish image on the cover with one hand. The picture looked back at her. It was a great wizard holding a crystal wand aimed at the sky in his right hand, his left index finger pointed to the ground. On a table just in front of his right hip sat the chalice of the psyche, the pentacle of the material world, the sword of knowledge, and the wand of passion. A glimpse at this image was all it took for Lilith's soul to quickly download the symbolic meaning of the seventy-eight cards to her cerebral cortex. She walked over to her mother. "This is what I want today, Mommy!" Lilith said, holding the package up.

"Really?" questioned her mother, taking the box of cards from her child's hands to inspect it. She gently put it back on the shelf and squatted down to get an eye-to-eye with her little girl.

"Let's go to the kids' room and have a look, okay?"

Reluctantly, Lilith complied and allowed herself to be led back to the storybook corner. But as soon as her mother let go of her hand, she spun around on the green carpet and walked back through the archway and onto the wooden floors of the adult side of the store. Winding to the back wall, she once again made her way to the shelf where the black cellophane-wrapped package nestled just at her eye level.

Again her mother kept a distance and watched as her little girl made an odd yet inspired move out of the kiddy books into the world of literature. Lilith's mother had an intense passion for books. She led book groups throughout Lilith's life and maintained a strong love affair with the written word. While growing up, a huge dictionary sat at the edge of the dining area of Lilith's family's house. Her mother was always ready to feed her children's minds when their bellies were full—something for which Lilith was forever grateful.

In the little neighborhood bookstore, what was about to happen would change Lilith's life forever. Once again, the little girl found herself in front of the shelf, staring at the Rider-Waite box set containing seventy-eight cards and a book. Once again, her mother followed and watched. Lilith took the black box off the shelf and held it to her chest. Once more, her mother came close and squatted down to fully assess her little cherub's expression. She lovingly placed her hands on her daughter's arms and looked deeply into her eyes.

"Are you sure, darlin'? Are you sure this is what you want?"

"Yes, Mommy. Please, I would like this today," Lilith replied, handing the box to her mother for another inspection. The deal between the two was that this was the day Lilith could choose a book of her liking to take home. Though this was a deck of Tarot cards, it did indeed have a book along with it. Her mother figured that the cards were pictures and served as a learning tool. Without a doubt, this complied with the pair's agreed bookstore contract.

Lilith held out her hands, ready to receive the little package of wisdom.

"Okay, sweetie," said her mom. "If this is what you want."

"Yes, Mama. This is what I want today."

"Are you sure, baby?"

"Yes, Mommy. Thank you! Thank you! This is what I really, really want!"

"Well, all right then! Let's go get it!"

The joy little Lilith felt was elevated, exuberant, and floaty. It was a feeling she would always have whenever she thought of her mother. In that moment, neither Lilith nor her mother knew that this would be the start of her true calling.

Gathering up the little package and Lilith, her mother checked out of the store and together they set off to find a perfect afternoon of lunch followed by some playtime in their favorite park. When they returned home later that afternoon, Lilith's mother peeked around the child's open bedroom door, observing. She watched as Lilith carefully removed the cellophane wrapping covering the little black box. From it she removed the small book, got up, and walked over to her bookshelf. Before placing the little paperback on the highest shelf she could reach, Lilith fanned through the pages. The book opened to a description of the Chariot, VII in the Major Arcana of Tarot. Years later she would use numerology to distinguish a person's soul and personality cards held within the deck. By calculating her own numbers, she would realize that this was the card of her identity. The number seven represented both her soul and personality.

Lilith had come into the world with a gift that the mainstream did not understand. In her effort to fit in, she had been through times of self-doubt which drove her to deny and renounce her unique abilities. Such incidents were behind her now. She had faced many challenges, and each test gave her an opportunity to trust in her gifts of intuition and divination.

"You can see into the bottom of a soul," sang Ambo Shanti with Saruk AUM in perfect harmony. "Your ability to divine is one of the reasons we love our assignment—watching over you." The pair disappeared and quickly rematerialized with a vina and tablas. They floated in the air, sitting on silk striped pillows, and began to sing in their unique language. The music produced intense orange light which cast a palpable sensation over the girl rocking in the chair. Her mood shifted to a blissful feeling of love and acceptance for herself and, in turn, for all living things. Lilith adored the times when the angels treated her to their celestial music. The sounds of their divine voices rang out, causing leaves on the giant tree to glitter. The currents in the air inspired a flood of iridescent froth to roll out of the great water and onto the shoreline of existence.

Little Lilith's ears perked up when she heard a faint humming. She realized her mother was in the hall outside her bedroom door, watching. As quickly as she had noticed, she drifted into a dreamlike place. Her body sat down and her hands began to mix the cards together in a stirring motion. Next, she placed thirteen of them in a formation, face up. It was the same motion she would use years later when mixing the dry and wet ingredients together to bake her signature flatbreads and desserts, and the same motion she used to spread clay onto a plaster slab for proofing when preparing to throw pots on a wheel.

Visions of art school flashed through her mind as she gazed out onto the limitless water. This moment drew her quickly through a vortex to the conversation at the Fortune 500 resort party.

"When I meet people like yourself," she said to the man, "the first question I like to ask is, what are your creative outlets?"

The perfect man with the perfect hair and perfect suit across the table from her stared blankly into space as if unable to see or hear her. He looked so numb and plastic. She wondered what could possibly make a man lose his humanity and become an empty shell. His answer to her question was "Golf."

Sadness overtook the dark cherub. Receiving a sport as an answer to this question from a seemingly nice person overwhelmed her with deep disappointment. So, as she always did in this situation, she leaned back, took a deep breath, and began to explain what a creative outlet is.

"I appreciate your passion for sport, but what I am asking is, what do you make? What do you create?"

A blank stare, numb and lost, blinked back at her. She took another deep breath and consciously curled the corners of her mouth upward. She decided to give it another try. "What I am asking about are your muses," she continued.

The sound of crickets chirping in the night filled her ears. The glazed face lost all expression and blurred into a glob of beige. Once again, the voice barely squeaked, "Golf."

"I truly appreciate your passion for the sport," she repeated, "but what I am asking you about is creativity. Do you understand?"

The bewildered face stared like yards of khaki fabric spread out into the distance. There was nothing, not even a head shake.

She continued to try to convince him that golf was a sport and not a creative outlet. "What I am inquiring about is creativity. Do you have a camera? Take pictures?" Nothing stared back. She continued, "Do you draw? Doodle? Write? Dance? Sing? Play an instrument?"

"I have a boat."

What she was dealing with here was so enigmatic that she had never seen its like. It was the epitome of saying, "I have it all in material riches, yet I am the poorest man in the world." Lilith felt so overwhelmed with grief for this being that she could barely curb the urge to sob uncontrollably.

"Keep it together," whispered Ambo Shanti, causing a piercing ringing in Lilith's left ear.

"I have you here in my hands, little one" purred Saruk AUM, moving the buzzing sound to her right ear.

Gently Lilith reached out and took the man's hand. She did everything she could think of to walk him back through time, back through his childhood history. She ducked into every possible corner of his past trying to uncover the idea of artistic expression, to help him remember what he had once loved. Usually in a situation like this, high school or junior high was the furthest back she would have to take a client in their mind.

The angels grinned listening to Lilith muse. "In rare cases, I have to travel into their memories of elementary school. Some lost their sense of joy in being creative when their blocks or clay disappeared. How sad it is for people to not have an outlet since toddlerhood! But this man could not remember. It was everything I could do to keep from weeping. How tormented to have a seemingly perfect life, yet be so miserable. How agonizing it must be not knowing what to do with your creative energy.

"People join together in couples and procreate. This becomes their reason to live. They lose themselves. They lose their passion for their mates and their passion for life. Why is this not dealt with more in our society? We are pushed to buy, acquire, strive—but for what? If we cannot use our co-creative power, what's the point? So, in the case of this man who seemed to have everything, I tried for half an hour to explain to him that the loss of his creativity was the reason for his unhappiness. I hope he got it. I even went out of my way to explain it to his wife later. I never found out if he discovered an outlet. I hope he did. Do you know if he did, Saruk AUM?"

"Does it matter now, little one?"

"I guess not," Lilith said, looking down into the sand.

"There have been plenty of times when you had magic moments, and even more when what you said helped people feel whole and healed. You don't need to witness every change; just stay in your good intentions."

Lilith noticed a sticky glaze over Don's vision.

"That is the look of memory," Ambo Shanti asserted as the three watched the holographic projection.

"I am able to see that so clearly now," said Lilith. "I only wish I could have given him more space in that moment. It was as if I could feel him swimming into his past."

Chapter 21

Occult

Shrunken heads and a wall of voodoo.

Lilith decided to shift the energy and head west up South Street. She reached out and grabbed Don's arm to pull him along with her.

"I thought you wanted to go to Fourth Street," he said, wondering what on earth was up this way.

"There's just a little something I need up here at Harry's," she answered. "It'll only take a minute."

"The voodoo shop?" screeched the Hierophant.

"I told you she is a witch," scolded the Altar Boy as he waved a thurible smoldering with frankincense around the Boardroom.

"This is gonna be cool!" added the Stoner.

"They have shrunken heads in there!" exclaimed the Nine-year-old, pushing his way to the front in order to get a good view out through the eyes.

"What on earth do you need there?" asked Don.

"You'll see," answered Lilith in a matter-of-fact way. "It's just a few blocks from here."

"Oh, I know where it is!" Don exclaimed.

"Have you ever gone inside?"

"Not since I was a kid."

"Well, it's become as much a museum as it is a shop. Did you know that Harry's was the first occult shop in the country?"

"Really?" Don marveled. "I would think there would have been one in the South earlier, like in Savannah or New Orleans."

"Seriously, let's ditch this freak!" pleaded Reason in an effort to get the teen contingent on his side.

"Seriously, let's hold onto her and never let go instead!" responded the Teen and the Stoner as they shoved Reason into his wingback chair.

"Yes, I have to agree with the young ones," added Casanova, pushing over to the window of the eyes. "I am intrigued!"

Don would have followed her anywhere at this point. "What's a couple blocks out of the way?" Casanova remarked out of Don's mouth.

"Exactly!" responded Lilith with a smile.

Harry's Occult Shop was founded in 1917. Up until then, the city had not seen anything that compared to what Harry Seligman, a pharmacist, was about to introduce. The decedents of escaped and freed slaves had found their way to Philadelphia by means of the Underground Railroad, led by Harriet Tubman. Years later, as the seeds of their Yoruba and Ibo traditions sprouted in the fertile ground of freedom, Harry's entrepreneurial intuition saw opportunity in the herbs and powders they sought. He quickly identified a unique niche market and, as if overnight, converted his little shop into a sanctuary for the new tribe. The dual mottos Harry devised are still the structural support of the store's work today. The maxim "We aim to help" sits on a sign above the counter and resonates through the many healing modalities offered by the shop. The original aphorism, "Light a torch for the good and cross swords against evil," is still displayed in the front window.

"I never understood the point of the crossed swords."

"Don't take them at face value," responded Lilith.

"How is it that we are supposed to take two huge swords, then?"

"Swords represent the element of air. So, all things air," she answered but, seeing that this explanation only confused him more, she continued. "Swords are communication, thought, and new beginnings. Two swords indicate a stable mind that is in balance."

"Oh," said Don as he opened and held the door for Lilith, and then followed her inside.

"Hi Lilith!" came a voice from the direction of a display case. It took Don's eyes a moment to adjust to the low light inside the cool dark shop. "I've got your candle right here, girl. Looks like it's already working," the blonde-haired woman said, winking, as she stood up behind the counter. "Best take the incense and oils, too!"

"I intend to, Marcia," Lilith blazed back with a grin.

"So, I'm guessing you used the floor wash?"

"Yes. And the powder!"

"Good. Well then," said Marcia, ogling Don as she bagged up the items and quickly rang up the bill, "here you go." She tossed a small container filled with orange dust into the bag just before handing it to Lilith.

"What was that?"

"Just a little something for later!" Marcia teased, winking again as she handed Lilith change for the fifty dollar bill she was about to pull out of her purse.

"Thanks!" said Lilith, handing her the cash. She tugged on Don's sleeve to signal she was finished and headed toward the door.

"What the heck is in that candle for?" questioned Reason.

"Hey, Lilith," Marcia called, causing her to stop and turn in the doorway.

"Yes?"

"Can you do readings in the shop on Monday? Sandy is going to be out of town."

"Sure! I'll see you then."

"Great! Enjoy the rest of the weekend!"

"We sure will!"

"She said 'we'!" The Horny Teen danced with the Nine-year-old on top of the Boardroom table.

"Well, that was very interesting," Casanova opined. "I wonder if that dust is an aphrodisiac?"

"What was that little container she threw in the sack?" asked Don.

"Oh, that's a really nice incense that Marcia knows I love. We can burn some later."

"She said we again!" sang the kids in unison yet again.

"Where to now, milady?" asked Don.

"Milady? Really? This is what you are calling her? Why not get a hat with a purple feather and start prancing around in velvet knickers!" screamed Seduction as he stormed into the Boardroom. "Poofter!"

Lilith blushed coquettishly.

"Look at this! She likes it" purred Casanova, motioning Seduction to clam up and join the boys near the eye windows.

Any fear or apprehension that Don had carried into Harry's Occult Shop quickly melted away, revealing a new layer of confidence.

"God knows what is in that sack of hers!" bellowed the Hierophant.

"Shut it!" scolded Seduction. "She's ours!" he yowled with Casanova.

"Shall we head down toward the river now? Perhaps get a bite to eat?" Don asked, offering Lilith his arm.

"Sure! Sounds like a great plan," Lilith agreed, smiling as she entwined her arm with his. "Let's cross over and walk in the sun now." The two walked across South Street and headed east.

"You mentioned Savannah and New Orleans earlier. Have you been there?" asked Lilith.

"Not to Savannah, but yes, I've been to New Orleans. How about you?"

"Yes to both," answered Lilith. "What great cities."

"Which one would you return to?" asked Don.

"I've already been to New Orleans a few times, but both could easily pull me back."

"And Savannah?"

"I was in Savannah last October. It was amazing how many adventures I had in such a short span of time. The first day I was blown away by how gorgeous the historic district is. When I first arrived it was a warm evening, like yesterday. The following morning, the weather began to turn from the sweaty heat of summer to the cool crispness of autumn. It was simply delicious. After breakfast, I headed out on a long walk from the bed and breakfast where I had a room for a couple nights. Savannah was a stopover on a road trip. I was on my way to Asheville, North Carolina, thinking that would be the place which would capture my heart."

"I want to capture her heart" hummed the Romantic.

"You stayed at a bed and breakfast?" asked Don.

"Posh!" commented Seduction.

"Yes. It was named Roussell's Garden, and it was located just on the edge of the historic district—at least that's what it said in the description. When I told my friends who worked at the Mansion on Forsyth Park, they just rolled their eyes and acted like I was staying in a crack house. Sure, the neighborhood was more than a block off the edge of the park, but it was so beautiful.

"Roussell's Garden sits at the bottom of the DOT loop, right at the turnaround on Henry Avenue. If you're fussy or paranoid, you could think there are some questionable buildings on the nearby corners. But if you look around closely, you can see the character and history in the empty structures as they wait to be transformed. Roussell's Garden has a charm and a sense of peace in spite of its surroundings. I believe that whole neighborhood is in its renaissance."

"What is the mansion?"

"The Mansion is a bohemian Marriott. I love those. They're smaller

and have really nice artwork and amenities. I have a really great friend who manages the front desk."

"Couldn't she get you a room?"

"I let her know too late. So, for my stopover in Savannah, I booked the bed and breakfast even though she'd made me an offer to stay at her place. I just didn't feel right putting her to all that trouble. She did give me a great deal on my way back, though.

"That first morning, after breakfast, I spent some time in the gardens with the owner of Roussell's. He'd grown up in New Orleans and had created an amazing oasis with ornate iron arches, flowers, and fruit trees. It was so inspiring."

"Did you draw?"

"I did! I had a sketch book with me and did a bunch of drawings, as well as a little writing. Then I took off to enjoy the people and colors and sounds of the Saturday afternoon. The cooler, late October air had everybody feeling so happy. As I walked up through the park, I noticed that every dog I passed was in a costume."

"A costume?"

"Yes! Apparently they have a designated day in early October to dress their dogs up for Halloween. In every square, you could hear the tickling sounds of giggles blended with the sweetness of friends meeting, and children playing under the cool shade of huge live oaks."

"I've seen it in movies. I imagine it's quite beautiful."

"It is."

"Did you have a favorite park?" asked Don.

"Don't ask me why, but they call them squares in Savannah," Lilith responded. "I walked through a lot of them that first day and, of course, wanted to see Monterey Square."

"That was the one in *Midnight in the Garden of Good and Evil*, right?"

"Yes it was, but the first time I was there, I didn't realize it. I stopped right in front of the Mercer house—that's the name of the mansion—to have a drink of water from a bottle in my pack. It felt so nice in the cool shade, and I was enjoying soaking in all the rich architecture. It's so different than here."

"I bet. So what did you see?"

"Every square had artisans selling crafts. There's a little association that allows them to vend. It's kind of a cool setup. So I was in Monterey Square and I saw a woman crocheting. On her head was a spider web of bright purple with a huge rose. She had fashioned all of this out of the cheapest yarns. It was so intriguing that I felt compelled to go talk to her."

"Why is that?"

"Because I love to crochet. I've been doing it since I was a child. My grandmother taught me. It is like counting mala to me."

"Mala? As in prayer beads?"

"Yes! You know what that means!"

"We are well-versed in eastern ways!" sang the Guru, his head shaking side to side as he floated on a puffy little cloud, just above the center of the Boardroom table.

"Yeah, apparently we do," added the Stoner, blowing some smoke which added to the fluffiness.

"Apparently we do!" chided Reason, causing the Boardroom to buzz with murmurs and humming.

Lilith waited to continue until after Don gave her a small yet knowing nod. "I walked over to get a full-on look at this woman. She had a style I had not seen in the previous artisans that day."

"What was different?"

"Most of the others were wearing a regulation blue denim shirt and making flowers and other little forms out of palm leaves. Low overhead, you know."

"I feel that!" The Stoner elbowed the Accountant's side.

"Tell me about the purple spider webs," Don encouraged, genuinely interested in artists everywhere in the world. Their unique styles fed his creativity through an exchange of molecules and electricity.

"Well, first of all, it was the purple color of the cheap acrylic yarn. It was the type of stuff you give a kid to play with. The same I used to buy at the five-and-ten store when I was little. This woman was making the most unusual pieces from it," explained Lilith, using her hands to augment her words. Don felt like he was watching a dancer express a painter who was illustrating an enchanted forest.

"It fascinates me to see another artist working in one of my mediums and doing something completely different with it," Don interrupted.

"Absolutely! I wanted so much to talk with her but she was really shy. I decided to give her a tip in exchange for allowing me to take her picture. This was all it took to loosen her up a bit. I offered to show her the pictures I'd taken. They were really quite flattering, but she was embarrassed and didn't want to see them. So I asked if I could sit down next to her and show her some pictures of hats I had made for friends. She was so blown away by my crocheting that she started calling me the master! It cracked me up. I told her, 'No! No! I am not at all a master. You are!' She contested that. We laughed and talked about what we liked to make out of yarn. After a few minutes, she felt even more relaxed and decided to share her signature stitch with me. It was so unusual. That's one of the cool things about crocheting. You can just invent as you go along!"

"Seems like that is exactly what this girl is doing!" cut Judgment.

"Screw this! I'm hungry!" said the Stoner.

"Hush up, all of you!" ordered Romance. "I like her and I want her. Look how she glimmers—I can see her light!"

"Oh, here we go!" buzzed the Boardroom as they adjourned for a hiatus, leaving Romance alone to gaze out through the pupils of Don's eyes. It was obviously all going downhill from here.

"Yeah, and too late to intervene," snorted the Stoner. "Let's go eat," he pleaded, scratching his crotch as he got up and headed out.

"Ooh, big words from mister intellect over there," blurted Judgment.

"I stayed with her for a while," Lilith continued, "and then I decided to get back to my adventure. I wanted to see more squares, and continued toward City Market. It's a shopping area kind of like Chestnut Street. I stopped in a few galleries and shops along the way. My feet were getting tired, so I decided to give in and hire a pedicab."

"What's a pedicab?" asked Don.

"It's a rickshaw hooked to a bike. I never knew that name for them, either. I always called them bike rickshaws, but in Savannah, they're called pedicabs. A few blocks later, I found a little group of them waiting to seduce potential fares. I made eye contact with one cabby and just knew he was the ride for me."

"Yeah, I would like to ride her!" jibed the Playboy.

"Like you can!" overlapped Reason.

"Hush, now!" implored Romance with a distinctly southern-infused accent. "What can I say?" he continued. "It must be the South, y'all!"

Lilith continued, "After I made it obvious that I was choosing him over the other cabbies, we were off on a positively splendid meandering tour of the historic district. Savannah's architecture would make you swoon! It's the best of the brickwork you love here mixed with the ornate ironwork of Louisiana. It has a unique charm, and though it hasn't been very long since I was there, I want to go back again. I bet you'd be inspired by it."

Chapter 22

Southern Hospitality

Ghosts in the attic and rattling bones.

There was something about the Victorian buildings and the huge live oak trees in Savannah that sent Lilith into another world. The phenomenon was similar to her experiences in other historic cities she had visited; they seemed to enhance her psychic abilities, making it easy for her to tap into the unseen and the unknown. This happened when she'd traveled to the French Quarter in New Orleans; Paris, France; and Oia, on Santorini, in Greece.

From the moment Lilith got her license as a teen, she loved the sensation of driving and looking at the landscape drifting by. Every year she would get the itch to travel.

She'd decided to take a break from Philly and grabbed her journal, packed up the car, and hit the road when the leaves began to turn. Her mom had given her some money to book a room in a bed and breakfast for the getaway. Lilith was excited by the idea of sitting on a big southern porch, writing and drawing. Originally she had planned to meander down Skyline Drive in Virginia, but something pulled her further south to Georgia.

Savannah was so much more than she'd ever imagined. Walking along the tree-lined streets, Lilith felt as if a dormant part of her psyche woke up and drank the soma of inspiration. In the afternoons, she walked through innumerable squares and went to museums, which took her all over the historic district.

City Market bustled with modern shops behind antique store fronts. The merchandise was secondary to her fascination with the beauty of the architecture and signage. She fell in love with all the colors and textures.

It was on a corner just off a walking plaza of shops and brew houses that she spotted a group of pedicabs waiting for fares. The driver in the center caught her eye, and she was pulled to his cab as if by a giant magnet. The others melted away.

"I would like to hire you for the afternoon," said Lilith matter-of-factly to the young driver. "What's your name?"

"George," the wiry young driver answered. He looked tired or sheepish—she wasn't sure.

"Can I do that?" she asked.

"Hire me for the afternoon?" George responded. "Sure, sure. Hop in," he said as he jumped in the saddle and backed the cab out of its slanted parking space.

A couple of blocks away, George stopped and twisted around on the seat to look her in the eyes. She had been so tired when she climbed into the throne-like seat that his adorable face had been hidden by the mist of her exhaustion. Lilith sensed the young driver wanted to cut a deal, and she was open to anything. For the moment, she was just thankful to be off her feet and in a comfy place where she could make some notes in her journal.

"I just want to say…" George began, causing Lilith to look up from her purple pen laying an inky image of a tree against the thick, textured paper of her book.

She smiled as if to say, "Yes?"

"We're not supposed to do this," George continued.

"Accept a fare?" questioned Lilith with a smirk.

"It wasn't my turn, but my buddy who was next in line said okay, so I got you."

"Well, thanks! It's nice to be gotten!" replied Lilith, grinning. She shifted in the seat to get a more straightforward connection with her charioteer. He was super skinny and genuinely cute. *Too bad he's way too young for me*, she thought, and then asked "So, how does this work?"

"Well," George said, "you can pay by the run, the hour, or…"

"Can we make a deal?" she cut in.

"Sure. What are you thinking? Where would you like to go?" he asked, smiling.

"I don't have a specific place in mind, but I do know that I'd like to see a bunch of squares and some interesting architecture. I seem to have missed the Mercer House, and I promised my mom I would see it. You know, the whole movie and book thing."

"Yeah, of course I do! Okay, well, that's down near Forsyth, and there are a lot of squares to see on the way—both on this side and the east side."

"I'll leave it up to you. This is your town," Lilith said. "Let's visit the ones you think are cool, and make lots of stops. If you can add some storytelling, I'll hire you for an hour or so. How does that sound?"

"Good for me," responded George. "Let me call in to let them know I have an extended fare." He pulled out a decrepit phone that looked as if it had met the macadam a few times, flipped it open, and dialed his dispatcher.

Lilith sat and wrote while he chatted, not really paying attention to what he was saying. When the cab began to move, she realized he was done with the call. "So, where are you taking me first?" she asked.

"Here's my idea," George began, stopping the cab and swiveling his sinewy body around to meet Lilith's eyes as he spoke. "Our first visit will be Ellis Square." She grinned, closed her book, and capped her pen to give him her full attention. "There are so many squares. It would be

impossible to see them all in one afternoon."

"We can go for more than an hour. I just want to make it to the health food store for a juice before it closes. You know, the one at the bottom of Forsyth." He nodded, and Lilith continued, "What is your hourly rate?"

"Sixty dollars," George stated without skipping a beat.

"What kind of deal can you give me?"

"How about I charge you eighty for two hours?" offered George.

"Okay, let's go for two hours. I'd like to see some of the east side, and I trust you to make the choices. I'm in it for the adventure! What do you say?"

"Here's what I propose," said George. "I'll choose some on this side, and then take you over on the other side of Bull Street before I take you down to Brighter Day at the bottom of the park. That's the name of the store you want to go to."

"Perfect! I don't want you to rush. Take your time, stop, tell me stories. Let's enjoy this glorious weather and this day!"

And with that, they were off. The rickshaw was a smooth ride, and Lilith was so happy to have found a great driver. The first stop was Ellis Square, a site that George explained was known as having been the marketplace for the slave trade. "It's now a popular spot for concerts," he explained, pointing out the brand-new performance hall that had been built over the old trading structure.

There was a quiet little wedding going on under the trees in the center of the square as the pair approached. They decided it best to not disturb the scene.

George pointed out a few little tidbits as they headed south on Barnard Street to Telfair Square. As they cruised around the Jepson Center for the Arts, Lilith had a revelation about the layers of civilization in the south. She imagined how the buildings were constructed on the ruins of others by relentless settlers who never gave up—like ants, they just kept going. A flash of Cemetery Number One in New Orleans blazed through her mind.

George's sweet voice cut into her daydream. His explanation about how the historic district of Savannah had gone through exactly that type of building and rebuilding flowed like a river of honey into her ears. She flipped open her journal to make some notes and a quick sketch, imagining the workers and rocks and dust that lay invisible under the foundation of the city.

George turned his attention forward to watch where he was guiding the bike. They cruised down York Street and, as they passed the glass windows of the Telfair Cafe, they saw white enamel chairs set up for a reception.

"That's some wedding! I wonder where the people are?" Lilith mused.

"Yeah, how 'bout that!"

"What a perfect afternoon to get married!" exclaimed Lilith.

"I know, right?" George agreed. "This is the first cool day of the season!"

"We all picked it!" returned Lilith.

As they approached Telfair Square, they spotted the wedding. The crowd was frozen with anticipation awaiting the ceremony. George peddled tentatively over to the edge of the square and parked by a security guard who was giving them a stern look. George assured him with a glance that they would remain quiet and polite.

"The bride is about to walk. Can you feel it?" whispered Lilith.

"Yeah," George responded.

"There she is!" said Lilith, pointing to the back stairs of the museum. "Let's watch her before we take off."

Their timing was perfect. A saxophone player began swooning "Besame Mucho" to the quiet crowd. The two sat in silence, watching as the father led his beautiful daughter down the aisle.

"I used to sing at weddings," Lilith interjected.

"Really?"

"Yeah. I always made the fathers cry."

George smirked a little and jumped back in the saddle to peddle them to the next location.

When the light at Whitaker Street turned red, George stopped and asked over his shoulder, "Do you want to see the most haunted house in Savannah?"

"Do we have to? I'm kind of sensitive," Lilith confessed, shifting in the seat.

"Really? In what way?" George inquired, completely fascinated.

"'I see dead people,'" she said, quoting a movie.

For years she had been talking to deceased and disembodied spirits. There was a time when she cleared them out of houses for pay, and it had taken a toll on her health. She'd seen her share of crazy and knew better than to walk right into it knowingly. Her highly attuned sense of the unseen realm caused her to develop an ultrasensitive meter, warning just how much insanity would be okay to take. She sensed that this would be way over the limit.

"See them?"

"Well, I can always smell them and feel them and hear them and—yes, I can usually see them."

The look on George's face was enough to tell her that this needed some explaining, so she decided to tell him about some past experiences.

"I've always been different. I wasn't like other children" she began.

"When did you realize it?"

"I've known from the time I was a little kid. I used to talk to aliens."

She could see that George was trying to keep cool and not interrupt her. He seemed to be warming up and open to more conversation.

"The most intense energy I've ever experienced was in New Orleans. Have you been there?"

"No, but my dad is from there. I want to go some day."

"You should! I've been there several times, and each time my senses and experiences are more intense than the previous visit." She could tell George wanted her to continue, so she decided to lay it all out.

"The first time I was there was with my parents. We used to meet up in different places at least once a year for a vacation. They lived in Florida at the time, and my dad loved road trips. So I flew to meet them and we stayed in a really haunted hotel on Canal Street, right at the edge of the Quarter. I had so many visions and experiences in that place that it was almost too much to take."

"Like what?"

"Blood dripping down the walls, bodies jumping down the elevator shafts. But that was nothing compared to…"

"Compared to?"

"One night, after eating po'boys and listening to jazz on Bourbon Street with my folks, I took off to go on a walking ghost-tour. I met up with a large group of folks outside Reverend Zombie's Voodoo Shop on St. Peter Street. That's where you buy the tickets for the tours. You should check it out when you go for a visit."

"For sure."

"Anyway, I bought a ticket and stood on the street with a group of people while the guides, who are obviously actors, divided us up. It's way better to have a theatrical guide, don't you think?"

"Definitely," George responded as he continued to peddle. *He's a really fun choice for this excursion*, she mused.

"These guides have a true interest in what they do. I think it's a cool way to get an acting gig. On this first tour, I had a particularly great one. He seemed to be one of those guys from SCA—you know, the Society for Creative Anachronism. They dress up and reenact things from European history that took place before the seventeenth century all over the country. Lots of them do Civil War reenactment

and Renaissance Faires."

"Yeah, we have them all over here. They do ghost tours and Halloween shows," George agreed. "How did it go in New Orleans?" he asked, wanting the nitty-gritty.

"Well, we started off at an old Irish bar named Pat O'Briens. Our guide René led us past the bar area through a breezeway into a typical French Quarter courtyard garden. He gathered us in a semicircle and began telling us the story of the original owner of the establishment. René explained, in great detail, the story of the gentleman who had owned the building, and a terrible argument he had with his wife. As I looked up to the top of the building, the evening light and all the colors changed. I realized I was watching it all play out. It was as if I could see right through the walls of the second floor above the bar.

"The sound of René's voice faded into the background, and all at once I was watching the original scene. It was wild! I saw the fight and could hear the yelling. I saw the man hit the woman and knock her out. He dragged her down the stairs from the attic to the second floor, where a row of large windows looks down over the courtyard. The man opened one of the windows and tossed the limp body of the woman out. I felt it thunk against the brick paving of the courtyard. Then I flashed my gaze around the group for a moment and saw that everyone was still engaged with the voice of our guide. At the same time, I realized I was watching a live reenactment of the original scene.

"In my vision, the man ran down the stairs and came storming out the back door of the private side of the building. He reached the body of the woman, lifeless on the ground. Then he grabbed a shovel propped up against the back wall with one hand and her arm with the other, and started dragging her toward me."

Lilith noticed George had stopped the cab and was curled around in the saddle, completely enthralled with the story. She grinned and kept going.

"They were coming right at me, and literally went right through me. It was so cold, like opening the door to a dank, damp cellar. It was all so real I couldn't believe that the people on either side of me didn't feel the chill."

"Wow!" said George, his exclamation enough to say keep going, please.

"René asked us if we knew what came next. No one answered. There was just the sound of crickets." George got the joke and giggled. "I waited, and still no one tried to answer, so I raised my hand. René nodded and I started right where he had left off—or at least I thought he had. I described the fight, the head clunking, and how the man dragged the limp body of the woman down the stairs to the second floor. I went on about how he shoved her out of the window and how she landed and appeared dead, then the way he picked up the shovel and took her by the arm and began to drag her across the courtyard. I continued to explain what I had been seeing in the vision up until the pair was right there, right where I was standing, and I saw an apparition of the man digging a hole. The people all looked so confused, unsure if I was really a tourist or part of the theatrics of the tour."

"I bet!" George exclaimed.

"Our guide tried to bring it back and questioned me. 'And then what happened?' he asked, raising an eyebrow. A young boy, about twelve, came over close to me and stared right up into my face. I looked right back at him and kept going. 'Then he dug a hole right here,' I said, pointing at the bricks to my right. 'And?' asked René, sure I was done. 'And she wasn't dead! She began to scream as he was burying her alive. But he just kept going, covering her with dirt, slowly deadening and muffling her screams with each shovelful!'"

"Whoa!" George exclaimed.

"Yeah, right? At that point it seemed I'd thrown the guide off his game a bit. As we left the site and headed up the street to our next destination, René asked me if I had been there before. I assured him I had not and, on top of that, added that I had not read anything about any of it. I pulled out one of my cards, which says that I'm an astrologer and read Tarot cards, and handed it to him. He glanced at it before putting it in an inside pocket of his vintage overcoat. He asked me if I'm psychic. I grinned and asked, 'How am I doing so far?'

"The young boy overheard our conversation. As soon as René moved to the head of the group to lead the pack further, this kid decided to cling to me. At first I was really annoyed; it had not been my intention to spend the evening with a twelve-year-old. But he asked me all sorts of questions and seemed really interested in what I had to say, so I let it go.

"He walked to the next spot with me. René once again gathered us, this time on the sidewalk in front of the Delphine LaLaurie house on Royal Street. I didn't even want to be on the same side of the street with the creepy vibes. The kid could see I was feeling something and whispered, 'What is it? What do you feel?'

"It was then that I started to have a change of heart about this kid. He seemed to get me, and understand. As René began to talk about Madame LaLaurie, I decided to whisper some of the impressions I was receiving to the boy.

"'Ask Lilith,' he chirped when René looked around for input. I could hear the air move as everyone whipped their heads to look at me. I added a little about the tutelage of Madame LaLaurie and some wrongdoing involving the torture of slaves. The heads spun back to René and he grinned his approval.

"'She's psychic, for sure!' yelled the kid. He was instantly a fan and became so excited.

"As we walked on to the Provincial on Chartres Street, he began to ask me off-the-map questions about aliens and other extraterrestrial happenings. I could smell decay and hear wailing cries as we turned the corner, leaving Ursulines Avenue behind us.

"'What is it?' asked the kid. 'Is it really gross?'

"'Yes,' I responded, 'it's awful. They're cutting limbs off soldiers unnecessarily!'

"'Aggh, gross!' he said. 'Lilith knows what's going on!' he shouted, and everyone scurried over to me.

"This was becoming really embarrassing, but René had joined in by now and was encouraging me, 'Go on, Lilith. Tell us what you're picking up.'

"So I detailed what I was sensing, and once again it turned out I was right. The stops became a game. René would tell a story to a dangling point; then everyone would look to me and I would finish it."

"Unbelievable!" George said, though he sounded just a little skeptical.

"During those tours, there's a stop at a bar for a drink and a break. As we headed to ours, a British gentleman joined the kid and me, walking. He said, 'Okay, Miss Psychic. If you are really psychic, you can answer anything, right?'

"I was a little nervous, but said, 'I'll give it a try.'"

"Good answer" George interjected.

"So when we got to the bar, he sat down across from me in a booth. He reached into his shirt pocket and pulled out a business card. Then he placed it on the table facedown. He kept his finger on it and asked me, 'Okay, Miss Psychic, what do I do for a living?'

"The letters CPA flashed in my mind. I blurted out, 'Certified public accountant?' half questioning, as I didn't know if that's what they're called in England. The guy turned pale. His jaw dropped and he flipped the card over and handed it to me. Sure enough, there was CPA' next to his name."

"Amazing!" George said, hopping back into the saddle and beginning to peddle the bike once again. "Ha! Well then, we'll have to test your skills!"

"Oh, boy!" said Lilith, wondering if she had overstepped a boundary. "Where are we going?"

"The most haunted house in Savannah—423 Abercorn Street!" George replied.

As the pedicab got closer to Abercorn Street, Lilith felt a piercing pain.

"I can feel it already," she moaned. "It's stabbing me here, in my liver," she continued, holding her right side. "Let's not go!" She groaned, doubling over in the seat of the cab.

"Really?" said George, turning around for a second to look at her. He peddled around the corner onto Abercorn and parked the cab along the side of the square, opposite the house.

"Ahhh, oh God! Something awful happened there. I can feel it!"

"Tell me! Tell me everything you see."

"It's more what I'm feeling right now," Lilith began as she gave in to the sensation. She said a silent prayer of forgiveness and protection, then dove into the images of the vision.

"Oh my God! Something heinous happened here. A man killed his child, a girl child. I can't go near it. Get me outta here!" she screamed, doubled over.

"What else?" asked George. "You sure? Nothing else?"

Somehow Lilith gathered her strength and went back into the sensation.

"A single father—angry, angry for so many reasons. He loved a slave and it tortured him to the point of torturing his own child. The child loved the slave's children; she just wanted to play with them. But the father was so frustrated that it drove him mad. He tied his own child up. She sat up there," Lilith said, pointing to the window to the side of the grand entryway which looked over Calhoun Square. "She wanted to play with her friends. They were here, in the square." A tear fell onto her cheek.

George thought to stop her, but the roll of energy was overwhelming; there was no turning back. She jumped out of the cab and stood in the street, fully taken by the vision. Her arms moved in the air as she described the events.

"He felt so bad—so guilty—but he couldn't stop himself. He was doomed to fade away slowly in the agonizing pain of self-loathing..." For a moment Lilith surfaced out of the vision, but was pulled to continue.

"Next, there was a family with several children—girls. It was the play that killed them. Once they would play, the anger of the dead child's spirit possessed the youngest and...aggh! I can't stand it! It's awful!"

She took her water and splashed some on her head. "How am I doing?"

George was keeping a straight face, but inside he was truly blown away by her precision. *This is the real deal*, he thought as he watched her.

"There's more! Something happened in the yard!" Now her curiosity took over. "Come on, we have to go over there! There's something in the garden!"

She felt it and took off running across the street. George followed, leaving the cab and all her things behind. He watched as she was pulled magnetically to touch the metal of the garden fence. The trees spoke to her, and she continued.

"A deal gone bad, the slaughter of innocent slaves in the shade of that balcony." She pointed to the second-level veranda running the length of the house. "Government officials making bad deals, a card game." The images were coming so fast. She whipped through a rapid succession of scenes like the cards being thrown down in the play she was witnessing through the thick back wall of the tan house. Suddenly she saw where she was. "Get me outta here! Now!" she screamed into George's face. He turned and ran back to the cab with her just behind him.

Lilith stood for a moment, grounding herself, and then reached into the cab, grabbed her water bottle, and poured some of the clear elixir of life into the cupped palm of her right hand. She leaned her head over the liquid and chanted an audible AUM as she witnessed the geometry of the prayer in her mind's eye. She then took the vibrating water and splashed some on George's crown and then on her own head. She dabbed some on her third eye, and then his.

"So how did I do?" she asked, taking a deep breath and flopping onto the seat of the rickshaw.

"Unbelievable!" exclaimed George. "Not only did you nail the stories, you did it chronologically!"

"Really?" Lilith questioned, furrowing her brow.

"Want to go to Saint John's Cathedral?" asked George.

"Perfect choice. Let's go!"

The further they got from the Abercorn house, the better Lilith felt. As the cab slowed down in front of the huge cathedral, she leapt out and bounded up the steps. The sign said there was a mass going on, so she took care to open the door into the main sanctuary quietly. Once inside, she went straight to the font of holy water and scooped some into her hands. She blessed herself like a proper Catholic, nodded to a guardian who was seated in the back pew, and stood quietly for a moment to take in the splendor of the carved statues and gilded paintings.

That was all it took. She scooped up another handful of water and bounded out the door and back down the steps to George, who was waiting in the street with her chariot. After she splashed some of the holy water on George, the two were off to the next square.

As they crossed East Liberty, Lilith was blown away by the beauty of the architecture. If there hadn't have been a time constraint, she would have wanted to look at every property on every single street. She lay back in the cab, resting and regrouping from the ghostly encounters, feeling grateful to connect once again with the trees and gorgeous afternoon.

George peddled them north to Columbia Square, and there they encountered a third wedding.

"Another wedding. Can you believe it?" George asked.

"Wow. I'm not sure how to take this!" said Lilith.

As George circled the park, they watched a military groom wait for his bride at the garden altar of trees.

"And we're watching another bride walk. Incredible!" exclaimed Lilith.

George pulled the cab over to the sidewalk just in front of a pinkish house on the west side of the square. "Do you feel anything here?" he challenged, tilting his head.

"A little," she answered, happy to not feel the malevolence of the Abercorn house. "It's a lot more playful than before! You tell me the story. That last one wore me out!"

"You're right; this is a much more playful ghost. She likes to climb in bed with men who stay here. It's an inn now. You can go look inside if you like. Check out the parlor in the front," George suggested as he gestured at the bay windows to the left of the front door.

Lilith complied and walked up the unusual-feeling steps.

"Everything is iron!" George responded to her quizzical expression when she looked back at him from the grand porch.

The iron felt good and grounding. She stood still, feeling very grateful, allowing it to reorganize her molecular structure before going in to have a look at the sitting room. When she returned, George was on the phone finishing up a call.

"That was work. They want to know where I am."

"What did you tell them?"

"That you booked me for the afternoon and that I can take a fare after five o'clock this evening," he said over his shoulder, pushing a couple buttons on his ancient flip phone.

"Sounds good to me," Lilith said agreeably, looking back at

her journal.

George turned slowly in the saddle, causing her to look up and flip her book closed. He stared deeply into her eyes. "I'm a little psychic, you know," he related.

"We all are, darlin'. We all have the gift. It's just that some of us are able to tap into it more freely than others. Why do you bring this up? Are you picking something up from me, here?"

"Have you been married twice?" George asked, folding his arms and looking very self-assured.

The sound of his words stopped time dead in its tracks. There was a tunnel of energy, and she swooped back to a point when she had been married—the one and only time she'd taken that plunge. Back then she had a dream one night, so intense that it seemed the prophetic words were hanging in infinity all her life, up until this moment. And though this scene was different than the dream, the time right here, right now, possessed the identical energy of the dream, and it hovered in the air above and around the little cab.

"I can't believe you just said that, that you asked me this!" exclaimed Lilith.

"I'm right, right?"

"Well, not exactly. But the way you asked me is a moment from a dream I had a long time ago."

The feeling of getting it wrong didn't sting as much as it normally would have, and George looked quizzically at the little woman in his cab.

"What, then?" he pressed.

"Well, to answer your first question, yes, I was married once, and there was a very significant second relationship. But no, I was not married twice—and I can't believe I just said it this way!" She waved her arms into the air. "Wow!"

George's stare deepened as she continued.

"I had a dream. It occurred shortly after I was married and really threw me off balance. I have intense and often prophetic dreams." She could see that George was following her intently, so she continued.

"I dreamt I was on a road trip to Asheville and I had stopped in a café that was lined in very natural-looking wood. I sat in a booth with a man, and he asked me about being married twice—exactly like you just did! That's what blew me away a moment ago. It was the exact rhythm and timbre of the man in the dream."

"Was it me in the dream?"

"I don't recall. It wasn't so much the face of the man, but his voice and the trigger of the question. In the dream, I answered as I'm about to; this is the truth of this life. I was married once for ten years. The first four years were great, but the last six were a big lesson. I stuck it out through addiction and betrayal, through therapy and healing. After that was over, there was a very significant relationship with a guitar player who became and still is my best friend. He lives out in Arizona, where we'd moved together."

"And now? Do you want to get married?" George queried.

Lilith thought, *This can't be the guy for me—he's so young. But how cute of him to ask.* She looked over at the soldier who was now reciting his vows to a blushing bride in front of a very quiet, very unemotional group compared to the two weddings they had witnessed earlier. She weighed what was to come from her mouth next.

"I am open to a relationship, definitely. But, will I marry again? I doubt it. Marriage is a financial contract, a business agreement. But love—love is a sacred vow that needs to be renewed yearly. Love is what I'm open to as a commitment. But the legality of marriage, no. I don't think so."

Part VI

Flash

The only one we need to really get to know is our true self.

Chapter 23

Passage

All roads up the mountain lead to the same view.

Lilith stopped for a moment, prompted by Don staring down at the sidewalk, just after the pair crossed Eighth Street. He was wondering how she knew he loved brickwork. Embedded in the grey concrete square were a few small glazed clay tiles.

"Do you know what these are?" asked Don.

"Clay tiles," Lilith answered.

"Yes, but what kind of clay tiles?" Don returned.

"Small, bluish-greenish clay tiles," Lilith returned as she knelt down to point directly at the cluster of sparkling little shapes.

"We got her," screeched Intellect.

"Hook her now!" jabbed the Playboy.

Don began to explain, "These are Mercer tiles—"

"Henry Mercer's tiles!" Lilith cut in.

"Oh geez! She knows about these, too," cowered Low Self-esteem.

"Just give up, dude," suggested the Stoner, exhaling a huge cloud of smoke.

"No! I want her," said Lust, standing to reveal tight-fitting, shiny sharkskin pants.

Don continued, "So you know about Henry Mercer?"

"Of course I do! I grew up in Bucks County. We went on school trips every year to the Moravian Museum to see the pottery and tile works factory. My school required that the students learn about the process he used for manufacturing. It was definitely one of the things that influenced my decision to go to art school."

"Oh crap," screamed the Stoner.

"She's out of our league, dude!" added the Teen.

"Get out of this now!" begged Low Self-esteem.

"I believe we've got this," said the Playboy, kicking his heels up onto the Boardroom table. He leaned back in his plush chair to light up a Cuban cigar and then offered one to Casanova, who gladly accepted.

"Extinguish those this instant!" scolded Reason. "You're obscuring my ability to navigate these waters."

"'Scuse me, sire, but I believe we are talking about mud here. Would that not be the shoreline?" politely corrected the Student.

"Sire! Ha, ha, ha," laughed the Stenographer, pausing to read through the recent minutes. He squinted as he lifted the seemingly endless tape of paper flowing from his archaic little machine. Then he pushed back from the huge mahogany table to have a good belly laugh.

"Let it go, dude!" implored the Stoner. "You're getting nowhere with this chick. Let's just go have a doobie and a glass of wine. Then we can head back to the home studio to do some abstract painting."

Reason screamed, "All of you, clear out! I am handling this." He swung his chair around to peer out through Don's eyes. "Stay quiet and smile. Not too big!" he ordered.

"Yeah! Do the look!" yelped the Stoner.

"That'll melt her!" added Casanova.

Don cracked the look—one eyebrow up and a smile just a little wider on the opposite side of his mouth. The entire Boardroom fled the table to watch what was happening. It worked. Lilith's heart skipped a beat, and they could all feel it. It was like a leap of faith and an off-guard knowing all at the same time. It was the same heartbeat that she'd experienced when sitting in the pedicab in Savannah.

Don's eyebrow gently melted back in place, causing Lilith's full lips to flash her million dollar smile.

The original stardust of creation sparkled and flashed, causing Great Mother to sneeze a cloud of golden light. It washed through the branches of a maple tree across from where the couple was standing on South Street. Future moments merged into the present moment, forming a burrito fold in the fabric of time.

"Have you ever seen a hay ball?" asked Lilith, breaking the suspended silence.

"A what?" choked Don, completely confused as to why the look's effect had failed to last longer.

"It was something I saw in Savannah while I was having a snack at Forsyth Park. That's the big, famous square in the historic district."

"What kind of snack? Ask her, numbskull!" poked Logic at Don's grey matter.

"Yes, yes, this is an opportunity to figure out how to close the deal," added Casanova.

"A snack?" asked Don quietly. "What kind?"

"Good one, buddy!" said the Horny Teen, high-fiving Casanova.

"I was eating a pomegranate and some nuts I'd gotten in a health food store. They had some cool little iron tables outside, and I was sitting at one, enjoying the late afternoon air after my pedicab tour around town."

Reason stared at the Stenographer for notes. The Stenographer immediately reached for the trail of paper and recited, "Rustic, iron table, health food, outdoor café…" Looking up, the Stenographer remarked, "I am paraphrasing and adding, I know, but we need all the help we can get."

"Listen to him. He's onto her!" yelped the Horny Teen, adjusting his jeans.

Lilith continued, "Up pulled a tiny car with a giant ball of grass on its roof. A pair of women with thick southern drawls started cackling about it at the next table. They began to chide and heckle like the two old fart characters in the balcony from *The Muppet Movie*."

Don chuckled, getting the joke, and she continued.

"This nondescript guy hopped out of the car as the mocking went on. One said 'What's this all about?' The other said 'What's that on the car? Is that a big ball of grass?' The first one added, 'How is that big ol' ball of grass hangin' on there?' They went back and forth like this until the guy walked toward them. He passed me first, and I saw that his t-shirt read 'Hay Ball Tour,' and had a list of cities he had visited. Then I realized the car had a matching sign. I wondered, 'What the heck is a hay ball tour?'"

"The grass ball on the car, right? That's hilarious!" Don laughed.

"Wow! Look at her face! It is lit up like an offering candle. She gets that we get her!" screamed the Altar Boy. His outburst caused the entire Boardroom to shove forward, tilting Don's head a little closer to Lilith's face.

Saruk AUM brought his head closer to the face of his Apsara, inspiring her to smile. The two crouched, watching, as they perched on a high branch of the tree across from Lilith and Don.

Divine Father held his invisible face against the earthy cheek of his Goddess. A trilobite stopped to look into the round eyes of a fishy counterpart. The moment snapped like an overly tightened guitar string, twanging in surrender. This caused the burrito of time to fold in on itself snugly, like the French seam of a well-made pair of jeans.

Lilith and Don started to walk again down South Street and crossed over at Seventh. When they got to the ornate alcove of the Garland of Letters Bookstore entryway, Lilith hesitated.

"Oh, geez," cried Low Self-esteem. "Here comes another story!"

What is it going to be this time?" he pleaded.

The Divine Father beamed a golden ray of light at Don's forehead. Deep in the center of his skull, the pinecone-shaped pineal gland lit up and began to sweat a shimmering milky liquid. The sweet nectar overflowed down through his throat and then into the center of his heart. There it blended with the fire of vitality. Without realizing what he was doing, Don opened his arms to the tiny goddess facing him. He watched as her eyes drifted closed.

Lilith felt an irresistible magnetic attraction and leaned into his embrace. She smelled patchouli and wool blended with the distinct aroma of goats, which she associated with male energy. This drew her in deeply, and she melted.

"Tell me," whispered Don. "Tell me what you're feeling, standing here."

"I remember how I felt when I used to spend time in this building upstairs," she responded. "It was where I once practiced kung fu and had a family."

"You had a family?" asked Don, wondering what she meant.

"Yeah. The students and our teacher, we were like a big family. We had classes every night. On Friday evenings, when we were finished, we would walk over to Chinatown for dinner."

"Dude, we're getting really hungry!" reminded the Teen.

"When was this?" asked Don.

"It was back when I went to PCA, right when the performing arts college cut off all ties. The separation of the two schools made it really hard for me to minor in dance. There was no physical education of any sort at PCA, so I had to find my own form of exercise. My first semester was okay because I was studying with a great jazz teacher. Second semester, I was blocked from my first choice and gave up. That is how I ended up here on the mezzanine floor. There was a little kung fu school up there. I was just remembering the day I began painting silhouettes of

each student on the walls."

"What types of shapes were they?" asked Don, causing Lilith's smile to widen.

"Look! Look at how her energy shifted!" cooed the Guru, floating in on a cloud. "You are receiving her now," he said, his head shaking side to side. "This is very good," he gestured with a wave of his hand, "very, very good!"

Lilith began to describe. "They were dark shapes, classic shadows. I beamed a light on each student posing in positions from the forms we were learning. Our teacher chose the poses that he felt exemplified each student's animal nature."

"What colors were they?" Don inquired, easily visualizing the images.

"The walls were a golden-yellow, and the paintings were black enamel. I used a cheap light to flood the shadows on the walls and then outlined them in pencil. It was really easy. I did all of them in one afternoon. Over the next few weeks, I painted them—filling them in with the thick black gloss. It was really fun." She smiled at the memory.

"Was there one of you? What animal were you?"

"I bet she was a tiger!" growled Lust.

"Yeah," responded Lilith. "Mine was a classic Bruce Lee pose. Our teacher did the tracing. He used to tease me and call me 'Little Bruce.'"

"That's hilarious!" laughed Don, wrapping an arm around her. He finally felt in charge and somehow completely able to let go, all at the same time.

Don took Lilith's hand and began to lead her down the sidewalk. They walked on quietly. Just before crossing Sixth, he stopped to submerge himself into the depths of her eyes.

"Dude, it's getting way past lunchtime, and it is time to munch," insisted the Stoner.

"What's your favorite type of food?" Don asked.

"Well, I'm mostly vegan, though I sometimes stray a bit and eat cheese or put cream in my tea. I guess living in the Market makes it too easy to eat dairy."

"That explains The House of Cheese!" said Don, who was beginning to feel a little high as he rode the vibrations of being with Lilith.

Don felt the shape of her hand in his. Consciousness noticed how sentences were being formed and how soft his gestures were. The morning had given way to a splendidly cool afternoon.

"Let's cross back to the other side of South," suggested Lilith. I'd like to see what the Art to Save the World Gallery has on display. I heard there are some new pieces."

"Sounds good to me," Don said agreeably.

The textures and colors of fiber weavings and sculptures bounced in the window as the two paused to look around.

"What do you think of these?" Lilith inquired, pointing to little *nichos*-style altars made out of paper and clay.

"Very nice," said the Artist, inspecting the construction.

"Impressive," Don mused as the Artist evaluated the materials and techniques.

Chapter 24

Ancestors

You are the myth your ancestors told around the fire at night.

Ambo Shanti leaned forward and whispered into the ear of the quietly contemplative Lilith. In turn, Lilith blinked and looked sincerely into her female guardian's eyes. The giant chair squeaked a bit when the rocking motion halted.

"It feels like so much of me already has been stripped away, Ambo Shanti. Will it ever come back?"

"No, child, I am afraid it will not."

"Perhaps I should gather some branches and build an altar to my missing parts."

"Nothing is missing, sweetie," consoled Ambo Shanti. "You are still you."

"I don't feel like it. I feel—"

"Transformed," interjected Ambo Shanti in an effort to lift Lilith's spirit. "You are morphing and ever-changing."

Lilith shifted out of the chair and wiggled her toes into the sandy earth.

"I think I will make an altar something like the ones I had to honor Día de los Muertos. I want to show my gratitude for this sacred space."

Lilith had built her first altar when she was living in Bucks

County. It was inspired by her many visits to the Kripalu Ashram in Sumneytown. The small Kula Shala compound spread across a beautiful hillside ridge in a very old forest. A variety of buildings where residents lived, ate, practiced yoga, and devoted themselves to their guru were tucked between the huge old trees. The idea of a large community living together in harmony fascinated Lilith. It felt so natural to be there among the devotees. She was sure that she had partaken in a similar practice over the course of her many past lives.

Her first experience with communal living had been as a boarder in high school, but being at the ashram was a much different form of community than she had experienced at school. In an ashram, people perform a variety of daily practices. They ingest the same food together, both alimentary and spiritual. Devotees breathe the wise air of their guru's channeled teachings and the wisdom of the enlightened masters of the lineage. Lilith fell in love with different daily practices, like meditation, listening to the guru speak, and the study of ancient writing.

During her weekly visits to the Kripalu Ashram, she enjoyed walking in the woods, taking yoga classes, eating vegetarian food, and having plenty of time for meditation. Her favorite place to engage in quiet contemplation was at Muktidham, the house that the guru of the community, Yogi Amrit Desai, had built for his teacher Swami Kripalvananda, known as Bapuji, when he had come to stay in the United States.

The great saint stayed in Muktidham for four years of total silence. Each morning he taught the community through smiles and chalk board notes interpreted by his loving disciple. Then he would retreat to his bungalow where he immersed himself in his own personal *sadhana* practice. Just after the swami returned to home to India, he left his body in *mahasamadhi*, the great enlightenment, his final practice.

The residents honored the small house as a living altar to their teacher's teacher. It was kept locked, and they only gave the key to serious seekers. Lilith loved to walk up the path in the saint's footprints to sit in his space and meditate. Everything in the house had been kept just the way it had been when the master lived there. The residents maintained it spotless and intact.

Lilith could feel the incredible energy of Bapuji's devotion in the space. Whenever she needed to feel connected, she would book an hour or two in the little house and, after a hike through the woods, disappear into some magical time visiting the gap between thoughts on the altar of the great one. This always gave her a deep sense of peace. It remained the most amazing ancestral shrine she had ever experienced. It was not just a diorama on a shelf, but a full-scale place she could be inside of. She supposed some people experience this sensation when houses are passed down in families, and certain furniture, pictures, and knickknacks with sentimental value are kept.

Lilith knew that in Asian cultures, there are specific places and often separate rooms in a house designated for devotion to one's ancestors. *It's unfortunate*, she thought, *that in our society we're so busy focusing on the future that we tend to trample all over the past.*

"It's true," said Ambo Shanti. "Many people starve in their need to feel connected. They yearn for spiritual linking. They desire to fit in."

"Perhaps it is because they run away from their roots so fast," Lilith mused.

"Granted," Ambo Shanti continued. "Not all energy from the past is what we want to take with us into the future. We must learn to sort through the layers."

"I doubt whether westerners are really able to truly experience personal shrines."

"Those who are able to discern and identify what defines them can see what is toxic and needs to be released, dear one. They are the few who honor their roots."

Lilith floated into a memory of her studies with shamans and medicine people. She learned to clear the negative energy that was brought through the experience of birth, which delivers us into the light. She believed infants were a whole lot closer to clear than adults but, similar to the ancient ones, she had a deep knowing that we all come into our first breath in need of a lot of cleanup and healing. To her, it was hilarious to think that society views babies as perfect and pure.

"It is not about immortalization, but rather acknowledgement," said Saruk AUM, agreeing with Lilith's musings. "To have an altar honors the bits of the ancestors residing in you."

"So many people have twisted ideas about their family history," Lilith stated flatly. "Most people don't have a clue about where they come from. They have no idea how their grandparents met, nor can they tell a story about their parents."

"This is part of the foundational breakdown of society," Saruk AUM said.

"Do you know where you come from?" asked Lilith.

"Yes," smiled the Gandharva. "When we are sprung into this job of guardian, our heritage is sung to us for what translates as one thousand and eight earth years. It would be wonderful if humans would do the same for their children," added Ambo Shanti, completing her partner's thought.

"I am certain that some indigenous cultures do this," Lilith noted.

"Imagine if your parents sang you the story of your conception or how they met," Saruk AUM posited. "Perhaps then a great wrongdoing of society could be righted."

"And the greater would once again experience the sense of being a part of a village," Ambo Shanti added.

"We all work so hard to have a space of our own, even if it is less than thirteen feet from the boundary of a neighbor's," Lilith observed. "People struggle to get out of their family's house and go out on their own. They spend so much time working on disconnecting from their roots."

"This removes the essence of the ancestors from the DNA," Saruk AUM said. Lilith felt he was looking so intensely into her that he was able to isolate tiny chromosome strands. "Then," he continued, "not that long ago, people lived with several generations of their family under one roof. In some countries this is still found, but not in the West. Western culture is unusual in that it seems to try very hard to get away from the original family. The children are extremely disconnected. Many are being raised by single parents, and often suffer from a variety of emotional problems as a result of this lack of village."

"You were raised by both of your parents, little one. You had the luxury of your maternal grandmother living with you."

"I know," said Lilith, remembering what it was like to share a room with her Nanny. She continued, "Thank goodness for grandparents. They are the great spoilers of us all!" She remembered her grandmother's way of giving and nurturing.

"It is her love that wove into your psyche, sweet one," Ambo Shanti chimed in. "She grew up very connected to the thread of her grandparents and knew their stories and songs. We have watched so many immigrants try hard to lose their past. They changed their names, adopted a new language, and renounced their ancestry. Look at what this has done to the greater as a society. It has destroyed the sense of belonging to a village."

"It is said that it takes a village to raise a child," added Lilith. "Who is raising our children? This job is in the lap of the teachers who are underpaid and less than acknowledged."

Chapter 25

Nourishment

The fine art of pie.

"What were you majoring in at art school?" asked Don as he turned away from the gallery window.

"Fine arts and teaching," Lilith replied. "And you?"

"Fine arts also," answered Don.

"I doubled in teaching," Lilith added.

"What on earth for?"

"My father thought teaching was a worthy profession. He had no belief in my ability to make it as an artist and earn a living. After beginning the classes, I started to believe him and thought that it would be a good idea. After receiving my bachelor's, I returned to the little boarding school I'd graduated from to be a teacher. They offered me a few classes each week—and floor sweeping."

"Floor sweeping? Are you kidding me?"

"Yes, floor sweeping and no benefits," Lilith reported.

"Sounds like a job in a third-world country!" laughed Don.

"Art-teaching positions were few and far between," Lilith responded. "I was bravely embarking upon the employment market, using the help of teacher placement agencies. I hit so many dead ends. The agencies told me that the only way to find a job as an art teacher in public education was to find a school where there was a very old art teacher or one who was pregnant. I was further instructed to circle around like a vulture and wait for them to get ready to leave, and then pounce on the administration for their job."

"Oh my God! That's so morbid!" Don exclaimed.

"One agent laughed and told me, 'The only way to get a teaching job in art is to find a teacher who is dying. Then go and get their job.' I tried sending out all the papers and letters that you do when you're looking for a job. I soon realized that public education didn't need me, so I turned to private schools. I was even willing to relocate and live at an all-girls school, taking on non-art-related responsibilities. Thank goodness I had no luck there either."

"That sounds like a nightmare," Don remarked. "What changed?"

"I was standing in my parent's kitchen one winter morning. I wasn't really sure what I was going to do. I was still living here in Philadelphia and was just home for a short visit. The phone rang and I picked it up. It was my high school sculpture teacher, looking for me. We were both excited and shocked that I answered the phone. That's how I was offered the underpaid job."

"It's starting to sound a lot better!" Don offered, smiling assuredly.

"I became chief of my own small village and started figuring out how to raise teenagers."

"Wow. I'm sure I could never handle that. How did it go?" Don inquired.

"I learned a lot about using love and humor. They taught me many things, the most important of which was that I didn't need to make babies and raise children of my own."

"How long did it last?" asked Don.

"Just a few years," Lilith answered. "When it ended, I tried teaching some adult courses. It was then I realized I preferred raising adults."

"I prefer raising myself!" Don laughed. "So now you're here, back

in Bella Vista?"

"Yeah, but it's different this time," Lilith mused.

"How so?"

"Well, moving back here and living in Valentine's palace is so inspiring. The vibe of art and creativity permeates the bricks. It's nothing like it was when I lived over on your side of Bella Vista."

"I can imagine," Don replied. The pair paused in front of the old Grendel's Lair on the corner of Fifth Street. Lilith melted into an intense déjà vu. She flashed back to the feel of her roller skates carrying her up the twisting staircase to the second-floor dance space in the old club. She remembered how cool it was that they let her in with her wheels on.

"So you eat pizza but not cheesesteaks, right?" asked Don.

"Ugh, I'm kind of over pizza for now."

"How can that be? Are you not a South Philadelphian?" he teased.

"I used to eat pizza every day!" groaned Lilith.

"No! That's overkill!" Don cautioned.

"Tell me about it!"

"The only way you could possibly eat that much pizza is if you worked in a pizzeria."

"In South Philly, we call it a pizza store. Yup, you got it, and it was the greatest job I ever had."

"Greatest job? No way!"

"Yes indeed! Working in the pizza store was by far the best job I've ever had. I delivered pizza on roller skates in South Philly. Back then I lived up on Eighteenth and Spruce. My crazy roommate Sarah got me the job. I wonder if you knew her; she might have been in your class. I think she's your age."

"I don't think so. What was her major?"

"She was into design."

"Nah, no way. I only rubbed elbows with the ones in fine arts."

"She was hilarious. I guess it ran in her family because she's

the cousin of a bunch of famous comedians. It was pretty cool living with her."

"What did she look like?"

"Kind of like a big Barbie doll with reddish hair. She had a thing for spandex and super-high spiky heels."

"No, I don't know her. How the heck did she come up with pizza on skates?"

"We'd both come back from winter break with roller skates. It was right at the beginning of the craze, but before roller disco took off. We used to skate down at Penn's Landing with a huge group of roller-dancers called the J-Walkers. Sometimes we performed during parades or at the art museum."

"Really?" said Don.

"Oh good grief!" said Reason. "Thank God she is talking in the past tense on this one."

"For real! There's no way we're getting on skates. Not even for a squeeze!" added the Horny Teen.

"But gentlemen, think of the spandex! Stretchy tight little outfits are very good!" added Lust.

Lilith continued, "A skate store opened up near Headhouse Square. As soon as we heard about it, we claimed it as our territory. The owners liked us to skate around the street in front of the store on Third, picking up beginners to teach. They loved having the hot skater girls helping out the tourists who were renting their skates."

"Yes, I can imagine!" said Casanova, who had become interested, his words coming out of Don's mouth.

"One day a handmade poster showed up on the wall inside the skate shop that read 'Looking for Good-Looking Girls Who Skate.' Sarah tore the flyer off the wall and claimed it for us. She was so bold that she rolled over to the counter and demanded to use the phone. She instantly got us the gig."

"Dang, that Sarah was a go-getter!"

"Yeah, she was. When she announced that we were going to deliver pizza on skates, I was skeptical. I told her she should take the job and I would wait to see what happened, so she went first. It all seemed a little fishy to me. She took off for South Philly, and I skated home alone that afternoon.

"That night she rolled back to our apartment after a couple hours with sixty dollars cash and a free pizza. I was amazed and felt a little foolish for not trusting her and going along. She insisted that I accompany her the following Saturday night, at the owner's request. She said the delivery was to a little card game, and that it would be a single run if the two of us did it together. She explained that the following week would be a bigger group, and that they would want double the order she'd delivered earlier that evening. There was no way she could carry so many pizzas by herself."

"Why is that?" asked Don.

"The steam starts to break down the boxes, and they can't hold up under the weight of the pies."

"Ah, that makes sense. So you went for it?"

"Yeah. The following Saturday afternoon, we skated across town to the Italian Market and on down into the depths of South Philadelphia. The shop was on the corner of Ninth and Emily, near Tasker Street. I skated eagerly, following Sarah through the Market and past Pat's Steaks. I'd never been down that far. When we got to the store, a funny little cartoon of a man greeted us. He said his name was Vinnie Eyes."

"That is so South Philly!"

"I know, right? He quickly offered me a slice of his artistry, a very impressive Margherita pie. Then he scurried off to complete the order we would take to the same destination Sarah had delivered to the previous week. I could feel the cash filling my thin wallet.

"Vinnie pulled two pies out of the oven and brought four more boxes out of the back kitchen. He said they were filled with mini stromboli. Each of us stacked a pizza on top of two of the stromboli boxes and, loaded up, we headed out the door and north on Ninth Street. I was so happy, singing the whole way! Sarah had told me very little, but tonight I trusted her judgment. When we swooped around the corner of Reed and Seventh, I noticed a bunch of cherry-tops glowing in the early evening light. It seemed odd, but I figured it was South Philly, so I didn't say anything at first, but then I asked Sarah, 'Hey! What's the address where we're going?'

"She said, 'It's just up ahead.'

"'Up ahead where?' I was beginning to feel really creeped out.

"'Just up there,' she said, pointing with her free hand.

"'Where all the cop cars are?' I asked.

"'No, don't be paranoid!' she scolded me.

"'Don't be paranoid? Are you crazy?' and I was thinking, *Look at all the cherry-tops!*"

"You still trusted her?" asked Don.

"Yeah, I still trusted her, but my instincts were yelling, 'Get the heck outta here!' Ignoring my inner voice, I followed her to the blue-green door on the west side of the street. She raised her hand to knock, and the door mysteriously opened. Inside the tiny front room were two police officers, a SWAT-team officer, and three FBI agents. An arm reached out and grabbed Sarah. Another reached a little further and pulled me and my pizzas in as well. It was all so bizarre and happened so fast that I didn't have time to be angry at Sarah."

"What happened inside?"

"They grilled us, asked us a bunch of questions—who we were and what we were doing there.

"'Delivering pizza!' Sarah snapped, 'what does it look like?'"

"Whoa! That Sarah has a brass pair!" Don exclaimed.

"I started feeling a little queasy, thinking her big mouth was going to get us in a lot of trouble. I was sure this was why I hadn't wanted to go with her the week before. I was starting to get really paranoid, thinking, 'We'll never get paid,' and that Vinnie the pizza guy was going to think we'd robbed him. How could this ever turn out to be good?"

"Holy crap! What a story!"

"The chunky FBI agent asked our names, and we made up aliases on the spot. Honestly, I had no idea what was in the boxes, and I heard murmurs coming from the back room about something being hidden in the little pies. Then the FBI guy pulled out a small pocket knife and took the center box out of Sarah's stack. He set it down on the corner of a table that was decorated with huge towers of cash. Two agents had come into the tiny front room where all of this was happening and started to count out bills. I realized that this was a big deal card game, and we were in the middle of it!

"The FBI agent opened the first box, revealing two dozen perfect little stromboli. He then systematically stabbed and examined each and every one of them."

"Looks like he's done surgery on Italian food before!" chirped the Defiant Teen.

"I couldn't believe it," recalled Lilith. "Then, out of the back room came a crime scene photographer, aiming his camera right at us. Impulsively, I covered my face with my forearm. I guess somewhere in the archives of the FBI is a picture of me with my arm over my face and three pizza boxes on my shoulder!"

"Was it scary?"

"Yeah, kinda…but on the other hand, it was completely surreal. I get an adrenaline rush when I think about it. Anyway, they took my boxes and made us stand in the corner as each was opened and every little stromboli was stabbed. 'Clean!' the guy barked. I was screaming, 'What the heck!' on the inside.

"Then the FBI agent began to chow down on a stromboli, and

handed a few out to the other agents. I couldn't believe it. It was like a skit on Saturday Night Live—totally unreal. While all the jaws were chewing, Sarah bellowed, 'You're going to pay for those!' as she pointed at the stack of boxes. She was fearlessly staring deep into the bottom of the FBI agent's soul.

"'Sure, I got this,' a second agent said, flipping through some bills. 'How much, doll?'

"'Ooohhh,' I thought, 'Sarah is going to smash him for that.' The look she flared back in his face could have been an A-bomb. The agent shrunk back in his chair and stretched so we could see his chest holster.

"'Oh, brother,' growled Sarah, not trying to hide her disdain. She was a warrior princess, staring right into the eyes of an FBI agent. Her invisible spear was pointed right at his cheek, full of the gooey stromboli.

"'Got any sauce?' he asked.

"'Oh, you've got to be kidding!' I thought.

"'Gravy!' Sarah corrected.

"'Gravy?' he questioned, then sunk back in the chair, acting as if we didn't exist.

"Sarah pointed to the last box of the six that the other agent was finishing stabbing. How sad for the little crispy pies to be victim to a relentless switch blade. 'In there,' she directed, 'In those little cups. That is where you will find the gravy.'

"I was blown away by how in control Sarah was. This was super freaky. We were at a major bust and in spite of it, I felt cool, calm, and collected because Sarah was such a badass!"

"She sounds like a total badass!" said the Stoner, his words coming out of Don's mouth.

"I think I want her!" blurted Casanova, standing up and heading to the door of the Boardroom.

"Where is he headed?" bellowed Reason.

"Groin, I'm guessin'," responded the Horny Teen.

"He must be headed downtown. It seems the humidity just went up," added the Stoner, unable to get a light on his current joint.

Don's mouth filled with saliva, and his body temperature began to rise.

The arms of the Divine Infinite stretched to the edges of time and space, welcoming the Great Goddess into the crook of his invisible shoulder. There she snuggled and purred like a kitten contented with a bellyful of warm milk.

Reason struck his gavel on the table with a loud crack, causing light to fragment and shatter. The floor of the Boardroom was suddenly covered with multi-colored dust. Deep in the still waters of the Great Mother, fish formed from the gentle trilobites. They sprouted tiny hands and began to play with shiny little pebbles.

The FBI agent negotiated the cost of the pies with Sarah. She pushed hard for a tip while Lilith backed into a corner and wished there was a way to escape the small room. Her eyes scanned every inch of the cramped space. In her mind she quickly summed up the huge stacks of money and organized the sad-looking gangsters, who sat handcuffed to chairs and an old radiator under the window.

Lilith was sure there would be no tip, and only hoped to break out of this scene. Somehow, Sarah managed to get paid and scrape up a meager, gratuitous five bucks each. She dropped one last stinging comment as the pair, finally freed, exited the house. On the skate back to the pizza store, Lilith whistled and then sang a little Reggae tune about police and thieves. Back at the store, Sarah gave a full report to Vinnie. She punctuated the story by announcing that they were through for the evening. Vinnie agreed and said he would be in touch. He wasn't freaked out at all by the story.

That night, skating home, Lilith imagined what it would be like to live in South Philly.

"Do you think he knew what was going on at that game tonight?"

asked Lilith.

"Oh yeah, I'm pretty sure of it," Sarah answered.

"Geez, he fed us to the lions!" Lilith added. She had a brief twinge of knowing the future, and saw herself living in Bella Vista. It felt as if it were already happening in the now.

When the roommates arrived at their brownstone apartment near Rittenhouse Square, Sarah declared that she would negotiate a deal with the pizza man, Mr. Vinnie Eyes—a.k.a. Captain Pepperoni—to reinstate the two skaters as a regular delivery service. Her enterprising mind was already calculating the tip possibilities and she was sure that, no matter what, it would come out way better than a standard waitressing job. Sarah knew the minimum wage for a waitress was around a dollar an hour, so she figured she would ask for three under the table. The next morning, Lilith awoke to Sarah's voice ordering Vinnie around over the phone. She was cutting the deal. Listening to her strong, self-assured negotiation was a foundational stone in Lilith's autonomy, and she took indelible mental notes. Sarah orchestrated the two working deliveries on the weekends, and alternating on the slower weeknights.

Vinnie said yes. He had a weakness for Amazon women pushing him around. For Lilith, it turned out to be the best job ever! The two pulled three times the standard pay for waitresses, and steadily received huge tips. They were free, skating all over South Philadelphia, jumping curbs and going their own way down one-way streets. Everywhere they went they won the affection of the neighborhood and scored a ton of free pizza. For two years, they reigned as South Philly icons, and Lilith continued for another two after Sarah moved had on.

On Fridays, as the two girls skated out from their uptown apartment, they chatted about art school, concerts, and boys. Skating through the entrance to the Market when they crossed Christian Street was like entering a completely different world. The energy shift was palpable. As they rolled down Ninth Street, vendors called out, "Yo, pizza girls!"

One night a fruit vendor tossed an apple to Lilith, just like the iconic scene from the movie *Rocky*. By the time Lilith moved to the Market, she already had an enclave of admirers and a following. Her pizza fame earned her a place "in the family."

She loved working at the pizza store. TV and news shows taped her twirling, skating into the lens of a camera, and smooching as she swooped in with pies stacked on her shoulder. It was an easy choice for her to quit her other job waiting tables at the Armenian grill down near Headhouse Square on South Street. She'd worked there with her best friend Owen. The separation caused her to miss him, so she decided to rent a trinity house on the edge of the Market so they could be together. This became a haven for them while she finished art school.

"So," Don observed, "you were worshiping at the altar of pizza!"

"Yeah, I guess I was, for a few years. It was sacred."

"It must have been the oregano!"

"And the cheese!" Lilith smiled. "And the sauce. My boss was so hyper about his sauce recipe. He locked himself in the back kitchen and stuffed a rag in the keyhole on days when he made it."

"Don't you mean gravy?" Don asked with the cutest quizzical expression. The two laughed so hard they had to stop and catch their breath.

***

"Isn't it odd that women go out to eat by themselves?" asked Saruk AUM of Ambo Shanti as they perched on a rooftop watching Lilith and Don down on the sidewalk.

"Yes, they sit at fancy bars eating upscale food alone while guys go out in packs to drink beer and scarf pizza and wings," she responded.

"Good point, love. It's a wonder how any of them ever get together."

"Each wants a partner, but neither is able to partake in the ways of the opposite," Ambo Shanti added.

"It is a mystery, indeed, my darling," said Saruk AUM, gently touching his consort's face. "Each being has free will. We all have choices to make. Many people ask how to manifest what they want. They ask how to get another person to act or do as they wish. No matter how much we want something from or for another person, we cannot change their ways. The other being's free will is always stronger for them. Even the Divine cannot change us. We are all co-creators, and therefore have this freedom of choice. Our own will is stronger than the imposed free will of any other."

"Maybe he does get you, sweetie," Ambo Shanti whispered in Lilith's ear. "Bella Vista was a chip off the bigger hologram of South Philly!" she added.

"Like I get you, my darling," purred the infinite space as he wrapped his great unseen arms tightly around the globe of rock and water. He cradled it into his ever expanding chest.

***

"Did you used to frequent Grendel's Lair?" asked Lilith.

"I did!" Don answered. "I saw so many bands there. Did you?"

"Sure! It's an easy skate down here from Bella Vista."

"Bella Vista is the best!" Don smiled.

"It was and it is!"

"What was your first place like?"

"My first place was a stereotypical Trinity house. My next-door neighbor Anthony was a classic Italian prodigy. His mom lived in the house behind his, and owned the one behind mine as well. She did Anthony's cooking, washing, and cleaning. What a life! I had no idea what sustained him. Every morning, like clockwork, Anthony would sing Start Me Up' as he toweled off from his morning shower. That cracked me up!"

"The Rolling stones song?"

Her smile answered yes and she continued, "That was back when I lived with my roommate Owen." Don snarled and Lilith quickly added,

"Who is a gay man."

"So you lived with a fruit?"

"A fruit?"

"It's a joke!"

"No, it's not!" she retorted. "It sounds more like a phobia! Are you afraid of being gay yourself?"

"What?"

"Back out!" screamed Low Self-esteem.

"Maybe your fear is causing you to find disdain with the lifestyle?"

"No, that's not it at all!" Don pleaded in an effort to make things right.

"You know," Lilith countered, "fourteen percent of the male population is documented bisexual. Imagine what the real number is."

"Oh please!" howled the Hierophant.

"Yikes!" yelped the Altar Boy, "I can't believe she is spouting statistics!

"I never thought of it that way," choked Don. "I give up. I guess you called me on this one."

"We are straight!" screamed the Lover and Casanova simultaneously. "Tell her we are straight!"

"It's unfortunate that people are unable to relax around this subject. So many of us are influenced by our elders and end up taking on their habits and belief systems," Lilith opined more calmly.

The Boardroom clamored around the table for a swift parley about what to do. "Blame it on the family!" declared Reason.

"Yeah, come to think of it, the macho men of my family really dissed the gay population," offered Don.

"It happens," Lilith said with much more understanding. "So now you have the opportunity to change that familial pattern…"

"I assure you that I am 100 percent straight!" Don exclaimed.

"…and practice acceptance?" she questioned hopefully.

"Here comes a pregnant silence," whined Fear.

"Say something brilliant, dude!" pleaded the Horny Teen. "Make her smile!"

Don closed his eyes for a second, gaining recall. "Tell me more about Anthony, your hairy neighbor, and your roommate Owen."

Lilith smiled. *He remembered their names*, she thought.

"Nice save!" commended the Referee, making the safe signal with his hands while giving a tweet on his whistle.

"See, he was listening to you," Saruk AUM said, pointing to the blips on the screen.

"What?" Lilith asked from under the giant tree where she had gone to search for fallen branches.

"Please, tell me about Owen," Don asked with even more sincerity in his voice.

"We used to race each other to the tiny bathroom window on the second floor of our house to watch the tight-bunned, hairy-chested Anthony. He would come out of his morning shower, wrap a ridiculously small towel around his hips, and wipe the steamy bathroom mirror with his hand. Then he would sing."

Lilith remembered their daily, early-morning banter.

"Do you think he sees us?" giggled Lilith.

"How could he not?" countered Owen. "I know he sees us! I know he wants me! Get out of my way, you hussy!" he squealed, playfully tickling his best friend's ribs.

"Yeah! Right? Well, you're probably right. Besides, you deserve him! You deserve each other. He is your type, after all. You love those big hairy bears!"

The two carried out this morning ritual for a little over two years.

"Why did you leave that house?" asked Don.

"Owen eventually moved out, and the house was more than I needed. The timing was perfect, so I moved on."

Chapter 26

Seeds

Dormant potential slumbers awaiting
the perfect moment to take root.

"Tell her a story, fool!" the Jester begged, jingling the bells on his *marotte*.

Don decided to open up a bit. "I was forced to be an altar boy when I was little."

"Where is that coming from, you idiot?" howled Casanova.

Lilith smirked.

"Shhh…she likes it," said Reason

"Let it ride!" decreed the Lover, waving his hands as if smoothing the air.

"It was the last thing I wanted to be," Don admitted.

"So it's true. Every Catholic mother wants her son to be a priest?" probed Lilith.

"Well, maybe. But in my case, I think it was to just to be a good Catholic boy."

The Altar Boy tore off his robes and threw them down at the feet of the Hierophant as he stuck out his tongue and gave him a raspberry.

"Get off this corner, man!" urged the Stoner. "It has a bad vibe."

"Let's keep walking," said Don.

"Ask her a question, dude," prodded the Horny Teen.

"Light her up again," begged the Artist.

"What was the religious weather like for you as a kid?" Don asked.

"My parents showed me their religion, but they but never forced it on me. I was born into Judaism, taken to synagogue on important holidays, and sent to the Jewish Sunday School every week. When I was little, I went because I thought I had to."

"So you left at some point?"

"Yes. I was moved to a Quaker school at age seven. The Quaker philosophy is to encourage students to develop their own ideas about spirituality. By the age of nine, I began to question the stories and theories I was being fed in synagogue and Sunday school. This caused me to become disillusioned with all of it, and one Sunday I raised my hand to be excused from class so I could go to speak with the rabbi. Anytime a kid wanted to leave to see the rabbi, they were allowed, during his office hours. It was a way to get a free pass out of the room. So I did. I went to see him."

"That seems pretty bold for a nine-year-old."

"It was," whispered Ambo Shanti to Saruk AUM as they giggled, perched on the telephone wires above the couple's head just near the corner of Fourth and South Streets.

"I left my classroom and walked down to his office. When I got there, I told his secretary of my desire to speak with him, and sat down to wait my turn.

"He came out his office door and looked right at me, calling me by name, and then invited me to come in and sit down. I remember the room was dark, with rich wooden furniture and a bookshelf filled with really old books. The whole thing had an ancient feeling."

The entire Boardroom had moved to the front and was now staring out through Don's eyes, hanging on every single word.

"This is quite an amazing story," offered the Philosopher.

"I could use a glass of wine," interjected Casanova.

"I'd really like to do her!" added the Horny Teen.

"Shut up!" yelled the Collective as they turned back to absorb more of her story.

"So what happened?" asked Don.

"I proceeded to ask permission to begin studying for my bat mitzvah."

"Doesn't that happen when you're thirteen?" Don inquired. "Didn't he think you were kind of young for that?"

"As a matter of fact, yes. He leaned back in his giant chair and laughed at me. I felt humiliated. I imagine there was a look of puzzlement painted on my face."

"Paint! Yes! Let's paint her!" screamed the Artist.

"He shook his head and told me that he did not perform bat mitzvahs for girls, only bar mitzvahs for boys. He went on to say that I would have to wait for my confirmation at age sixteen before I would receive any acknowledgment or rite of passage from his organization."

"That sucks," said the Altar Boy as he kicked at his crumpled robe under the table.

An expression of sadness, blended with disdain, shadowed Don's face.

Lilith felt supported and went on. "I thanked him for his time, informed him that I would not need anything more from the establishment, and went back to my classroom. This was my first awareness of the necessity for equal rights for women. The rebellion for women's liberation had already been established, and this was my initiation into it."

"Geez!"

"Back in my classroom, I took a long, hard look at the people around me. My middle-aged, overweight teacher had squished her bulky body into a lot of white vinyl reminiscent of the seventies. She looked like a shimmering snow-sausage. I remember a huge oversized silver and white watch on her wrist. I took it as a sign that it was time to go. I thought that it would be no great loss if I walked away and never returned. So I patiently waited for the end of the class and left to catch my ride home."

"That's amazing! I've never heard such a story. What did your parents say?"

"She is so not like any of the other kids!" ribbed Saruk AUM.

"I went home that day and announced to my parents that I would not be returning to Sunday school. I told them that I had spoken to the rabbi and made this decision on my own. I never told them what the rabbi had said to me, to spare them the humiliation I had experienced. Instead, I said I was tired of listening to the same stories about dead people, year after year."

"And that worked?"

"I have no idea why it worked, but it did. My mother said okay."

"What about your father?"

"My father didn't really care. They weren't that devout and usually only went to worship if there was a high holiday or a bar mitzvah or wedding. I guess, in my own way, I was letting them off the hook."

"Amazing! You—at nine—had the wherewithal to even come up with all of that!"

"I'm sure it was as a result of the encouragement I was receiving from the Quakers."

"It had to be more than that," Don said. "How does a little kid figure all that out?"

"I guess it's because my mother always let me try things on my own without getting in the way. She'd let me fall and fail without interfering. After a failure, she was always there to help me up and dust me off, but she never got in the way. She always allows me to figure things out for myself."

"I wish more mothers would learn to do that. You're so lucky."

"Yes, I'm so grateful for that quality in my mother, and I love her for it. The simple act of letting me find my own way has always been her way to teach me. It's a great gift that nurtures my growth. To put it in Tarot terms, to me my mother is the High Priestess."

"Okay, you just lost me," Don said, puzzled, offering his hand to Lilith so they could continue walking. "Can you explain that?"

"Sure. In the deck of Tarot, there are two separate decks. The portion known as the Major Arcana is numbered zero through twenty-one, and is represented with Roman numerals. These are the trump cards."

"Interesting," Don observed. "I bet that's where the idea for blackjack came from!"

"You may be right. There's no known source for it."

"I wonder if we're onto something," Don said.

"Perhaps we are," Lilith mused. Then she continued, "There's one school of belief that says the Tarot cards came from the Italian game *Tarocchi*. Some believe it is the other way around. I agree with the latter." She could see that Don was genuinely interested and kept going. "The rest of the deck, the pips, are just like regular playing cards with the addition of one extra court card per suit."

"By court card, do you mean the Jack, Queen, and King?

"Yes. In the Tarot, there's a Page in the people cards as well. This second deck is called the Minor Arcana."

"I had no idea."

When Don said this, Lilith smiled from the center of her heart. She loved the cards intensely.

"Some readers consider the Fool card a separate deck from the Major and Minor Arcana decks."

"Why is that?" Don asked.

"The Fool represents our journey in life. He is the ultimate significator. His symbol is the hoop of eternity, the zero."

"And the High Priestess, what does she represent? What is her number?"

"She is II. In the image on her card, she's sitting on a throne, holding the book of law. It's traditionally depicted as the Torah. Unlike the many mythical characters who show up in the deck, she's considered to be an historical figure. The High Priestess is wise and knows all! Behind her is a wall of juicy pomegranates, bursting open with ripe seeds of potential."

"Like you, my celestial deity!" thought the Divine Masculine as he rocked his ever-transforming Goddess.

"I often see my mother's potency as that of the powerful High Priestess—encompassing a perfect balance of masculine and feminine energies. In ancient times, the High Priestess was also known as the Papas."

"Like a pope?" Don asked as he stopped and faced the tiny philosopher.

"Yes, like the pope. It is believed that there was once a female pope, and she was said to have reigned in the early thirteenth century."

The Stenographer stopped clicking on his device and reached out to look at the ribbon of paper pooling on the floor. It was definitely time to take a break. He looked over at Casanova and said, "I agree. Let's give this a rest and get some wine!"

Chapter 27

Harmony

Polarity is the realization that seeming opposites are in fact entrained.

Lilith's rocking chair creaked to a halt. The reverberation of sound echoed across the water, creating rings to infinity. Ambo Shanti and Saruk AUM flapped down for a landing. The two angels sat silently, looking at Lilith, who had just completed a small image of a male and female from sticks and leaves she had gathered.

"What does she need from us now?" asked Ambo Shanti of her partner.

Saruk AUM's look was questioning, and the two decided to just sit in honor of the moment. Lilith sensed their presence and began to speak as if to no one in particular, but to everyone at the same time.

"So many times I have begun the journey with only part of myself. It takes so much discipline to really get my entire life moving on the spiritual path. I yearn for more, and the desire is eating away at me and creating emptiness inside of me. I have been looking at the addictions I have had to material objects, and I have been trying to get other people to fill the aching hole inside me. I long for someone to save me.

"I have come to realize that many women I have known searched for a knight in shining armor. For me, it was easy, as I had never lived on my own when I was younger. I was either with my family or living with roommates. My parents raised me to believe that one day I would be married, and a man would take over my father's financial support and provide me with a home and an allowance. I managed to manifest the man and the home, but I had a gaping space yearning for emotional and spiritual connection and passion. The man who materialized was nowhere near my fantasy.

"I looked around at my friends, my colleagues, my acquaintances, and I saw them doing the same thing. Many settled on some of what they wanted because they were afraid to be alone. They were tired of the continued search for what the ego told them is perfect. Most people do not really hold the hope that their ideal life can exist, and so they settle."

"What does she want that is any different from what any of us want?" questioned Saruk AUM of his partner.

Ambo Shanti crouched, pensively preening, smoothing her sleek wing feathers. As she did, an iridescent sparkling dust floated on the breeze and landed in the water just offshore. A group of fish saw the light change and swam toward the colored cloud. As they made contact with it, their scales changed from dull greys and browns to vibrant rainbows of color.

"The yearning to connect centers from deep within us," responded Ambo Shanti. "It is our constant craving to couple and our strong desire of wanting to merge."

The Divine Emptiness puffed his invisible chest and then softened in a galactic exhale of green wisps. His Goddess cuddled in the vast, vacant void of his being. She responded with a sound of deliciousness and nestled deeper into her consort's embrace.

"I have an uncontrollable yearning to be one with her," the Divine Emptiness whispered, "and the magnetic force of Shakti impulsively attracts us to one another. It is irresistible."

"It is amazing to me how many people numb themselves in an effort to escape growth," Lilith pondered. "It must be the fear of pain and the hollowness of dissatisfaction."

Ambo Shanti smiled so warmly that the Sun Disk dripped honey on the great water, painting orange and yellow streaks upon its surface. She offered, "This is the beginning of addiction. It doesn't matter what you are hooked on. All fixations are formed from the same desperate feeling of emptiness and the perception that you are completely disconnected. This feeling leaches all of the power of positive energy from your core. This in turn masks your ability to see that we are always connected with the Great Divine."

"No one can magically come into our life and change it for the better," said Lilith. "I am beginning to understand! The work needs to come from inside our own being. It is becoming clear to me that we must focus on ourselves. It is not about 'What do you have for me?' or 'How can I change you to be better for me?' but rather 'What do I have to present to this partnership?' and 'What am I bringing to the table?'"

"Yes, and you have worked so diligently on changing so many things, your diet and thought patterns and habits. It takes an immense amount of energy to eat healthily, think healthily, and use the body in healthy ways," Ambo Shanti encouraged.

"Think back to your training in Chinese medicine," Saruk AUM urged gently. "Remember that, in the Oriental philosophy, there is a description of Yin and Yang that is a lovely metaphor for the male/female relationship. It demonstrates Yang as a straight line with a coiled line around it like a stretched-open spring—the kind of toy you loved to play with as a child. When drawn in two dimensions and viewed from the side, this image appears as a sine curve, undulating along a centrally fixed line. The horizontal, fixed line is the Yang line. It is steady and direct. The curving line is the Yin line. It is mutable and changing. The two appear to intersect continually as the Yin line seems to ripple above and below the steady support of the Yang line. The ancients implored us to look at this model from a different viewpoint, shifting to the angle of where the two lines might originate. When we change our perspective, we see that the model image would appear as a dot for the end of the Yang line, surrounded by what is perceived as a circle, formed by the Yin line. The two never touch. The Yang line is straight and goes off into space; the Yin line is a spiraling continuum and never makes contact."

"Is this how relationships really are? This explains so many feelings. Some days I wonder if any of us ever truly connect!" Lilith chuckled.

"As a model for the feminine and masculine energies, this explains a lot about the spiraling dance women do and the straightforward progression men seem to make. This simple metaphor explains why in such a beautiful way. Even though the two appear to interact and connect, they never are able to come into full contact."

"Where are we going to take her?" questioned Lust, breaking the silence in the field of Don's mind.

"Tick-tock!" grumbled Casanova.

Where shall I take her? Don pondered. *A woman like this has seen and tasted so much and, after all, we both live here. How can I possibly impress her?*

"Take her to Jon's. They have an early happy hour this afternoon. We can get her drunk and have our way!" chanted Lechery and the Horny Teen in unison.

"Oh, no. This flower needs to be coaxed open slowly," countered Casanova.

"I know what she wants! I got what she needs!" howled the Italian Stallion, reaching into his tight leather jeans for a scratch.

Don asked, "Would you like to get a drink?"

"Sure. It seems like the perfect time for a glass of wine," Lilith answered.

"We are in, baby!" sang the Horny Teen. "Let's walk past Zipperhead and drop by Condemnation. We can see if she likes glow in the dark with ribs!"

"Oh, no you don't! That's not going to cut it!" came shouts from around the Boardroom table.

"Do you recall the last time we trusted you on that matter?" bellowed the voice of Reason. "That poor girl went out screaming, barely pulling her clothes on before she fled. All she got was a fleeting glimpse of the sausage in that eerie yellow-greenish one that we let you pick out!"

"Okay, okay. Let's let him guide the ship," said the Horny Teen, slinking back into his chair and pointing at the Teen Angel.

"Splendid idea!" purred Casanova, spreading a velvety maroon tablecloth over a café table.

"Where shall we go, Lilith?" Don queried.

She stopped. Her eyes widened as she looked up and responded, "How about Jon's on Third? My old roommate runs the kitchen. I'm sure he'll make us a great snack, and they have a decent wine list."

Don looked baffled.

"You remember! Owen, the one I told you about, who shared the house with me years ago in Bella Vista."

Don sighed and smiled, then drew her in close, holding her tightly as they continued.

"Do you have to work tomorrow?" Don asked. "Do you have a job now?"

"Not right now."

"Pay up!" the Stoner said, holding his hand out to Reason.

"I've been doing commissions and reading cards. I haven't worked a steady job in the city since just after I graduated from PCA. After the pizza delivery job, I worked in an antique shop up on Pine Street, just across from Dirty Frank's. I used to hang out there all the time."

"Of course you did! Everyone from PCA did, and we all ate at—"

"Layla's!" Lilith finished the sentence with him. "I love the falafel

there. I eat them all the time," she sang.

"Me too," Don rejoined.

"Have you ever met Dave there?"

"No, I don't know any Dave. Does he work there?"

"No, he just likes to hang around the creative types and mooch sandwiches. He's kind of crazy, thinking artists have enough funds to feed him," said Lilith. "He seems to have a knack for knowing who has a rich daddy, and he latches onto them. Dave is one of the strangest people I've ever met. He can be insightful and kind one moment, and totally hyper and completely overbearing in the next."

"Why would you even hang around a guy like that?"

"He was like a mascot of my sophomore class. I couldn't get rid of him, so I just had to give in. He used to call me the Egg-i-mo,' alluding to my somewhat Asian-looking face and making a crack on the name Eskimo. He seemed to think it was hilarious. The whole 'what's your ethnicity?' thing is old news. One of the most popular questions people ask me is, 'What are you?' Where do they come off? Why do we have to make everything fit into a little box with a label?"

Oh God! What is she? Now I need to know! Don thought as he maintained a sweet grin.

"Anyway, Dave was out scouting around for old items one day with his favorite art buddy, Chaz, whom he'd identified as a rich kid. They came into the store. I recognized Chaz as someone I'd met at an attic party. Did you ever go to one?"

"Sure," Don responded. "Did you date Chaz?"

"Yeah, for a brief second. It's so weird that I never met you before," she commented, scanning her memories of attic parties for Don's face.

"Tell me about Chaz."

"Dave told me I needed to get out and have some fun. I'd been cooped up in my studio painting a lot, so I took him up on the offer. Dave really liked the idea of me being a cushion when he was with

Chaz. The selling point that tipped me over the edge was when Dave told me that Chaz was a catalyst for the obscure."

"So what about Chaz?"

"I tried making it with him, but he often freaked me out."

"What did he do?"

"Do you want me to just skip to the weirdest example?"

"Yes! Say yes!" implored Reason. "We don't want to cross her boundaries!"

"Please," Don requested.

"Okay. It's kind of strange. He wanted to have sex inside a huge kiln at the clay studio where he worked. When we were in there, he proceeded to get my foot stuck in his mouth."

"What?"

"I know. I blame it on Dave. After all, he introduced us."

"That is just too crazy for words!" screeched Lust.

"We have much better techniques!" added Casanova.

"It makes me wonder if Chaz ever came down off of the acid we dropped around the time all that happened," Lilith added.

"Sounds wild," Don commented.

"I have to admit that I don't regret any of it. But the foot fetish thing still has me feeling a little wiggly," Lilith conceded. "Are you sure you don't know these guys?" she asked again, then went on. "Dave had been a gardener for a famous new age spiritual leader. After working at his California mansion for several years and witnessing the darker side of power, Dave decided to leave the West Coast and come to Philly. Dave and Chaz met at a self-help seminar where they tried to heal the wounds of their childhoods."

"I do know these guys," Don recalled, smiling. "Chaz is a few years younger than me. I vaguely remember Dave hanging around the college studios with him. So what did you get out of it, since the foot swallowing wasn't your thing?"

"I felt like I was getting stagnant. Dave was tired of my complaining. I was grumbling about how the roof had caved in on the pool where I'd been swimming at the Jewish YMCA up on Broad Street, and that I was in bad need of a fitness program. I was frustrated because I'd been taking dance classes at the performing arts school, but they wouldn't let me have the teacher I wanted since I was only part-time. So I just gave up. I hadn't had physical contact since the human shoe incident with Chaz and was feeling horny. Dave was tired of both subjects and decided to create a solution. He told me that he had a friend who was teaching martial arts."

"Oh crap!" yelled the Horny Teen. "She was banging the martial arts teacher from above A Garland of Letters!"

"He also said this guy was a hunk, so then I became interested. Athletics and a squeeze, all in one. I thought, 'This could be my lucky day!'"

Don started turning distinctly green as Lilith continued.

"Dave said this guy's name was Ricky Chong and that he was a bouncer at a bar down on South Street. You remember? Back then, it was the happening area for pub crawling and pickup lines. Though Dave wasn't a drinker—one of his only saving graces—and he was dance challenged, he offered to go there with me and get the ball rolling with Ricky. I accepted. I figured I could drink a beer, spin around the dance floor, and leave if it all sucked."

Don tried to keep cool, although he felt the temperature of jealousy rise a few degrees.

"We got to the bar and, to my surprise, this Ricky guy was a gorgeous mountain of Asian and Latin blood. He was The Rock before The Rock! I definitely wanted to dance with him, vertically and horizontally."

"I can't take it!" yelled Low Self-esteem.

"Hush!" scolded Lust. "Let it be a teaser. Look around. Who is she with right now?"

"Exactly!" added Casanova.

"It is just a story man! Let her tell it. We'll get some wine in her, and badda-bing, badda-bang," added the Italian Stallion. "I'm just sayin'."

Don squeezed her into his side a little tighter and turned his head so he could look into her eyes. Somehow he managed a little grin.

Lilith continued, "Ricky Chong's skin was like coffee—smooth and rich, the kind that pleases a French palate—blended with foamy cream, like a delicious latte. He's a Pisces, born on the Ides of March—a warning from the Romans—and in the year of the dragon. I thought it was fate due to the dragon tattoo on my left buttock. I am the year of the pig, so I roll over and let dragons consume me."

"You have a tattoo?" Don blurted.

"She rolls over?" drooled the Horny Teen.

"Several," Lilith darted back, then went on. "We danced intermittently that night while he watched the crowded bar and did his job as a bouncer and the doorman. It was a quiet night, so he spent lots of time with me. I tried to play it cool, but I wanted him badly. The night melted to an end point, and we left the club. Out in the quiet middle-of-the-night street, we looked at each other and decided to go to the place where he was staying. We arrived at the third floor walkup just off of Headhouse Square. I saw that he had no bed. I didn't care—I would have stayed with him in the middle of the road and felt like I was in a five star hotel. I was mesmerized."

Just when Don was feeling a little sick from imagining Lilith with another guy, she kept going.

"I gassed up at his station…"

"Why is she doing this?" cried Libido. "I'm shriveling!"

"…and I was disappointed to find that his nozzle was smaller, proportionally, than the rest of the pump."

"Ah, the punch line!" Casanova said, and then spritzed some breath freshener into his mouth.

"Badda-boom!" The Italian Stallion added as he spritzed a cloud of Versace Eros around his head.

"I learned that day that all the myths about hands, feet, and noses are a crock. I decided, after we broke up, that the only way to know how big one is, is to grab hold of it and feel it for yourself."

"Is she suggesting...?" questioned Lust.

"I believe she is!" answered Casanova. "And all this before a drink? Fascinating!"

"I got what you need, baby!" punctuated the Italian Stallion.

Don was relieved to hear this and smirked a bit. He wished she would check out his goods, knowing that his Sicilian ancestors had provided ample plumbing on his lean frame.

" Who cares?' I thought," Lilith continued. "Though I was wounded for a long time when we ended it," she lamented. "The relationship went on for two years, until my father broke it up. I had let Ricky Chong into my inner circle, my sacred space. I'd let Chong devour me. He was in every creative thought and every breath."

A horse whinnied and the sound of hooves approached the Boardroom. "Dive in and save her, lad! The drawbridge is down and so is her guard!" implored the Knight in Shining Armor as he led his trusty steed into the assembly room.

Opportunity, thought Don. The Sleuth coaxed him to ask, "What did he give to you? What was right about Chong?"

Lilith thought for a moment. "Chong began to teach me martial arts, along with a handful of devotees. At first we met in a rich older woman's house. She had Asian décor in her living room, so it was a great setting for the classes. He taught us the movements of cranes spreading their wings, monkeys picking fruit, dragons whipping their tails, and tigers crouching. I was instantly hooked. It was exactly what I needed at the time."

Don could imagine the tale illustrated in Chinese-style watercolors on gossamer-thin rice paper. The bold brush strokes of hand-ground inks gently danced on the filmy sheets in his mind.

To fan the flames of his curiosity further, he asked, "What else did you do together?"

"We practiced in the flickering shadows of Chinese lanterns and celebrated life as a family of misfits," answered Lilith.

"A family of misfits?" Don echoed.

"Yes, I told you earlier," she responded. "We shared meals in Chinatown around a big table—you know, family style. Chong's energy was as big as a lion's. Our chopsticks clicked as we laughed and felt like furry little cubs, part of his great pride. And his ability to make people laugh was epic."

Lilith slipped into a misty memory of busting a gut one day along with Jesse, who was Chong's roommate and lifelong best friend. There were days she laughed so hard, doubled over, that she begged Chong to stop. Jesse's favorite bit that Chong acted out was called "The Tales of Mr. Doot Dot." He would strap a couple of couch pillows to his bum and perform a skit a la Jerry Lewis.

Chong and Jesse had come south to Philadelphia, leaving behind their home in upstate New York. They were in search of Jesse's father, Philly J., who had dropped his seed and moved on, as musicians do. By the age of twelve, Jesse was able to play the drums at a professional level, and his mom was forced to tell him the truth about his father. Lilith was eternally moved by their brotherhood, and how Chong lovingly called his buddy Little Jesse Jay.

Lilith snapped back and continued telling the story to Don. "Eventually Chong got enough money to invest in the loft space above A Garland of Letters. He named it the Silent Spirit Kung Fu School. The core group was very devoted to our teacher and the art form. We trained every night. I quickly moved up in rank and became second in command as an assistant instructor. Then I began teaching classes for

women and children on my own. Eventually Chong decided to enter the entire school in competitions."

"Grr, a spicy one!" growled Lust.

So you must be really feisty, thought Don.

"And possibly deadly," Reason interjected, as Don's mouth said, "Sounds impressive."

Completely absorbed by her memory, Lilith kept going. "On the weekends, we would get together and hike up to Market Street to an X-rated movie theater that showed a triple feature matinée of imported Chinese fighting films. We sat on trash bags and newspapers that we brought along for fear of what was on the seats in that place!" She remembered the dank smells of the theater and the way the light carved out the incredible angles of Chong's face. She wondered if she would ever really let go of how she felt about him.

In the cool blackness, the kung fu students and their majestic *sifu* escaped the city's hot summer afternoons and studied the classic moves and comedy of Bruce Lee and Jackie Chan. Lilith cut her hair short, emanating Bruce. She ate, slept, and dreamed the dance of katas and fighting postures.

Chong trained her to be ready for anything. He used to hide inside dumpsters or in alleys and attack her as she walked home from selling trendy shoes and fluorescent miniskirts on South Street. The two would start out really fighting, and soon Chong would change it to a tickle torture before ending it by sweeping her off her feet and holding her by one ankle over something gross like a grungy puddle or an overflowing trash can. By this point, the two would be in complete hysterics, with onlookers on the street completely confused. Had more people owned cell phones back then, the pair would never have been able to carry on in this way. Cops would have been called, and the two would have had a lot explaining to do.

Chapter 28

Truth and Integrity

Acceptance is more potent than forgiveness.

"You love him," soothed Ambo Shanti's voice. "He is forever a part of you."

"You're right," sighed Lilith, looking up from a detailed diorama of skeletons dancing. She had constructed it from bits of bark, mud, and moss gathered from under her giant tree. "He deserved fame. He was so amazing. When he sang, I melted."

"To pursue fame is to make an agreement to lose oneself," Saruk AUM commented from above her. She had forgotten where he had been perched. "It is easy to become caught up in a title or achievement. There is danger in this alone. Even scarier is what happens after."

"What do you mean, dangerous?" asked Lilith.

"Fame brings with it a loss of self," continued Saruk AUM. "Many exchange the wild ride happily for what little they knew of themselves prior to its arrival. To deal with the loss of privacy, one can opt for extroversion. This will ease the invasion for a while."

"But what do they do when it is over?" Ambo Shanti asked.

Lilith sat down on the sandy shore of the little island and put her chin in her hands. The thick, gummy goo of sadness coated her face.

"To lose one's self is to create a time bomb," continued her guardian.

"But isn't this what we are trying to do? Lose ourselves?"

"It is the mind which needs to be lost!" Saruk AUM responded vehemently.

"It is the ego which needs to be managed, love" added Ambo Shanti in a much silkier lilt.

"It is very easy to ignore the creation of this malignant force until it is too late," Saruk AUM went on as he consciously adjusted his sound. "To achieve a title, to win an award, or to become the greatest in your chosen category takes a great deal of determination, willpower, and work. No one gets it with total ease. No one wins it without work unless a clear choice is made.

"To pursue and to maintain fame or a title forces a person to find their edges. These boundaries do not come into the light of awareness until the fame fades or the title is taken away. Then the intensity of recognition crashes like a tidal wave. An individual caught in this pattern often makes choices hastily. Those around them are swept up in the current as well, and everyone loses perspective."

"This is what happened with you and Chong, sweetheart," said Ambo Shanti as she touched down by Lilith on the beach and wrapped a wing and an arm around her tiny folded body. Then, to Saruk AUM, she pleaded, "Lighten up! There is no need to crush her!"

"It is the ego that crushes!" he retorted with a crash of thunder. "With fame often comes fortune. The danger is that the individual is often ill-prepared to handle it. When a child is thrust into fame, there are adults to guide them. The trouble with adults is that they often do not have a clue of how to handle it or perceive the best course of action. We all believe we must drive ourselves and strive."

"Even you? Even the Gandharvas and Apsaras?" asked Lilith, straightening up as her eyes widened.

"Indeed. Even our culture has created a non-bloodline royalty though, unlike humans, we have no combination of the rich with the famous. In your realm these dangerous icons fool the young into thinking they must struggle for the same. It is a blade that severs our connectedness to one another. Once the disconnecting occurs, we drown in deep depression.

"A symptom of the prima donna is the belief that tasks belong to others and not one's self. It is important to learn to take responsibility. At very early ages, we must be taught integral tasks. We learn how to care for our bodies, and should be educated to care for our minds and spirits."

"You both have taught me this well, Saruk AUM and Ambo Shanti. For this I am grateful."

"We feel your love" said Ambo Shanti, giving Lilith a full arm and wing hug, and then settling down so they could listen together to Saruk AUM.

"If you are not taught to value your fellow beings, the result will be a lack of interest, accompanied by condescension. You will become obstinate and hateful. Pride will be your greatest emotion, and pride is the root of all evil. It takes a strong spiritual shovel to dig out and destroy this type of root once it grabs hold."

Lilith imagined the things she could do with a shovel but, realizing it was just an attachment, went back to listening as her guide continued.

"To have a great deal of pride is to seek attention and honor, which puts one in direct competition with God. Vanity is the more superficial aspect of pride. Pride comes about through spiritual blindness and ignorance. It is so powerful a poison that it will eat you like acid and leave you sizzling in the dust."

"How, then, do I check my level of pride?" asked Lilith.

"Do you see pride in others and need to make yourself better in your own mind? That is a toxic indicator," answered the Gandharva. "Are you competitive beyond necessary levels? If your happiness depends upon beating others and being better than others, then you are very much in the throes of pride.

"Pride is fueled by conceit, anger, and ignorance. It manifests in impatience and intolerance. It forces us to refuse to submit to anyone else. Pride is sarcastic, caustic, and biting. It grows when focus is narrow. It feeds on aggression."

"How does it take form?"

"Pride can take form in the physical, the mental, or the spiritual realities. All aspects are equally damaging and dangerous."

"Can it be healed?"

"Yes, you can heal this. You must learn to practice gratitude and realize that there is no need to have superficial jealousy. There is no need to feel like you are the ruler or the best. To be a winner without humility is to imagine yourself as an idol. This is by far the most dangerous of sins we can commit upon ourselves."

"Is there a specific action, a karma that is prescribed?"

"Indeed! Performing service for those less fortunate is the best way to overcome pride. This puts you face-to-face with the opportunity to find and polish your facet of meekness. In modern society, it is very difficult to see the equality of beings."

"Oh! I get it! The facets of the soul, right?"

"Yes, you've got it!" smiled Saruk AUM, floating down to join Lilith and his divine partner on the tawny ground. "The edge of that particular facet is where Nine becomes Ten. It is integrity."

"Integrity! The angel cards! Did you have something to do with that?" questioned Lilith. "Integrity…" Lilith murmured under her breath.

"What is she mumbling about now?" jibed Lust.

"Let it ride, dude," insisted the Stoner.

"This is giving much insight, sure to bring her home tonight," the Guru chanted, causing most of the Boardroom to break into peals of laughter. Don did his best to keep a straight face. He had her in his embrace. "Integrity?" he asked gently.

"What?" asked Lilith, realizing where she was.

"You just said integrity. What's that about?"

"I did? I guess I did! I was thinking about a little deck of angel cards. I pick one every day. This morning I drew the card that reads 'Integrity.' It's been a while since I've seen it."

"Insights coming," said Lust, motioning for Casanova to come help him move the Stenographer to the front of the Boardroom.

"Type!" they commanded in unison.

"Tell me about this card," Don asked, completely captivated. "When was the last time you saw it?"

"It's not so much about the very last time…" she replied, drifting off for a moment.

"I make it a practice to draw a card as a theme on the eve of each new year. When I celebrate with others, I invite them to join me and make it a group happening.

"There were three years in a row I drew the angel card of Integrity. The first year, I really felt disjointed by this. I felt insulted. I've always had a great deal of integrity in how I behave and conduct myself. People tell me this all the time. One of my friends told me that it's my middle name. In spite of this, when I drew the card, it took me the entire year to accept the word and its concept."

"That would scare the bejesus out of me!" screeched the Altar Boy.

"The next year came," Lilith continued, "and several of the friends who had been with me the prior year joined me again to celebrate. There we were, staring at the little angel card deck. This had now become a joke theme for the previous year, and it was on me. I always let my guests go first, which only added to the tension of my draw.

"We were in my humble third-floor walkup apartment in Mesa, Arizona. We could all feel the looming tension, as if the San Andreas Fault line were ready to let go in neighboring California. It wasn't necessary to have a drum roll. There we were, all sitting on the floor

around my little tatami table on pillows, just staring at the deck.

"Floor seating," announced the Stenographer.

"Make a side note of Moroccan or Japanese for later!" called Casanova as he turned his gaze away from the eyes for a moment.

"It was my turn to pick. Everyone was encouraging me and teasing at the same time. The cards were all spread out, and I ran my left hand over the array of facedown messengers. All the eyes around the table stared at the energy coming off my fingers. I searched for my new annual ambassador of awareness. We all steadied our breath. No one spoke. The air was thick with anticipation. I chose. We smiled, and my best friend encouraged me to turn it over.

"There it was again—Integrity. I felt like I needed to lie down. I felt depressed and wanted to curl up in a ball. I got fuzzy, but I can recall exclamations of, 'I can't believe it!' and 'Two in a row!'"

"Intense," Don commented, giving her a little squeeze of support.

"'What had I done wrong?' I questioned. Had I not learned integrity in the past year? I reflected on the many modifications I'd made over the months. I thought about all the changes I'd instilled—to better myself as a friend, a teacher, and an artisan. 'Where have I gone wrong?' I cried to my friends.

"I didn't feel like partying. I felt like I should go join a monastery and figure out what was wrong with me. I looked up to the mantel at a collage I'd made the previous year with the giant word Integrity' across it and thought, 'Here we go again.'"

"How did you handle it?" asked Don.

"I did my best to make it through the night, and then I laid low for a couple of weeks. It took me a few months to accept this omen of Integrity once again. For a while, when the topic came up, I joked with my friends, and even denied it. But the word ate at me every day. As it turned out, I spent that year chipping away at my own ego and didn't even know it.

"One day, I was complaining to my friend about having two years of the same theme. She was so sweet, and said, 'The reason why you pulled the Integrity card again, Lilith, is because you're filled with it!'"

"You really think we can handle her?" sniveled Low Self-esteem to the rest of the Board. The Collective flashed looks of disdain, causing him to fade into mist and disappear. Don cracked a small understanding smile.

Lilith went on. "This helped me to accept the word and its concept even more. But I often felt an annoying fission going on. I didn't really believe it. I made it through the year, and then another New Year's Eve was upon me."

Don's eyes widened.

"This time I was celebrating with a bunch of people at a friend's yoga studio. I figured it was best to get away from the angel card ritual and be in a different environment."

"Sounds like a good move," Don offered.

"The studio had a little lobby area and a great room just off it where classes were conducted. We gathered early so everyone could go to parties after. Having had the influence of Integrity for two years running, I'd made a commitment to myself to be sober and stay conscious all night. I even decided to fast all day. My plan was to attend this gathering and then go home and meditate on the coming year in peace."

"She is a very, very good girl," said the Guru. "I like her standards very much!"

"So, there we were in the little lobby," said Lilith, imagining she was really there. "Everyone was showing up and sharing pleasantries while we were waiting for the time to go into the studio for our get-together. I needed to go out to my car to get a drum I'd forgotten to bring in. When I returned, the facilitator called out for me to take a moment and reflect on the last year, then draw an angel card and come into the studio with it. I could see there was no hurry, as people were getting pillows and blankets and building little nests for the opening meditation. I heard them sharing their angel cards, excited about their themes for the coming year. The voices in the other room sounded so happy. I heard the words 'Openness,' 'Hope,' and 'Trust.'

"I stared at the angel cards, praying for something sweet like 'Joy' or 'Beauty,' and laughed nervously to myself. There they were, a deck identical to mine, sitting there in a little ceramic bowl like cosmic cereal. I was sure they had followed me to the event. I'd been teaching community drumming at this studio for a few years and knew they were there on the desk all the time. It was all so surreal. What I didn't realize is that they would be playing a new joke on me that evening."

"Okay, this is a crazy story!" exclaimed Don. "So you…"

"So I sat down in the big desk chair and closed my eyes to meditate for a few minutes. I prayed that I would be guided to pick the card that was for my highest good and the perfect focus for the coming year. I gathered all my energy and stirred the contents of the bowl, trusted, and drew a card. There it was— 'Integrity'!"

"What did you do?"

"I almost crapped my pants. I freaked out and threw it back into the bowl."

"And…?"

"I stirred, I became a kid playing a playground game, and in my mind's voice I screamed, *Do over!* I pretended it didn't happen.

"I prepared myself and drew another card. I turned it over and there it was again—'Integrity.' I'm pretty sure I said 'Holy crap' out loud, and most likely they heard me in the other room.

"This couldn't be, I thought. I stood up and put the bowl down. I shook it off and turned a slow circle in the middle of the lobby, remembering the words of one of my teachers: 'Spinning around is good because when we complete a full circle, at some point we are magnetically connecting to the place where we were born, the source.'

"So I did this. I spun around and acknowledged the direction I had come from. I picked up my drum and headed for the door to the studio. I decided if I picked a card in transit I would be given a lighter one, like 'Peace' or 'Laughter.'

"I walked over to the bowl, freed my mind, stirred, and chose a third time. I practiced positive thinking, smiled, and turned the card over. There it was for a third time, twice over. 'Integrity'!"

"Amazing!" Don said.

"I know, right? I walked into the studio with the card and decided not to get into a big story about it. I acted like it was the first time I'd ever drawn it. I figured since none of my friends who knew the story were there, my relationship to the card could be kept incognito."

"What do you think it means?" Don inquired.

"That was the beginning of my understanding. I started to get that integrity is about acting with the sincerity of newness. I realized in that third year that we cannot use the past to be present with integrity. We can draw from the outcome of the past experiences, but we must be in the moment with all our good practices and good intentions."

"Many years have passed since then," reminded Saruk AUM.

"And many theme cards," Lilith smiled.

"What happens when it shows up again?" asked Don.

"I plan to not freak out when my buddy Integrity' shows up in the future. I draw a card from the deck every day, so I've seen it since. But when I see it again as a theme for the year, I will take it as a loving wink and reminder rather than a slap in the face. I'll know that I have the fortitude to work on it again for another year."

Lilith and Don stopped near the Theater of the Living Arts.

"Have you always lived in Philly?" she asked.

"Yeah, I have—in one neighborhood or another. I've traveled a bit, but have never lived in any other place. It seems like you've lived in a bunch of different places, though."

"I have, but I seem to keep coming back here."

"Why, do you think?" Don inquired.

"I'm not sure. My first astrologer said that the East Coast of the United States draws people to stay the length of their lives more than any other place she'd encountered in her years of doing readings. I really didn't think I would end up here again, but here I am."

"Where else have you lived?"

"At one point, I lived in south Florida, taking a break from everything—the city, the galleries, art, and music. I just needed to make it all stop. Life became the beach, the sun, and a big bowl of tropical fruit. These qualities reflected in the quirky personalities of the locals.

"At first I spent a lot of time watching the rain fall and the leaves on my ficus hedge grow. Having lived in the desert, it was an impressive phenomenon to see that much water drop from the sky. It seemed to rain for three months straight. At least, that's how I remember it."

"Moving from Arizona to Florida must have been a huge change."

"Yeah. When I got to Florida, I became completely fascinated by rain. In the weeks after my move, I sat on the floor, carefully unpacking my life from of a pile of boxes, watching water fall from the sky and wondering how it is that a person can accumulate so much stuff. My entire life seems to be a grand magnet of attraction."

"I'll show her some attraction," rumbled Lust.

"The house I moved into seemed to be the most challenging one I've ever decorated. I'd moved so many times, but my furniture magically knew exactly which wall it wanted to rest against. This was not at all the case in this house. Instead, I felt like I never quite got it in order. Perhaps it's a reflection on my self-perception. What do you think?"

"Perhaps it's because I'm a guy," Don began, "but it doesn't seem to faze me much when I move. I don't have that much furniture. But as far as a workspace goes, I guess I can relate. In my studio, everything has to be just right for me to create."

"Well, there you go! That's what I'm talking about. And have you ever just landed someplace, and you knew at a gut level—perhaps even at a cellular level—that everything was going to work out and was meant to be, but no matter what you seemed to do, you couldn't make it happen?"

"Sure. My entire childhood with my sisters felt like that."

"How did you handle it?

"I just let go and let it sweep over me like a huge, unexpected wave, I guess." In that instant, Don recalled a flash from his dream the night before when he had become unglued and subsequently flushed down the cosmic toilet.

"How do you handle it?" he quizzed.

"I surrender," Lilith said.

"Surrender?"

"Yes. I just completely freakin' let go."

"You let go?"

"Yes, I let go. Why are you repeating every single thing I say?"

"Everything you say…" He was transfixed on her cherubic lips again, the whiteness of her smile, the way her tongue moved inside her mouth when she spoke. For a moment he thought about making a film of it, but shook it off as it seemed like a notion no one else would get.

"Perhaps paint her in four panels, like a Warhol," suggested the Artist.

"Cut it out!" she scolded, holding her index finger up to his mouth. "Don't speak!" She squinted into the sun, maintaining the universal shush symbol against his lips.

Don quivered. She was touching him, and then she placed her hand back into his and they continued to walk. The two joined and became a third phenomenon as the dynamic of "couple" emerged. This third-dimensional magnetism shifted everything.

It felt good and right as a Möbius of energetic infinity traveled through the helix systems within their DNA molecules. Electrons jumped back and forth in a frenzied exchange. Nothing could ever be the same.

Don broke the silence. "Last night, I had the strangest dream."

"Really?" said Lilith with true interest. She felt that dreams were the holy grail, filled with healing nectar from the psyche, and that they connected us with the collective consciousness. "Please tell it to me!" she pleaded.

"I wish I could, but I can only remember little bits."

"Share the fragments with me, then. Anything."

"Okay. Well, for some reason, when I heard something you said earlier, I remembered feeling stuck to the ground and then getting picked up by a big wave."

"And..."

"That's it." Even though it was a tiny shard of consciousness, she still seemed really interested, so he added, "If I remember any more, I'll tell you."

"Promise me," she said, extending the pinky of her right hand and waiting for him to wrap his around hers for a commitment.

A pinky swear, thought Don. *I can't remember the last time anyone asked me for one of those. This girl is too much!* He indulged in the tiny ritual with her, which inspired a beaming smile.

"So, tell me," said Don.

"So, tell you...what?"

"Tell me how you let go."

"I can't say exactly," Lilith began, "but I can tell you about some ways I've done it in hindsight. The great yogis talk about living in the moment, and lots of people talk about going with the flow. I guess the key that I've discovered is to not do anything at all. It's not that I become apathetic, it's just that I create space to not have an agenda, to let go of being the doer."

"I think I'm following you."

"Ah. But, you see, right there—that's already doing. Get my point?"

"No, not exactly."

A new wave emerged from Lilith. It was a fiery goddess with a thousand arms and a thousand weapons and, like the Great Mother Durga, she was suited up and ready to put an end to ignorance.

"How about," she offered, "I tell you about a time I just trusted and went with the flow."

"Okay."

"Okay, then. I was in Florida, struggling. I was having a really hard time trying to figure out what I was supposed to be doing. It seemed like everything I tried just backfired."

"Was it sabotage?"

"It was a type of sabotage, but not the type you're thinking."

"How can you tell what I'm thinking?" Don asked.

"I just can."

"Pretentious," said Judgment, filing his nails while peering over little pince-nez spectacles.

"Finally, I just gave up," Lilith recounted. "That's when I learned that the more I tried to do and make things happen, the more life pushed against me."

"Lose her," suggested the Stoner, taking a long hit off a joint. He choked as he held it in, and then slowly released a huge cloud of smoke.

"Oh, hush up," scolded Reason.

"Let's watch," cut in the Voyeur, getting the gist.

Chapter 29

Illumination

Enlightenment by pizza.

"Why do we leave relationships and commitments after so many years of perceived happiness?" Lilith asked into the empty space as her chair creaked to an abrupt halt.

The Great Mother squeezed her warm body into the Father's embrace, and from her shoreline a massive set of vines grew into the perpetual sky. Ambo Shanti swooped down from the only wispy cloud in the distance and perched on a leaf high above the questioning sprite.

"People and the demigods—avatars and guides—are like vines that grow upward to the Sun, high into the heavens," said Ambo Shanti. "The ascent is inspired by the seeking of a deep connection with the Great Divine. When we are attracted to others, we are drawn to a celestial spark that is a reflection of our own true beingness. This is often mirrored in the people, places, and things to which we are magnetically pulled, and those which are irresistibly attracted to us.

"Life is our spiritual climb upward. Our journey is unique, like each of these vines. We meet and intertwine with others, just like the twisting creepers that throw feelers and furry feet to anchor themselves as they brave the winds of change. Sometimes we are separate and grow in our own unique directions. This is our individual yoga."

"Yoga?"

"Yes. I have taught you that the word 'yoga' means, literally, 'relationship.' You remember?"

Lilith nodded, eyes wide, drinking in the beauty of this luminous being's wisdom.

Ambo Shanti continued. "Often we travel together through many events and years with the same spirits. Sometimes the motion needed to reach a precise point in the space-time continuum takes many lifetimes. Our travels carry with them many lessons that teach us through karmas."

A question mark appeared on Lilith's face, then a dawning of understanding. "Oh," she said, "I get it! Karma, as in action!"

Ambo Shanti grinned ear-to-ear with the pleasure of a mother, a sibling, and a best friend all rolled into the loving expression. She continued, "Relationships color our future lives as they complete our past lives."

"All at the same time?"

"Yes! At any given moment, a plant can shift direction, bloom, or die. When a beautiful relationship comes to us, we must be grateful for the reflective quality of unconditional love. This is the steady and vibrant glow of divinity. Therefore, it is important to always be in the present moment."

"But what of the endings?"

"When a relationship ends, we must recognize that the letting-go is perfect. If a partner or friend leaves us, it is a time for opening and understanding. This is perceived through bodily felt sensations."

"So the mind is left out of this?"

"Exactly! There is no need to understand the why. This is an opportunity in the lesson of acceptance. The sadness or confusion that takes place is best utilized as a mirror. It is an invitation to practice the art of self-acceptance. In the seeming gap of endless nothingness, we are able to really see and feel our connection to the oneness of the greater. Through this, we come to understand that we are perfect and that the universe is perfect. Just as we are, and just as it is."

"Why, then, do we struggle?" said Lilith.

"Because we feel so out of control. But there is no such thing as control of a situation. If we try to do this, our efforts turn back on us in negativity. Life is like a rushing river. If we fight the current, we are drawn under, and then drown in our own emotions."

"What about a repetition of the pattern?"

"There is no possibility to step into the exact same water of a river twice! Though it looks and feels like the same water, the molecules and structures are subtly varied."

"How can we save ourselves?"

"The true reflection of the Divine Essence is the only thing that can keep us afloat," offered Ambo Shanti. "When we realize our true self, there no longer is a need to identify by means of a single individual idea of 'me' or 'I' in any situation. This creates a deep connection to everything, the all that possesses a knowing and is the Divine."

"When does this happen? Is there any way to witness it coming?"

"Timing is easy to predict through the movement of the stars. The celestial bodies give the propensity of pure potential; it is easy to read their messages, interpreted by the many schools of astrology. But remember, free will is always at play in life. This gives us opportunities to make moves according to unique dynamics. Anyone, at any given time, can join or leave a situation or commitment. There are never any guarantees."

"Even between you and Saruk AUM?"

"Yes, even between the two of us."

"Doesn't that freak you out a little?"

"No, never! Our pairing is temporary, and not a marriage."

"Wow!" exclaimed Lilith in amazement.

"It is because of the understanding that lessons are needed for the evolution of the individual soul, as well as for the connection of the all to the greater. Do you get my point?"

"I do, but it still hurts," sighed Lilith, "and I feel so lost."

"Life is like a game of hide-and-seek with God. The Bhagavad Gita says, 'He who has no faith and no wisdom, and whose soul is in doubt, is lost.' This is why we need to learn to let go and surrender. The trick is staying in this state of mind all the time. Feelings like to drag you out and rub you in the gravel on the road of life. By staying in a constant state of surrender, the sensation of being lost eventually transforms into a sense of knowing. This guides you to find the state of just being."

Ambo Shanti's words reminded Lilith of a night when she had crashed on her skates while out on a pizza delivery.

She was carrying only one pie that evening and cruising really fast. Lilith knew the street well and was only half a block from the customer's door. As she turned the corner, she felt her wheels grab and bump and then hit gravel. The slow-motion fall of her body was saved by her agility and power. As she bounced, she felt the skin shear off her right shin and forearm. The last thing to hit the road was the pizza. Gathering her thoughts and evaluating the situation, she checked the box. The pizza was fine.

"I'm okay," she said, looking up, seeing a body watching her get up from the street.

"I'm not taking that pie!" yelled the silhouette looming on the dark stoop.

"Fine," retorted the wounded skater. "I'll go back and get you a fresh one."

She wheeled carefully back to the shop and explained to Vinnie what had happened. He checked the pie, threw it back in the oven for a minute, and then put it in a fresh box while Lilith dressed her wounds.

"What they don't know won't hurt 'em!" jabbed Vinnie.

Lilith stood up and rolled over to the counter. "Right!" she answered as she grabbed the pie and flew out the door, just wanting to get this one over with.

"Tell 'em what they wanna hear, babe!" Vinnie yelled after her.

She flashed a thumbs-up without looking back as she rolled away.

When she came around the corner that had eaten her wheels, she had a heightened sense of awareness. Suddenly she knew every stone and bump in the asphalt. This was followed by a momentary twinge of self-pity and doubt, which was in turn followed by a wave of wanting to cry and give up. It wasn't the road burn or the almost-squished pie, nor was it an ego blow from the angry customer assuming that she had trashed their dinner. It was something else.

She carefully negotiated the gaping pothole, swooped up on the sidewalk, and then ran up the stairs on her toe-stops to ring the bell.

"Back so soon?" quizzed the grumpy man, opening the door as the buzzer still rang.

"Yeah! We're so busy tonight that there was a fresh pie coming out of the oven when I got back to the shop. It's your lucky night!"

"Wait here!" ordered the growling man. "I want to make sure this one is okay." Grabbing the pizza, he trotted off to his kitchen. He returned almost instantaneously with a half-chomped slice in one hand and cash in the other. A string of mozzarella dangled from his lower lip down past his chin.

"Some kids did it," he said as he began to close the door.

Did what? she wondered as she skated back down to the corner. Lilith stopped and looked into her gaping nemesis, the pothole, thinking, *How could kids make a pothole?*

She turned her head and heard a very soft voice say, "Look over here," as a flash of orange light caught the very corner of her eye. Her vision adjusted to the dimming evening light, and she saw a roadblock tucked into a very tiny space between two walls. She realized that it had been removed from the damaged street.

Tentatively, she rolled over to the edge of the alley. A little deeper into the space sat a second roadblock, neatly placed against the bricks of the building. The whole scenario flashed in a millisecond. She saw the pothole and then the road crew placing the cautionary signs, followed by the neighbor watching the kids giggle while hiding the flashing warnings as he stood on his stoop and ordered pizza. He didn't even think to give a heads-up about the hole. Then she imagined her slow-motion crash.

Over and over at lightning speed, the events spun round and round in her mind like a hamster running on a wheel. She saw the kids and their prank, the witness, Vinnie and the second-chance pie. It all became confusing to the point where she cried out to the dark sky, "What should I do?"

"Complete the circuit," came the answer, sung in a soft, lilting voice.

As if watching a movie, she saw her body carefully take the road blocks and place them on either side of the giant holes to warn future traffic. She stood silently, staring at the hole and the orange flashing lights as they bounced off the gravel and broken asphalt for what felt like an eternity.

In an instant, she turned and kicked a skate to begin the glide back to the shop. In her ears, the voice said, "We are love. We always have been and always will be."

"How can I find peace with all of this?" she questioned aloud.

"You must find a phrase to halt the circle of *samskara*—the negative thought pattern. How would you feel when it stops?"

"Infinite!" she answered as she skated.

"What would infinity give you?"

"Space."

"There it is! That is your phrase. It is magic and will end all jumbled thought spirals and anger. Practice it. Repeat it until it is in your knowing and you no longer need to use the power of thought to find it. Let it just be!"

The skater stopped and slowly glided over to a smooth marble stoop to sit for a moment. In her mind she heard the sound of her own voice say, *Infinite space*.

"Yes!" sang the angelic voice, "Say it again, this time out loud."

"Infinite space."

"Again! Like you mean it, like you own it. Like it is the sacred key of vast wisdom and knowledge."

"Infinite space," Lilith said a little louder.

"Over and over! Say it again and again!"

"Infinite space, infinite space, infinite space…" She kept going until it became a sacred mantra. Then she was suspended in silent stillness. *I've got it*, she thought. *And the cool thing is that there is nothing to understand. This is infinite space!*

Part VII

Labyrinth

Once entered, the maze of existence seduces you to the center.

Chapter 30

Inertia

Lethargy and fear get you nowhere.

Deagadh took a deep breath and exhaled a great blast of air across the thick, greenish liquid bubbling in the colossal pot. He looked at Zahra with a penetrating stare and pulled her from his shoulder. The bird let out a tiny squawk, partly because of the pressure of Deagadh's hand squeezing against the back of her neck, and partly because she knew that her master was about to do something she might regret.

He pulled out a curved wand which had been tucked in the back of his belt and pointed it at his beloved grey bird while muttering, "*Tahged'han interceda va'acerte!*" In a puff of deep purple and blue smoke, the parrot changed into a black raven and flew through the mist and into the cauldron. Deagadh watched as she soared over the hills of Jaulan and touched down tentatively on one of the turrets of the king's castle. Zahra squawked and tested her new throat, unable to form clear words.

Crap. I'm mute! she thought.

"I can hear your every word in the silence of your thoughts, love," said Deagadh. "There is no need to talk. Stay very quiet, as I need you there for now. We are in touch and I am watching you. Now, go and have a look. See what is going on in that castle," ordered the alchemist.

Without a thought, the raven flapped her mighty wings and swooped around the massive stone wall of the castle. She felt the shivering chill of Jaulan's cold sadness and heard blistering cries echoing from the great hall. A small open window appeared ahead with a sill just wide enough to provide a touchdown for the powerful claws of the dark bird. She landed and cocked her head cautiously around the edge of the window, then shifted slowly to have a look at what was going on.

"I don't see a wound of any sort," projected Zahra, trying out her telepathic connection with her master.

"Patience, my love," said Deagadh. "I see through your eyes. Just sit still, wait, and watch for me now. You are right sweet bird," he continued. "It appears there are no signs of a physical wound. It is worse than I thought and as I feared, love."

The king's recent affliction that was causing him this excruciating pain was neither the cut of a sword nor a bruise of battle. It had been received in a most unusual way and, once incurred, he could neither live nor die.

He felt as though the walls of the giant hall were choking him. His armor from past battles, tarnished and darkened, seemed to be marching closer and closer, leaving no space for King Heron to breathe. In the tapestries which surrounded the humble bed where he lay, stories of his wars and the lady he had wooed were intricately woven. His pain made him unable to go to the upper level of the castle where his velvety chamber lay still and untouched for many years. He winced in agony and begged for salvation.

"This is terrible" Zahra squawked. "The kingdom is in such anguish. How will they go on?" questioned Zahra. "Can we help them?"

"Perhaps," came the thought response from Deagadh. "Perhaps, my love."

It hadn't begun in such dull bleakness. The warrior king had been born to loving parents who rejoiced in the birth of their first son. Though they were humble merchants, young Heron was treated as the king he would become. The lineage of this family was not that of royalty, yet they acted as if it were.

Heron was a ruddy, healthy baby—round, sturdy, and strong. He had an amazing sense of balance and superior fighting skills. Early on, his father decided to train his son in the art of battle. It was his desire for Heron to be a warrior, a leader—and nothing more.

Heron learned the art of fighting quickly and, by the age of nine, was sent away to a master for schooling. The succession of teachers was amazed by the boy's proficiency. Unfortunately, each one neglected to teach Heron the esoteric arts which were usually taught to young warriors of the time.

It became obvious at an early age that Heron would win many tournaments, capture treasures, and one day becomes a fierce leader. To keep him on target, his father insisted that he train only for competition. Heron was never allowed to share in playful games with the other young contenders that taught the boys chivalry. As a result, a great portion of his psyche was stunted.

Now he lay on his bed, shivering in the cold, drafty castle. The sky darkened further, causing him to shudder. Fever jolted his body. Hallucinations of his father's voice made him imagine that the dead man's breath was touching the tiny rosy cheek of his eight-year-old face.

In the musty vision, drops of rain bounced off the stones of Heron's mighty fortress. Zahra wondered if she should swoop down to him.

"No, darling," came the sound of her master's voice in the center of her head. "Just wait there for now."

Deagadh dove into the king's thoughts and tumbled back in time, back to the day when he had made the malignant vow which had brought on this dilemma. The toxic seed that took root in the center of his heart and had begun this negative spiral was created by his vow to always be a winner.

"Most unfortunate," squawked Zahra. "It doesn't look like that is an option now."

"Assuredly," responded her master.

Chapter 31

Sand

Clean every last grain of sand out of your shoe before attempting the ascent.

"A tiny flicker of doubt which is caused by a judgment is the pebble able to shift an entire mountain and bring it crashing to the ground. We must pick these pebbles from our feet," Saruk AUM sang in a lilting melody reminiscent of Kabir style Bhajan.

"Or move the barrier?" asked Lilith.

"Yes, little one. Or forgive those who place them, or unexpectedly move those that are necessary," Saruk AUM said. He blinked his large eyes and allowed them to focus deeply into Lilith's. It was as if he were extracting inspiration for the quintessential idea she needed to hear in this moment.

"We must wake up to the fact that the trials laid in our path of existence are but little compressions of feelings that cause necessary irritations."

"Like the grain of sand an oyster turns to a pearl?"

"Yes, exactly that!" he said, flapping his wings to lift off. Saruk AUM hovered carefully so he could gently kiss her forehead.

"The irritant is just a perception and something that we must own about ourselves. We must realize that what we identify as beautiful in our own gaze is really a reflection of who we are. This holographic deceit causes ripples which cloud the ability to see clearly. These mental disturbances confuse us and convince us that we are not God. But we must learn to still the waters and find a way to trust the fact that we are indeed one with the Divine."

"So," said Lilith, "what do we do with our judgment when it comes up?"

"Ah, there is the trick!"

"No kidding!"

"We must take care never to put these judgments on another. When we slip and do so, this is all it takes to rock the foundation of love. We must instead choose to pick the pebble out of wherever it has lodged, analyze it if we cannot resist, and then toss it away. It is just the compressed crust of the preprogrammed ego mind."

"How can I get myself to make this choice?"

"The first thing to choose is love. Be so passionate that you become singed by the flames. This burns away all poisonous perception."

Chapter 32

Time

Leaps, jumps, and warps.

Lilith had completely lost track of where she was. She was becoming aware of existing in several places all at the same time. As she landed once again in the body that was walking on Third Street in Philadelphia, she noticed her hand was in Don's. He was leading her across South toward Jon's. The patio gate was locked, so the pair walked around to the main entrance.

"Hi, Glen!" Lilith said with a smile as they passed the burly bartender. "Who's in the kitchen?" she asked as they wove through the bar to get to the outdoor seating.

"Your boy!" Glen responded to the back of her head. He watched her lean into the tiny pickup window of the kitchen.

"Hey, sugar buns!" she called in through the opening. A shiny face with thick curly black hair came to the window; hands shot out to grab her and lift her petite body off the floor. Owen planted a huge, smacking kiss on her lips.

"What's good for happy hour, O?" she asked.

"I have some lentils and arugula. How about a warm salad and some other nosh? Just pick your bottle. I gotcha covered! I'll send Jackie out in a few. Grab a list, you know where they are."

Lilith took Don's hand, grabbed a wine list, and tugged him down the narrow hallway to the patio. A corner deuce with a little sun shining on it was open.

"How about this one?" she asked.

"Who the heck is she not connected to?" cowered Low Self-esteem.

"It's all about the connections!" countered Casanova, shoving the others out of the way as he moved into a more forward seat at the table.

"Looks good to me," said Don, causing an adorable smile to form on Lilith's face.

She handed the wine menu to him, and he began to peruse it with help from the entire Board of Directors.

"Get her champagne!" said the Horny Teen.

"How droll," interjected Casanova.

"It's the afternoon, she's a girl, get something pink," offered the Nine-year-old.

"Out of the way, idiots!" shouted Lust.

"What then?" pleaded Low Self-esteem.

"Red! Dark, oaky red!" insisted Lust.

"A nice woody red with a hint of berries, right?" asked Don without even looking up.

"Yeah. How did you know?" Lilith purred.

"Best choice to stand up to the lentils and arugula!" he grinned.

She smiled in response, thinking, *Wow, he is really listening to everything.*

"Get the Malbec," insisted Reason. "Look at that year and price! It's a bargain."

"Really?" barked Casanova in response. "Do you really think bargain is the way to go?"

The Accountant quickly flipped open the books and started calculating what a week's worth of dates would run.

The Horny Teen skateboarded over and heaved the books on

the floor. "Really? You think skimping right now is gonna win her?" Everyone turned their heads around to watch him. "Get the Sangiovese! It's more complex. It's more like her." Mouths dropped open around the table. "And not too heavy," he added.

"Since when does he read *Food and Wine*?" asked Reason.

Looking up, Don asked, "What do you think of a Sangiovese to go with that lentil salad?"

"Sounds good to me," Lilith responded. "Owen will surprise us with the food, so no need to think about it unless there's something special you want."

"Oh, yeah. I got your special," groaned the Italian Stallion, rubbing his thigh.

"What wine?" asked a tall Malibu Barbie of a waitress who floated out of nowhere onto the patio. She flipped open a note pad as she came to a stop at the corner table.

"Hi, Jacks! How's it goin'?" asked Lilith.

"Good, good. The bar has me runnin' around, but O insisted I come out and be your waitress. No problem, though."

"This Sangiovese, please," Don said, pointing at the entry on the wine list.

"Good choice!" Jackie replied, smiling at Don and then gesturing positively with a wink to Lilith from behind him as she walked back toward the building.

"Did you go out to eat much as a kid?" Don inquired.

"Yeah, I did. When my parents would take me to restaurants, I enjoyed playing cards with my father while we waited for the food to come."

"Oh, God. She wants to play a game," whined Low Self-esteem.

Don responded, "Cards, huh?"

"Yeah. We never did this at home when I was little. When I was a teen, though, we would play cards with the neighbors after dinner on warm summer nights. It was a lot of fun sitting out on our screened in porch, sipping wine and listening to the crickets."

"In my family," Don began, "it was around the kitchen table in the late afternoon, sipping little cups of really strong coffee and eating biscotti my grandmother made. That was our thing. Sometimes we played Hearts."

"I never learned how to play that game," Lilith commented. "I would love to, though. Did you know there are thirteen hearts in a deck of cards?"

"I never thought of it, but now that you mention it, it makes sense, Lilith."

She loved the sound of her name rolling off Donny's tongue. It melted her.

"Did your grandmother cook for you?" asked Don.

"My grandmother didn't cook very often when she lived with my family," said Lilith. "Over time, I came to understand that it was because my mother was not very fond of her recipes and techniques. You're lucky to have grown up with homemade Italian food."

"I know. My grandmother's cooking spoiled me," Don confessed. "What about cookies? Did your mom make cookies?"

"No, my mom didn't, but my grandmother did. Occasionally, when my mama was gone for the day, her mother would take over the kitchen and embark on a baking adventure. My absolute favorite of my grandmother's food creations was when she would construct a simple cookie. It was something between a biscuit, a cracker, and a sugar cookie. Granny had a flair for making a mess in my mother's always-tidy, pristine kitchen. When mama would return home from her afternoon away and find her mother with flour streaked across her face, arms, and dress, and the counters stacked with bowls and cookies everywhere, all hell would break loose.

"My grandmother's recipe was simple and not overly sweet. Kind of like a biscotti, but solid and not as porous. She would roll out the dough, and then use a small green juice glass to cut the cookies into circles. Lacking patience and working at high speed, she would often have inconsistent shapes, ranging from perfect full moons to tiny crescents."

This was how Lilith had become aware of the progressive shape the Lunar Goddess makes in her journey across the night sky. She used to love to arrange the cookies so they illustrated the growing nocturnal light. A perfectly round burned cookie would represent the new moon. Then she would organize different-sized crescents to signify the entire progression leading to an underbaked, glowing, pale cookie that symbolized the full moon.

"I was blissed on those crazy cookie days," Lilith shared. "When the mess was finally cleaned up, I would slip back into the kitchen and make a big mug of tea or hot chocolate. I loved dunking and eating lots of the crunchy cookies!"

Though it drove her mother nuts when she would return home and find Lilith's grandmother on an alimentary adventure, she adored the cookies too.

"My grandmother never let anyone near the stove or countertops," Don said. "She ruled the kitchen with an iron fist!"

Jackie brought the bottle of wine and two glasses. Right behind her was Owen with a vase of roses and a candle. The two delivered their goods and poured the wine with visible winks of approval. They mouthed, "You go, girl!" as they giggled back to the kitchen for more.

A dip and homemade bread arrived on a large, handmade ceramic plate in the shape of a dark, purply apple. Lilith grabbed at the piece Don wanted first. She noticed his expression and took a bite. Then she held the remaining bit to his lips to feed him.

The laugh that fell from her mouth penetrated every molecule of Don's being. He was caught in a viscid web of passion. There would be no escape.

Chapter 33

Luck

Opportunity demands risk-taking and exertion.

"What to do?" Zahra squawked audibly.

"Quiet, bird!" scolded Deagadh, silently piercing the center of the raven's skull.

"Ouch!" came the telepathic reply. "I get it!"

"His eyes are shut now," said the wizard, waving his wand. "I am sending you in for a closer look."

The raven became smaller than a fruit fly and swooped over to the slumbering body.

"Look into his dream, bird!"

Zahra obeyed, perching on a hair near the center of Heron's forehead. She landed so lightly that the king did not even notice. Her eyes closed and she drifted into Heron's vision.

In the dream, young boys trained, playing knightly games of skill and speed in a meadow. They ran through the thick grasses, trying to catch rabbits by their ears. Zahra could see young Heron successfully capture one of the long-eared animals.

"That seems like an impossibility, boss!"

"Indeed," said the alchemist's assistant Alwyn, who had just shown up in the laboratory with a plate of dry biscuits and a steaming cup of strong tea.

"Nice of you to join in," Zahra responded psychically in unison with the alchemist.

"Shh, Zahra!" said Deagadh. "We don't want to disturb his dream."

Heron's youthful dream aberration of himself giggled with a wide smile, feeling the soft ears of the rabbit in his palms and the muscular wiggling of the furry creature. He held the impossible prize up for his teacher to see. All the other boys stared and cheered, in awe of his luck. The older knight praised him and then instructed him to take the rabbit home to his mother.

Heron proudly swaggered home, carrying the wiggling rabbit to share with his family. His mother greeted him and just as quickly as she praised the boy, she scurried around the back of the house. There she rapidly broke the rabbit's neck, skinned it, and began to prepare it for cooking. She never let Heron watch such things, and always protected him from the harsh reality of death.

When his mother was in the kitchen, Heron went into the yard and found a foot and the ears of the rabbit. He cleaned them and hid them in the small stone shed which stood just inside the sturdy wall of the family's garden. In the days and weeks that followed, he would sneak out to look at them and wonder if he would ever again feel the joy he had experienced with his first accomplishment.

Later that night, when his father returned home and the family sat down to dinner, Heron burst out in proud chatter about his ability to catch the rabbit and provide food for the family. Uninterested in the child's excitement, his father grumbled about his dislike for the stew.

Crushed and disappointed, Heron hardly ate, and then skulked off to his bed. Dreams did not come to him. He lay in the dark and stared into the nothingness. At times he felt like crying, but no tears leaked from his tired eyes. He could hear the rhythmic breathing of his brother and sisters through the wall as they slept in the next room. Gnawing

hunger ate at his insides. A crusty, leathery skin formed on the surface of his heart.

Chapter 34

Chaos

All change is good.

The speakers on the patio played a song from the 80s, and Lilith began to sing along.

"Do you know what key this is?" Don asked as he listened to the lilt of her voice.

"No, I don't," she responded.

"It's C sharp, the most tormented key in the circle of fifths."

"What makes you think it's tormented?"

"Listen to it; it truly is. It sounds like a howling hunger, and it's not just me, it's a fact. C sharp rubs you like a wire brush but, for some reason, you want to keep taking it in like one more peanut or another handful of popcorn."

"Yeah, I get what you're saying," she responded.

"Look," exclaimed the Altar Boy, "he's got her this time!"

"Holy smoke!" shouted the Stoner.

"Dude, that was a little loud!" scolded the Horny Teen. "Let's be cool. He's got this."

Don continued, "In the key of C sharp, you can hear the frustration we all feel when we try to make a connection. The song 'Heard it Through the Grapevine' is written in C sharp. It's so —tortured! It would never

sound the same in another key!"

Don swore that C sharp was more ominous to our auditory perception than any other. His reasoning was that C sharp used mostly the black keys of the piano in its scale. He said this gave the key, and songs meant to be played in it, a quality and message that the other keys missed out on.

"You're right!" agreed Lilith. "It's perfectly miserable."

Don lifted his head and experienced a flash of light. For a split second, his brain gave forth an image from last night's dream. The moment was all too brief, and he did not fully cognate the information being sent from the depths of his psyche. The Boardroom scrambled around, trying to recover from the power surge as the lights blinked off and the space went completely black and silent.

On the dark screen of Don's third eye, he imagined he saw a preternatural tree smiling through twisting lips. Bark was peeling off and falling to the ground. The deep crimson tongue in the mouth lashed a sound at the center of his skull that sounded like "Ah. Yeah. Hey." This was the closest he ever came to remembering the entire dream of the night before.

"More wine?" interrupted Jackie, as she reached for the bottle and then deftly began to fill the two glasses. "Ready for the salad?" she asked.

"Sure, that sounds great!" Lilith responded.

"That was weird!" Don exclaimed. "I didn't even see her coming. Did you?"

"No, I didn't either. It was chaos."

"Chaos?"

"A change out of our control."

"What was?" asked Jackie, topping off the couple's glasses.

"How I didn't see you coming up on us, I guess," Don responded.

"Oh, dude, keep your mouth shut!" screamed the Stoner.

"Yes, yes. Just hold the space for her!" said the Guru, emphatically causing the tassels on his silk pillow to sway.

"What the…" trailed Don

"To chaos!" toasted Lilith, reaching for the glass. She took a long inhale of the cherry-oak perfume of the wine and then an even longer, slower sip.

Chapter 35

Realization

It is okay that you are not like the other children.

Saruk AUM had been balanced on the back of the giant rocking chair and continued to sing the Bhajan.

Lilith interrupted him, questioning, "Are we ever really with another soul?"

"We are born of the union of two. But yes, it is true, little one. We are always alone. People seem to be constantly fighting against the possibility of being comforted by their aloneness."

"Yes, they sing that one is the loneliest number," she offered.

"It is sad that so many people strive so hard to be in union with another. The joke is that when they achieve it, they end up begging for their own space and freedom!"

"What is it about the idea of a couple that is so attractive, anyway?" asked Lilith. "Why do we try so hard to get into relationships and groups? What is this hunger?"

"It is a desire to feel accepted by the greater. What we all really need to do is to accept our singularity."

"How do we wake up to this?"

"First we need to question who we really are and where consciousness comes from," said Saruk AUM. "Do you remember when

you realized you had been here before?"

"I do," said Lilith, "but I always love to hear you tell the story! Please tell it."

Saruk AUM smiled sweetly as he began. "Your family was sitting on the couch in the den of your second house. It was a Saturday night, and National Geographic was showing an episode about the Dalai Lama and Lhasa. Do you remember?" he asked, knowing full well that she knew each and every word he always used to tell her this tale. "You were sitting on your father's lap, watching. Suddenly you began to cry and wiggle with a grumpy flourish.

"'What's wrong with you, Lilith?' your dad asked. Since you refused to speak, he had no choice but to release his hold on you. You slid off the couch and ran across to the television and hugged the screen. You ignored the static sparks and sensations of the electricity. Tears flowed down your cheeks and you began to sob uncontrollably.

"Your brother yelled, 'Get out of the way, squirt!'

"'What's wrong, baby girl?' your mother questioned.

"Do you remember what you did?" asked Saruk AUM.

"Of course I do!" smiled Lilith, quieting down once again to allow Saruk AUM to continue.

"You turned toward the group on the sofa, tears streaming down your little cheeks, and proclaimed that you wanted to go home!

"'Home where?' asked your mother.

"'You are home, silly girl.' your father said.

"'We live here with you—' your brother started to say when your mother elbowed him hard to stop him mid-insult.

"'I want to go there!' you said, pointing to the monastery on the mountaintop glowing on the television screen. 'Lhasa,' you said.

"That night I was assigned to you and came to your bedside. You were so angry about ending up in this family that your little spirit cried and argued with God all night. He had no choice and called in the bigwig—"

"Literally!" Lilith interrupted, giggling.

"Yes. Then that night you broke a horrible fever, and Satya Sai Babba himself came to you for the first time. He held your feet and prayed as he stood at the bottom of your bed. Do you remember what you used to call him?"

"Afro guy," Lilith said as she remembered the aberrational nightly visits from the saint.

"Later, your teachers could not answer your queries in school. You looked to your Sunday-school instructors and found that their feedback fell short as well. You went to the rabbi seeking information, and even he could not answer you. That was when you dropped out of Sunday school. You had a profound sense of knowing, and we had to intervene as there was no earthly being available at that time to mentor you. It was strongly apparent at a very early age that you were not like the other children."

Lilith giggled again. This was one of her favorite parts of the story.

"You were so much more sensitive. You never liked to play the way the other children did. You could feel things no one else could feel, and you could see the unseen.

"I left for a while until you were done with first grade and, when I returned, I was paired with my mate," Saruk AUM said, blowing a kiss into the air that invited Ambo Shanti to appear.

"You loved your parents, and we know that you are forever grateful for the vast array of culture they brought to you in your early years. We loved following you to the ballets, operas, and plays. We soaked up the movies and museums along with you as you developed and grew. We blessed the space where you slept and saw to it that your mother filled the atmosphere with jazz, big band, and classical music all the time. We came with you when you traveled to foreign countries, and watched as your father sought out local restaurants and cozy inns to immerse you in.

We encouraged you to taste and look and fully experience everything."

Lilith's family had lived in suburbia but, in spite of their white-bread surroundings, they had been diverse and aware. On her first foreign journey at the age of eight, her parents removed her little kid training wheels, giving her the first experience of life on her own.

"We whispered into their thoughts, giving them ideas which encouraged your oneness," said Ambo Shanti, landing lightly on the arm of the chair.

"I remember," said Lilith. "We were in a cute little low-rise hotel in Portugal. I had a tiny separate room to sleep in, attached to my parents' room. One morning I awoke to find they had gotten up and left me alone."

"We were so proud of you!" said Ambo Shanti.

"You weren't scared, not even for a second!" added Saruk AUM.

"I remember," Lilith continued, "there was a note near my bed, written in my mother's beautiful, scrolling script. She instructed me to get myself up, washed, and dressed, and to take myself down to the dining room. I was to ask the maître d' to please give me my breakfast. There was a moment when I was totally freaked out."

"That was nothing!"

"Hunger was fast motivation, and you followed the handwritten directions!"

"I remember getting in the elevator and pushing the button to take me down to the dining room. We had been at this hotel for several days, and the maître d' had been treating us like family. I walked past the hostess and she said, 'Bom dia.' I continued over to an empty table and the maître d' came to wish me a good morning as well."

"Then you politely requested cereal. When it came, you began happily chewing spoonful after spoonful."

"Just as I was feeling totally comforted and nurtured, my parents appeared. They said they had been out shopping. I felt so autonomous!"

"Later it was divulged that they had never left but were hovering nearby, spying to see if you could handle the task," Saruk AUM smiled. "Bless them for giving you this experience. You were empowered for life due to that little trial. It was the birth of your peace in aloneness.

"After that, you were unstoppable! By the age of twelve, you had been studying foreign languages. Your French was good enough to Sherpa your friend on an afternoon outing in Switzerland. By then your parents trusted you and were happy to turn you loose for a few hours at a time. You rode a bus and communicated *en français*. You and your friend were in search of a miniature golf course, but never found it."

"It didn't matter. I remember having a great time."

"You found a park with a merry-go-round, and rode it four times!"

"I did!"

"You realized an incredible sense of autonomy that day."

Lilith's father was not a great teacher. He did not understand how to break down information and explain it. This was the planting of an important seed in Lilith's psyche, making her quite the opposite. She was a weaver of the web, able to explain things and define them through story, much the way the ancients did. This flaw in her father became a cornerstone in her own foundation and taught her to be a teacher.

"Maybe a little too autonomous at that point!" blurted Ambo Shanti.

The look on Saruk AUM's face screamed, "Ya think?"

Lilith's face screwed into a scowl, a classic of her teen years.

"Now, now, don't go doing that!" chided Ambo Shanti, circling Lilith's face with her pointing finger. "You know what that does to the skin!"

Lilith responded by relaxing the muscles of her face and smoothing the energy of her thoughts.

"Much better, little one. What would you do if I weren't here to guard your youth!"

"My youth! You've got to be kidding! You know how old this

body is!"

"And you look fabulous!" Saruk AUM exclaimed as he jumped up, one hand on his hip, giving a snap in the air.

The three broke into peals of laughter. Tears streamed down their cheeks and just when one thought it was ending, another wave of hysterics took over.

"Stop! Stop! I can't take it—my stomach!" begged Ambo Shanti.

"Oh, my God. My cheeks hurt!" hooted Lilith.

"Oh, geez! Make it stop!" pleaded Saruk AUM, who had fallen off the rocker onto the ground, his wings kicking up a cloud of dust.

"Make it stop, make it stop!" implored Lilith.

"Okay, you asked for it," threatened Ambo Shanti. "Origami!"

The three went dead silent. An outsider would have never understood why.

When Lilith was at an early age, a neighbor's family took in a foreign exchange student from Japan. Lilith was fascinated by her. One day the exchange student was sitting at a desk on a particularly glum afternoon, intently folding the most unbelievably small origami cranes under the glow of a desk lamp. Lilith marveled at the colored paper and the precision of the girl's fingers. She drank in the joy of the artistry and the tranquility of the peaceful quiet. Lilith remembered the girl's smile and her saturated concentration. She wanted so much to learn from her.

The host mother came in and saw the little child's hands and chin leaning on the desk. Feeling overly protective, she barked, "What are you doing, Lilith?"

"I'm watching her, Mrs. Ewing."

"Don't disturb her! She's busy!"

Ignoring the command, Lilith turned to the beautiful Japanese girl. "What is your name?"

"I am Keiko," she responded.

"What are you making?"

"Cranes," came the matter-of-fact reply.

"Why are you making so many?" asked Lilith.

"If I make 101 of them, I will make happy," came the answer.

Up until this point, Lilith didn't realize that Keiko wasn't fluent in English.

Mrs. Ewing stood like a statue, arms folded across her chest, broom in hand, waiting for Lilith to leave. The little girl decided not fight against this or beg to stay.

"Would everything have been different if I had stayed there and refused?" she asked her winged guardians. "Would I have changed this destiny?"

The expression on the spirits' faces was the same given anytime the memory resurfaced.

Later that same day, Lilith ventured back to the room where she had been playing with the neighborhood kids and tried her best to fit in. The group decided to go outside and play in young Annie's playhouse. Lilith hated this sort of let's-play-house nonsense. She thought about going over to the giant magnolia tree in the yard, and wandered away from the tiny playhouse.

"You saw yourself in a particular scenario," soothed Ambo Shanti. "You wanted so much to be a part of the gang of neighborhood kids."

"We had to let you do it," interjected Saruk AUM.

"I was so miserable in that moment. What did I do wrong?" asked Lilith.

"Nothing. Absolutely nothing."

"I did nothing? Or I did nothing wrong?"

"You surrendered."

"You retreated. Think back. Walk through the memory in your mind's eye."

"Okay. I was not into playing house, and I walked out of the fenced-in yard and toward the big tree. Annie yelled for her brother to

come get me, and it had started to rain. Why do I feel like crying?"

"Keep going, you are finding it!"

Tears began to roll down Lilith's cheeks as she continued. "We went to Beth's house next door. The older kids started talking about playing school, and I wanted to leave."

"Tell it like it is happening now."

"Tell it in the present tense!"

"Be every object in the scene."

"Be every kid in the memory!"

"Like an active dream?" Lilith asked.

"Precisely!" said Saruk AUM as his mighty wings flapped, causing leaves to swirl.

"Repeat it in the Gestaltian style!" encouraged Ambo Shanti.

"Okay. I am protesting, arguing that school was not a game."

"Is not a game…"

"Begin again," instructed Ambo Shanti. Lilith was very familiar with this technique, but had not tried it with a waking memory. She was excited now to be a part of the experiment.

"Got it," she said, smiling at her angels. "The 'me' part of me is protesting, arguing that the 'school' part of me is not the 'game' part of me. The 'me' part of me is begging the 'other kids' part of me back to play with the 'Japanese girl' part of me. Then the 'kid' part of me locked the 'me' part of me in a 'closet' part of me and ridiculed the 'me' part of me. Oh my God! I get it!"

"Get what, little one?"

"That was the day I realized I didn't fit into cliques."

"And what else?"

"That solitude is an illusion!"

"What else?"

"The illusion I had let myself believe about fitting in or belonging to a group is ridiculous, because there is no such thing as separation."

"Good. And now, in this moment, what do you feel about the origami?"

"I am feeling so inspired by my vision of Keiko, the Japanese girl."

"How does it make you feel in this moment?"

"I feel so grateful for this solitude and for the peaceful outlets I am able to immerse my energy and creativity into."

"That was the day you truly were born as an artist!"

"The next time you were allowed to pick a book, we lead you to one about origami! Do you remember?"

"Yes, I do! The book came with a little clear square envelope of colored paper."

"That was when you retreated to your parent's basement playroom and dove into art projects."

"That was the day you first felt the spark of Divine Oneness."

"Oh, my God. I'm so grateful!" cried Lilith. Her tears turned from sad to a happy, joyful rain forming spiraling paisley puddles of bliss on the ground beneath her rocker.

Chapter 36

Birthing

We are continuously born and reborn,
reinventing ourselves again and again.

The Great Mother shifted in the arms of her consort, and the vibration of his infinite heart inspired her to create chains of islands in emerald and turquoise waters. The Boundless Father expanded even further, offering Great Mother more and more space in which to create. His gentle movement vibrated in waves as fruit trees bore and dropped their sweetness on her rich ground. This in turn invited small furry creatures to taste the goodness. Every rock and shell on the shores and every leaf on every tree shimmered in the sheer magnificence of being.

The sky changed, and clouds began to form. Wind swept across dry deserts, and grasses swayed in the savannahs of the Great Mother's giant body. In her ecstasy, the Goddess began to quiver and shake.

"I have you, my love," assured the Great Spirit. "You are safe."

"But I am scared, I am afraid," said Mother.

"Of what, my darling? There is nothing ever to fear. I am always here, and you are always a part of me. It is an illusion that you and I are different. We are two halves of the same oneness."

"But you are vast, empty space, and I am filled with earth and funk. If you look into me and see what I am made of, can you love me?"

"I will always love you. Trust in me. Surrender and let me be the support of all you do, all you change, and all you create."

The landmasses quivered and pulsated, causing frightful tremors to tear through the surface of the Mother. Water became displaced. Booming thunder blasted, giving forth searing bolts of light that scorched the landscape.

"This is a royal mess," sobbed the Mother.

"Why do you think this?" consoled the Father.

"I am ugly. How will you want me now?" she wailed, belching forth lava that threw clouds of cinder and soot into the skies.

"How could I not?" He coughed his reply through the smoky destruction and pandemonium.

Chapter 37

Collision

Realities shatter when we feel our own infinite space.

"You did the things that people thought you should do," Saruk AUM said as he gently touched Lilith's cheek. "You were so dutiful, and yet you managed to maintain your individuality. You wore the clothes you wanted to wear and had your own sense of style—never trendy," he added in an effort to soothe his tearful protégée.

"And you were never quite like the people you went to school with, remember?" Ambo Shanti reminded.

"You went to college for fine arts when everyone told you to be a scientist. You got a teaching degree to please your father."

"He used to say—" began Ambo Shanti.

Lilith finished, "That it was a good thing to fall back on. Why on earth would I want to fall backward?"

"He was goal-oriented. It was what he had learned from those before him."

"It is not your concern."

"Ask him the question, sweetie," urged Ambo Shanti. "Go ahead."

"I don't think so," Saruk AUM cut in.

"Don't listen to him!" Ambo Shanti said, elevating her tone.

"So," began Lilith, looking deeply into Don's dark eyes,

causing him to become even more absorbed in hers. "What brought us together today?"

"I want to shag her!" screamed Casanova.

"Duh!" interjected the Horny Teen.

"I'm with them, I think," added the Stoner. "Are there any cookies?"

Don answered, "Magnetics."

"Magnetics?" Lilith echoed.

"Yes," responded Don.

"He's right," whispered Saruk AUM. "Two souls come together by means of magnetic attraction."

"It is such a powerful and mysterious thing," added Ambo Shanti.

"But how does it work?" asked Lilith, creaking the chair to a stop and balancing precariously on the rockers.

"It starts with a collision of energies, like the magnetics of lightning or the sound pressure of thunder. In some cases, two people meet, dance, laugh, and intertwine, while others start slowly and build over time," said Don.

"You're right," Lilith mused.

"And some are reluctant and seem to never get going," added Ambo Shanti in a whisper.

"There are many relationships that appear impossible, and yet they begin in spite of ridiculous odds or the views and insidious comments of outsiders," said Don in an almost inward voice. This caused the entire Boardroom to back up toward the table. He added, "It's about quarks."

"Quarks?" asked Lilith. "Like in quantum mechanics?"

"Oh, here we go again!" screeched Low Self-esteem.

"Chill, man," commanded the Stoner. "He has this one! My boy knows some quasi-mechanics."

"That's quantum, you idiot!" countered the Nerd, stumbling into the Boardroom.

"Dude, where have you been all day?" scolded the Stoner.

"Busy calculating some—"

"Get to work!" interrupted Reason, pushing the Nerd to the eye windows.

"Oh, she's out of our league!" squealed the Nerd, trying to back away.

"Oh no, you don't!" bellowed Reason.

"Get in there! We need you now!" yelled the assembly.

Lilith sat staring at Don.

"Say her name before you go all science," said the Horny Teen. "She likes that!"

"Very astute," said the Guru.

"Quiet, everyone!" shouted Reason, causing a gust of hot air to tilt the Guru's pillow. His arms flailed as he tried to stay afloat. Don chuckled a bit, and Lilith's face turned a self-conscious pink.

"Lilith…" Don began, and as the Boardroom had hoped, the mere mention of her name caused a glow from her forehead. This light beamed brighter than the afternoon sun flooding the patio. He continued, "Something beyond chemical reactions and electrical circuitry is responsible for this. The great eastern mystics teach of invisible energy grids and cords that meet, mingle, and bind us to one another. Many of us are able to feel them. Some of us are able to see them. Quantum physics exemplifies attraction and the sharing of charges in its explanation of electrons and quarks."

"Touché!" exclaimed Casanova with a wave of an invisible foil.

"We are in!" squealed the Horny Teen as he high-fived the Stoner and then chest-bumped the Nerd into an open chair.

"Okay, I get how it starts," said Lilith, "but what do you think keeps it together? Once in a relationship, we become obsessed with connection."

"That is such a chick thing," said the Horny Teen.

"No, she is correct," said the Guru, righting his balance, then

drifting to the center of the table. "Just be yourself, boy!"

Don continued, "It's true. We desire a fusion and, somehow, within this coupling, we want to keep our independence and identity. The physical pull is strong, and soon we crave a link that's more permanent."

"Humanity's confused illusion is that there is separation in the first place, little one," said Saruk AUM.

"It is said that we begin to trade energy with our partners," said the Guru.

"Actual matter is passed back and forth," said the Nerd.

"When I breathe your breath, I become you," said Don.

The Boardroom rushed to the eye windows and witnessed Lilith melting like a Popsicle on the Philadelphia pavement in July.

"Nailed it!" shouted the Horny Teen.

"Call for the check, dude," said the Stoner, taking a much-needed draw on his joint. "But finish that wine first. It's worth it!"

"So I am becoming you?" asked Lilith.

"Yes, a little bit at a time," responded Don, "and I am becoming you."

The giant screened blipped and sparked over the water. Saruk AUM pulled a laser pointer out of his pocket and aimed a thin beam of light at the frozen image of Lilith and Don.

"It's true, you breathe in the air of another, and it is also true that you literally become one another little by little over time at a chemical level, but—"

"But what?" Lilith demanded.

Don wanted to stay suspended in Lilith's gaze. It felt like velvet and warm honey dripping all over his body. He decided to be silent and finish the last few sips of his wine. Jackie poked her head out of the doorway and saw that the bottle was kicked. Don gestured for the check, maintaining his steady stare into Lilith's transfixed eyes.

Jackie trotted over and broke the endless moment by placing the check down and clearing the dishes and bottle. Lilith picked up her glass, not sure if she was drunk from the wine or Don's deep stare.

Don reached for the check and Lilith slapped his hand away.

"You're kidding, right?" Don chortled. "There's no way I'm letting you pay for this!"

"I insist!" Lilith growled like a dark panther.

"Forget it!" roared Don.

"Come on, really! This was my idea," Lilith sparred.

"No, it wasn't, it was mutual," Don insisted.

"Okay, then we'll split it fifty-fifty. I won't take no for an answer!" Lilith snapped as she snatched the bill from his hand, slapping a pair of twenties down on top of it.

"Okay then, as you wish, my divine goddess," said Don, bowing ever so slightly.

The couple got up to leave, pushing their chairs back at precisely the same instant. Having both supplied a pair of twenties, Don decided to leave his share of the change, though it was a much bigger tip than his usual. He felt uneasy about getting into a match over it and decided this was a better choice. *Best not to rock her chair*, he thought. *Rock her chair? Where did that come from?* he wondered. *Okay, I'm losing it*," he thought as the two stood up.

She moved to his side of the table and swung her arms around him. Don was as happy as a six-year-old on a playground, imagining Lilith and an image of himself skipping over to a seesaw. She threw her head back in a wide open laugh, and he lifted her off her feet for just a moment in a caressing hug.

For the first time in his adult life, he felt completely open and trusting. The early autumn evening had a crispness that had not been there the night before, and it was as if the season had changed as a result of their meeting.

Lilith saw Owen poke his head out from the kitchen and blow her a kiss. She winked and quickly turned her attention back to the embrace. The wine buzz was perfectly igniting the couple's inner flames, and the inevitability of a physical union was becoming profoundly apparent.

As they left the patio, the iron gate clicked shut and a stiff breeze kicked up.

"Let's walk back up Bainbridge. What do you say?" Don asked as he wrapped his arm tightly around his dark prize.

"Sure, sounds good to me," answered Lilith, feeling caught in a sticky web of lust.

As they walked past the Famous Deli on Fourth Street, Don had a flash about going in and buying food for breakfast. He wondered if she ate bagels.

"Dude, you haven't sealed the deal yet," reasoned the Horny Teen. "You can't."

"My God, you are rationalizing so well! What's to come of my job?" joshed Reason, causing the Boardroom to crack up.

The sky was giving way to evening, the light dimming. Lilith didn't notice Don's confident smirk. She wiggled out from the arm wrapped around her shoulder and stopped. He turned toward her and found his eyes magnetically drawn to hers once again. The darkness was a little scary for a second. Suddenly he felt otherworldly vibrations from his dream of the night before.

Venturing into Lilith's eyes in that moment was like entering the sea in the darkness of a new moon. It was like walking into a haunted house. She looked deeply into him and through him at the same time. Her uncanny confidence and vibrant sexuality had him more than just a little off balance.

He took hold of Lilith with both his arms and pulled her tightly to his chest. Then he kissed her for the first time, softly and tentatively, as if asking, "Is this okay?" She responded by taking hold of his face in her hands and kissing him back intensely. He felt tiny in her arms in that moment, even though he towered over her by a good foot. He realized that he had yet to understand her full power and, instead of letting the Board analyze this, he chose to ride the waves and currents, just trusting. His body trembled with lust and excitement.

"Are you okay?" asked Lilith.

"Yeah, of course I am," he said, not really feeling okay at all. Don loved to swim in the daylight. When he would go down the shore, he would spend the entire day at the beach, mostly in the water. But this was a dark, murky sea. It was an unknown realm where he felt vulnerable and freaked out.

As a child, he went to see the movie *Jaws* with a group of his friends. The scene of the young woman swimming in the pitch blackness, being attacked by the great white, was indelibly burned into the fear center of his brain. Later that night, when he returned home after the film, he puked his guts out. It turned out that he had a virus but, despite knowing that he hadn't been sick from watching the movie, he was never able to shake the experience. Don's childlike love for the water remained as long as the sun was shining. This moment with Lilith felt exactly like that horrific night. Lilith was the dark, unknown aspect of the ocean, and her lust was the shark.

"You're trembling," Lilith observed. "Are you cold?" she asked, knowing full well that she had captured him.

"It's like a dark ocean," he said, drawing her into an endless embrace.

"You loved the water when you were little. Do you remember?" asked Saruk AUM.

"She still does! Don't you sweetie?" Ambo Shanti interjected.

"When you were a child and were left alone to bathe in a tub, you discovered what it was like lying in the water face up with just your nose out. You were so cute!" smiled Saruk AUM.

"I still love the feeling," Lilith said, "of being underwater, able to breathe, or floating on my back. In the watery environment, I can hear my own heart beating."

"That is because it is the sound of One, the sound of unconditional love."

"It's scary, like disappearing," said Don.

"What is?" asked Lilith.

"This feeling of being here with you. It's like treading water in the dark—kinda' exhilarating and totally freakin' scary, all at the same time."

"I love the water, especially in the dark!"

"Of course she does!" whimpered Low Self-esteem.

"Hush! Let her talk!" scolded the Lover.

"Dude, where have you been?" asked the Horny Teen. "We could have used you hours ago!"

"Yes, yes, yes!" murmured the members of the Board.

"By all means, take the controls," Reason said, offering his chair to the Lover.

"It is like a vibrational force, like unknown gravity," said Don.

"That was poetry!" Lilith blurted.

"It's like I am the moon, irresistibly wanting to be in orbit near you." The Lover continued to speak freely from Don's lips. "You are a magnificent goddess. It's as if you're constantly defining my phases, and these are reflected in what I'm feeling and what you see in my emotions."

The moon is how we feel about our mothers, how we see them. She is a cosmic interpreter. Luna is our emotions. It is pretty cool that he's using this as an example, thought Lilith.

"You must have loved your mother very much," offered Lilith sympathetically.

They separated from the embrace and stood for a moment, just breathing, before turning west. As they continued to walk quietly, Lilith wove her fingers through Don's. They headed up Bainbridge to Eighth

Street and turned south, following it until they reached Christian and the opening to the Market.

"Let's stay on this side," suggested Don. "There's less trash."

"Good idea," Lilith responded.

The pizza store on the corner of Ninth Street was still open. No one was near the window, and the chair in front was empty.

"Slow night," Don observed involuntarily, squeezing her hand as he continued to lead her back to his house. When they got to his stoop, they kissed again. Don wanted to pick Lilith up and carry her into his house as if she were his bride. He almost did, but something stopped him. They wrestled through the front door into the kitchen, and then up the spiraling stairs of his tiny trinity house, kissing and caressing. On the second floor landing, outside the bathroom door, they paused for a moment. Then they continued up the stairs to Don's studio on the top floor.

"Wait," he said.

"Wait? Wait! Wait for what?" screamed Casanova, the Horny Teen, and Reason together.

The Artist pushed forward. "I need to draw her before we make love with her."

"I can't believe this is happening," cried the Horny Teen. "I can't believe you're blocking me!"

"Chill, little dude. These older dudes know stuff," said the Stoner.

"Wait?" asked Lilith.

"Yeah, wait. Please wait. I want to paint you first. Will you model?" Don pleaded.

"Here? Right now? You want me to model?" asked Lilith. "You're kidding me, right? You realize you're asking me to work?"

"Yes, I realize I'm asking you to work," said Don, "and no, I'm not kidding. I want to paint you. I want to immortalize this moment."

"Well, since you put it that way, let's do it!"

"She said 'do it'!" howled the Horny Teen.

"Enough!" scolded Reason.

"Have a seat right here," said Don, tossing an oversized purple velvet pillow on the floor.

"Nice," Lilith murmured, kicking her boots off and flopping into the soft cushion.

Don flipped a podium onto the floor that had been leaning up against the wall. On top he centered a thick foam slab, and snapped a crisp white sheet over it. On the back corners he set some Grecian-style columns that he brought from an adjoining room, wound them with silk vines, and then draped them with lush maroon satin. As if flinging paint on a canvas in the reckless style of an abstract expressionist, he threw some green and purple velvet pillows of various sizes in the center, and then set a pot filled with iridescent peacock feathers and several arrangements of plants on the floor.

"I'll be right back," he said, bounding down the stairs. In seconds, he returned with a huge vase filled with fresh lilies and a waterfall of freesia.

This was a completely different Don that Lilith was watching. He was suddenly in his element, fully engaged and completely self-assured. He continued by climbing a ladder in the corner of the room so he could aim pink light at the space from a theatrical lamp which hung from the ceiling. Lilith looked around and couldn't believe how well-appointed this studio was.

"You have everything here, don't you?" she asked.

"Now I do," he said, flipping the light switch, which threw a warm hue over the entire scene.

She watched as he moved to the other side of the room and carried an easel into place. Next, he brought a small table, and placed a box of colored pastels on top of it. Finally he positioned a large drawing board on the easel that was already taped with an equally large piece of

warm-toned Canson drawing paper.

"What color—" Lilith began to ask.

"Moonstone," responded Don, continuing to set up.

When he had completed the preparations, he looked up. He'd noticeably transformed into Don the Artist. She was enchanted. Don nodded, and no words were needed to invite her to take off her clothes and lay in the temple-like still life he had created for her.

"And now…" he began.

"And now?" she echoed.

"And now, I will immortalize you."

"This is brilliant!" Casanova said as he slapped the Artist on the back.

"Simply brilliant!" added Lust.

Reason chimed in, "Kudos! Simply marvelous!"

In a flourish, Don skipped off down the stairs to fetch something in the bathroom on the second floor.

Where the heck has he gone now? she thought as she pulled her jeans off and undid the buttons of her sweater. She took care to drop them out of the vision path of the scene; her years of modeling professionally had given her great habits. After removing her top, she undid the hooks on her bra and slithered out of the matching *V*-string, placing them gently on top of the pile of clothes.

Just then Don turned the corner at the top of the stairs, returning to the cathedral-ceilinged space. He gasped at the glow of her skin and her naked beauty in the pinkish light. She was brown and sleek—a wild animal, tamed for only just this moment. She slowly climbed onto the platform and reclined, her hair spilling out over the pillows. She gazed off into space, comfortable in her skin, completely at ease with her entire being.

Don trembled as he walked closer to her, amazed at her magnificence. In his hand he held a very large white plastic container of

talcum. She looked at him like he was slightly crazy.

"I am going to powder you," he said.

"What on earth for?"

"So that you'll look like a marble statue."

Her eyes widened at the idea. *What the heck?* she thought, though she managed a demure smile. He placed the powder down near her, walked over to the stereo, and flipped it on. He then returned to the reclining goddess. She giggled as he began to rub the powder on her feet and legs and arms. She purred as he made his way up to her firm belly, gently around her breasts and nipples, and up to her glorious neck.

"May I put some on your face?"

"Sure, why not? I'm washable," she responded. "This is nothing compared to being laid in a tub of plaster by sculpture students!"

Don paused to kiss her deeply before finishing the white patina on her face. He was so gentle in the application that it hypnotized her. Don slowly smoothed the white powder around her nose and on her cheeks. He was careful to not get any in her eyes. He'd completed the task of transformation, and stood to admire his creation. What lay before him now was a sculpture of a goddess.

She watched him from the corner of her eyes as he backed away to take his position at the easel. Like a conductor readying an orchestra for its opening note, Don took up a piece of charcoal and began to draw.

With bold strokes and great power, the image came up on the paper. It was as if it were drawing itself, and a great force existed behind its creation. Twenty minutes went by, and the only sound in the room was the music coming from the speakers. An antique blues song by Robert Johnson howled warnings of going down to the crossroads at night as Don's hand moved like lightning, molding the image of Lilith on his paper.

"Let me see it," she begged, breaking the silence.

"No, Lilith. Wait until it's done," he commanded.

"Oh, come on, Donny! Let me see what you have so far."

"Stop talking and moving! I'm working on your face," he growled.

"I'll get up if you don't let me see it right now!" she screeched as she began to move her arm.

"Wait! No! Please don't!" he begged, holding up his free hand. "Here you go," he said, gently taking the board from the easel and turning it so she could see the image from her elevated position.

"Wow, I'm so impressed! That's really nice work! Okay then, I'll behave now. Is this where my head was?"

"Tilt it a little bit to your left," Don guided with his outstretched hand. "Chin down just a touch. That's it. Hold it right there."

He continued to create, and soon the original piece and two more were finished. Don was a pro. When he felt inspired, he could whip out drawings, paintings, and sculptures as prolifically as one of the ancient masters.

He stood up and spread the finished drawings out on the floor and invited Lilith to take a break.

"Do you, by any chance, have a robe that I could borrow? I don't want to get this powder everywhere," Lilith said, careful not to disturb the patina on her skin as she began to move.

"Sure," he said, bounding off down the stairs to fetch her something. He returned with an emerald green silk robe adorned with gold embroidery.

With pride, Don offered his hand and invited his subject to rise up off her podium to view his gallery of offerings. She slowly unfolded herself from the altar where she'd reclined and walked deliberately toward the display. Don wrapped the robe across her shoulders and she slid her arms into the sleeves and tied the sash.

Silently, she stood and really looked at each drawing individually. They were beautiful. She was right; he was worthy of her attention. As she absorbed the passionate curves and energies of his strokes and markings, she felt understood at a very deep level. This inspired a smile to curl her lips.

The images possessed a great play between the weight of her body and the space that held the chalky markings on the papers. The exchange of opposites was much different than the average Western mind could convey. It was like nothing she had ever experienced. The intensity of his expression and his ability vibrated in the pastel lines and shapes. He seemed to have a depth of perception that allowed the drawings to be in flux, in a constant state of motion. This was so vastly different than the typical attempt at life drawing which often cried out so desperately for perfection. Instead she believed that these images had a Far Eastern quality, one that sees the power and beauty in blending.

Her body stood in each piece as a mountain stands in the sunlight, one side drenched in a golden glow, the other worshipping and praising the darker spaces. His work rejoiced in the shadow's ability to give form and definition to the light. Don was able to show the validity and correctness of each, as if the rich shapes and lines on the warm-toned paper were singing in harmony.

For Lilith, the two—light and dark—had always intertwined. Long before she had studied Oriental philosophy, she felt insulted by the contrived Western idea that the only two choices are positive and negative.

"How is it that everything could be summed up and defined by just black and white or good and evil?" she had asked one of her teachers. "What about the infinite shades of grey?"

Lilith loved the act of mixing paint, and understood how to combine and blend colors together. For her, it was a mediation to commingle two pigments and watch them create many subtle tones. This was a beacon lighting her path of initiation into the understanding of the Far Eastern ways.

"The moon is present in these pictures," Lilith murmured quietly.

"What's that?" Don asked, causing Lilith to jolt in surprise. He realized she was deeply consumed in her admiration of his work. He had not meant to disturb her.

"The Moon Goddess, the soul and our emotions. She is present in your drawing."

"How do you see that? Please explain," Don said.

"You're able to capture the way light from the Great Spirit—our Sun—reflects upon our beingness, and how the Moon—our psyche—sometimes moves swiftly and yet, at other times, more slowly."

"Thank you," Don responded, impressed with her critique.

"It must be your love for your mother," continued Lilith. "I can feel it in these drawings, and even more so how you love the Great Goddess in all women. You must have been blessed with one of the greatest mothers possible, just as I have. My mother is a vast support in all ways, emotional and material. I adore our talks, and I love it when she really tunes into my sharing of philosophical ideas."

"I never had that luxury on a philosophical level with my mother," Don confessed. "She died when I was very young."

Unaffected by the mention of death, Lilith continued, "It's amazing to me how you capture the conversations and exchanges in your expression," she said with a wave of her hand over the drawings. It seemed as if she were receiving a transfusion of energy from each one, individually.

"And who am I in the scheme of what you perceive through these drawings?" asked Don.

"You are the center," said Lilith, closing her eyes to shut out the disturbances of the room so she was able to tune in to the vibrations more profoundly. "You are the source of love, like the Sun, the giver of nourishment to the ecosystems and environments. You are the container, inviting those who look at your work to bask in your rays."

Chapter 38

Battle

Face life's challenges and learn to accept, adapt, and accommodate.

The Alchemist leaned into the rippling fog that floated on the surface of his cauldron. "Zahra," he called, "fly into Heron's vision so we can watch what he is remembering."

The bird obeyed and found herself perched on a branch high above the field within the king's memory. She watched as Heron pulled the leather trappings of his sparring gear onto his upper body while his father lectured him on the challenge he was about to face.

"Your opponent is larger than you, Heron. You must use your wit and speed, boy!" he bellowed gruffly.

"Yes, Father, he is. Yet I am sure I can take him down."

"You must, boy. It is the only way for you to become a knight. Your mother and I can no longer pay for your schooling. If you win, you will be chosen to study with the greatest teacher of fighting and war. This is your chance, the only way you can go on."

Heron's eyes fell to the dusty ground. He knew this was true, and it tore at his heart.

"I promise, Father," he said, pulling on his boots and taking care to tie the laces tight.

"Take this, my son," said his mother as she handed him a scarf she had made the night before. Unable to sleep, she unraveled an old sweater and knit until dawn. Heron took the scarf, held it to his nose, and inhaled her distinctive scent. He tied it to his neck and tucked it under the stiff leather of his breastplate.

"We are watching you and cheering for you, my brave son," she said as she tried to hide her worry and concern.

"Do not fear, Mother," said Heron, kissing her cheek. "I will win."

"Of course you will, darling boy," she encouraged, returning the kiss to his forehead.

The family trailed behind Heron with banners as they marched to the fighting field. The opponent, a slightly bigger boy from another village, awaited his arrival. Heron's teacher met them at the edge of the turf. The villagers cheered at the sight of their hero.

"I will take him from here, sir," he said, reaching for the young warrior. He tugged at Heron's lacing. "Good job, son. This is snug and well done."

Zahra flew in closer and perched on the bough of a nearby elm tree.

"I am here, in his vision," she reported, unsure as to whether Deagadh and Alwyn could see her.

"We are with you, love," answered her master.

"Keep your mouth shut, bird! You will be found out for sure!" scolded Alwyn, inspiring a whack from Deagadh's stirring paddle to his rump.

"She is fine there," Deagadh bellowed. "Just another raven in a tree. Let her be."

"Ready your warriors!" shouted the officiator, who then introduced Heron and his opponent, Pauldrons.

As Heron looked over to where his family stood, he saw a thumbs-up from his younger brother and the forced smiles of his parents. Everything melted into the sensation of a dream. Heron felt as if he were outside his body, watching as it walked to the center of the field and began to grapple.

Everything slowed to an unreal time-warped pace. Heron saw his hands grab at Pauldrons' and wrestle him to the ground. The challengers thrashed and groaned as they fell to the earth, kicking up a cloud of dust.

The crowd cheered, giving Zahra the freedom to use her voice. "It is a close match, Master. I cannot say who is winning."

"The king wins this one," assured Deagadh. "Watch!"

Heron dodged a blow to his head and ducked to the ground. A swift sweep of his leg landed his competitor flat on his back. A roar from the crowd let Heron know he was the victor, but he awaited praise and love from the man he thought of as the king of his world. Instead, Heron's father slowly approached with a look of anger on his face. The boy's stomach flipped and twisted; sweat poured from his forehead as he rode a jolt of adrenaline. The sweet elation he had anticipated was squelched.

The screams of joy and praise from the villagers faded into the background as all the boy heard was, "If you ever lose, you will no longer be my son."

There was no pat on the head or shoulder. This was the first of Heron's profound wounds. His ears melted and his brain shut down. In that sentence, in that moment, Heron could see his path stretching into infinity. His quest was clear, and the route was paved with victory. There was neither a choice nor a secondary plan. In that moment he made a sacred vow to be a champion, and to devote himself fully, only, to winning.

As Heron grew, he was able to focus only on success. When he tried new challenges, if he was not the best, he quit. As a result, he never learned to do anything purely for the joy of the process.

The seeds of the pattern had been planted when he was a young boy. Heron and his brother loved to draw. The boys would make the activity a challenge, set rules, and race to complete their creations. They would run to their mother as she cooked or cleaned or wove to show her what they had produced. Though sometimes his brother would win, it was usually Heron who would succeed in gaining the charmed smile of their mother's approval.

The boys of Heron's village learned skills through many games over the years. One was played with stones colored black and white on a board painted with a grid. The game taught its participants the art of capture and resignation, useful skills when directing or being part of an army.

Unfortunately, instead of learning this art of war, Heron was trained only in the skills of fighting. This stymied his ability to function as a member of a team. Though it made him self-dependent, it isolated him. In spite of the admiration of the others, Heron felt sad and lonely. The time of playing in the field of his imagination quickly faded, and life became a contest.

Every four years, the boys of the village who had more than thirteen and fewer then sixteen winters were sent deep into the woods to seek out the ancient one named Alder. He was known far and wide as a great wise man and teacher of young men. Boys from the surrounding villages were directed to him for his clever teachings. There they would study the ways of the Great Goddess of the earth, known as Mother Gaia.

When it was Heron's time to go, he chose instead to immerse himself in rigorous training of sword play and combat. When the boys returned, he learned only bits and fragments of tales from young men who had spent time with the wise one.

While studying with Alder, the boys lived communally in the modest hideaway of the great teacher. They learned to honor each other as brothers, and were treated as Alder's sons. He taught them to identify plants in the forest, and showed them how to gather wild herbs to make them into medicine and potions.

At night, Alder would sit in a large wooden rocking chair in his cabin. All of the boys sat on cushions at his feet. They listened as he told the wondrous stories of his teachers and their teachers before them. This is how the old wise ones had passed on the secrets of the great lineage. A favorite story of the boys was about bees. In this tale, Alder introduced the young men to the concept of the Divine Mother. The message was to always honor each woman as if she were his one true queen.

Alder loved the insect kingdom and felt it held many magical messages. Another potent tale he shared was the secret of the ants. This lesson was conducted as a ritual rite of passage near the end of the tutelage. The boys were taken to a hillside to study the ways of the tiny insects and experience their wisdom.

Ants live in a nation, united and devoted to one cause—the survival of the nest. They demonstrate great order and discipline within their community. Each ant is born into a specific role and serves only his queen. Alder frequently reminded the boys that without women, they would not exist.

Alder had been taught by his masters that every woman is a treasure, a most beautiful, sparkling being, and a gift from the earth. The boys were taught to honor every woman as a reflective manifestation of the Great Mother Goddess. Alder's message was that the Goddess energy had brought them all into being. It gave them life, it fed them at all levels, and was to be worshiped with deep gratitude every single day.

Chapter 39

Weaving

Untangle the warp strings before interlacing the woof.

"I never graduated from art school," Don admitted. "I got into a strange rift with my professors. They threw me out a few months before the end of my senior year."

"Who cares?" Lilith said. "You're a brilliant artist. Ignore that, it means nothing."

"I try to…" Don began, walking closer to Lilith as he slid the belt out of his jeans.

"Just let it go," she coaxed, turning to look up at his face. "There's no sense in carrying a wound from the comment of a teacher," her voice soothed as her hand reached up to touch his face.

"I know. They were pollution to my atmosphere and clouded my creativity. I don't know how you or anyone sees it through to the end," Don scowled.

"I'm sure they feared your rays of brilliance," she said, twisting her fingers into his hair. "The rest of us have different needs, that's all. There is no comparison." Don's hands slid along the surface of the silk robe, entwining her like a vine. She responded by spiraling a leg around his thigh.

"I am not afraid to commune with the Sun, and I have no desire to remain pale in the darkness of their staunch ways. No, instead, I am willing…" He leaned in and kissed her passionately. As she continued to breathe, words came through on the exhales. "…able to transform…and grow with you." He kissed her harder and more passionately, winding his fingers into her thick locks.

Perched on the roof of the Bella Vista row house, Ambo Shanti nuzzled into the crook of Saruk AUM's chest, just under his wing, as he wrapped his arms tightly around her. He reached down to tilt her head so he could admire the way the moonlight glinted off her phosphorescent skin. He leaned in to kiss her with all of his heart. When he pulled his face back from hers, she asked, "Why is it that people who live on islands in fishing villages hate fish and are afraid of playing and swimming and boating in the water?"

"One of the great jokes of humans, I suppose," he responded, pulling her close once again.

"I feel most alive like this," Lilith cooed, allowing her eyes to close as she drifted into the bliss of the moment. She pressed her body into Don's arms. He lifted her up and carried her down the flight of stairs to his second floor bedroom. Her hair draped over his left arm and her legs molded over his right. Don laid her down on his duvet and backed up a few feet to remove the rest of his clothes. She tried to reach up to help him out of his jeans, but he motioned for her to lie back.

"Do you always get what you want, woman?" asked Don.

"Of course I do! I visualize it already happening. I see it as here and completed."

"That explains it," said Reason.

"Yes indeed," the Guru said with a wag of his head. "This explains a great, great deal."

Ambo Shanti wiggled free of Saruk AUM's embrace just enough to blow a wave of glowing bubbles into the air. They glistened in the night sky, reflecting the moon and stars. She imagined everyone receiving their wishes in the beautiful, floating, iridescent globes.

"You love to create in the bubbles!" exclaimed Saruk AUM.

"I love to watch as they float and dance on the air currents. It reminds me how to best get the energy moving for everyone. I place all my feelings and beliefs into the multicolored spheres. When they burst into tiny particles, I feel the wishes and prayers disperse into the sacred vibrations of the universe."

"And then what, my love?" asked Saruk AUM, floating in the air in front of his queen.

"Then, I let it go, knowing that it…just…is."

Lilith grinned and complied. Don's jeans fell to the floor, revealing his excitement. Surfing on a wave of anticipation, he dove into the worship of his goddess, kissing every part of her glowing glory. She moaned in delight and steadily grew to an explosive peak. Don pleasured her over and over before he allowed himself to plunge inside of her. As he readied himself for his target, she grabbed his shoulders, twisted her leg around his, and flipped him onto his back. He tried to flip her back over, but it was impossible. He tried to speak, but she placed her fingers to his lips.

"Shh," she hushed.

"But—"

"Don't speak," she ordered sternly.

"But—"

"No!" she scolded.

The lynx pinned Don's arms and mounted him like a bull rider. Excitement and fear rose in him simultaneously. It was more than he could take; he had no control. He exploded much earlier than he would have liked to. Disgusted with his inability to hold on, he turned away from her as she rolled off him, laughing and covered with sweat.

They lay in silence for what seemed like an hour before he had the nerve to turn and look at her. During that space and time, Lilith had drifted off into a dream. She saw herself standing on the beach of a tiny island in the morning light. All around her lay brilliant turquoise water and soft white sand. She walked the circumference of the entire island, returning to her starting point. Next to her beginning place, a large, twisted tree had grown. Its limbs looked like the curls of her hair. She pulled branches from the tree as it spoke to her in a foreign language. The dream body took great care when removing the pieces of wood. If she tried to take the wrong branch, the tree's voice elevated. This quickly taught her the proper method of receiving its offerings.

In the white sand of the beach, she began to assemble a large rocking chair from the harvested boughs. As she worked on into the afternoon, the sky grew pink and red with the sunset. She watched as her dream body climbed into the rocking chair and began to sing the song of the tree.

Lilith blinked her eyes open to find Don on all fours, looking down at her. She jolted awake, quite startled.

"What are you doing?" she barked.

"Why did you flip me over?" he growled.

"What's your problem? It's over!"

"Why did you flip me over, Lilith? What was that about?" snarled Don.

"What's the matter with you? Can't take a woman being on top?" she roared back.

"It's not like that. It's just that—well, I wanted to give to you, in a certain way. You know?"

"No, actually, I don't," she said, thinking *Are you kidding me?* as she rolled away from him and clutched the sheet up to her cheeks. *Maybe this is a good time to gather up my clothes and go,* she thought.

"What just happened?" asked Don. "Why did you turn on me?"

"I didn't turn on you," she said, rolling to face him. "I just wanted to be on top, in control."

"But like that, I couldn't hold on and I lost it," Don squeaked. "I lost control."

"But I deserve to be on top," commanded the Goddess.

"Sure, sometimes. But I…I wanted this all to go a different way," Don pleaded, sure that he was making a big mess of the situation by the look on her face.

"Selling your opinion when you don't mean it, robs you and depletes your power bank," jibed the Guru. "Doing this buys approval, but this approval is a form of prostitution. This type of selling out is a power drain."

"It's all good," drifted the Stoner, returning to the Boardroom in a cloud of smoke.

"Dude," began the Adolescent, mirroring the behavior of the Stoner as he accepted a half-baked joint from his hand. The Adolescent took a long hard draw on the spliff and held it in as if he had been doing this for years. After a small choking sequence, he released a cloud of smoke, blasting it over the entire Boardroom in the hope of creating a contact high for the Collective. "I think this is what she's talking about."

The sparring conversation went on like this for what seemed like an eternity. They argued and calmed like the tremors of an earthquake. Lilith tried to explain her desire for control; Don argued his right to it. Lilith laughed as if Don was a child; Don flared and charged like a bull stung by a bee.

"I give up," Lilith murmured, getting up to find her clothes. Don reached for her arm and pulled her into his embrace.

"Don't leave like this. Stay, Lilith. Let me hold you, please."

Too tired to fight the offer of his warmth, Lilith collapsed back into the bed. She snuggled her bottom against his belly and fell into a shadowy sleep.

Don listened to her shallow breathing change to the long and steady rhythm of dreaming. He wondered why he was such a screw-up. He analyzed the situation and recalled his momentary power when she was still and statue-like. He wished he could return to carving her image into paper with bold colors and weighty chalk marks. The voices of his three sisters mocked and ridiculed him as he drifted off into a restless sleep.

Don blinked in the darkness. He found it impossible to focus on anything as he groped around in the obscurity. He was on his hands and knees; the ground beneath him felt moist. He tried to stand, but hit his head hard on what seemed to be a ceiling. Crouching back down, his hands felt for the edges and boundaries of this chamber. Ever so tentatively, his fingertips followed the concave curve of his surroundings. Fear choked him as he realized he was in some sort of tunnel. Claustrophobia rapidly took over, and he wanted to run. Again he hit his head, this time much harder. He felt a trickle of moisture dripping from his scalp onto his neck.

Adrenaline pumped through his body. He dropped back to his knees and instinctively began crawling. He closed his eyes to help focus on the steady movement of his limbs. He cursed his luck and the situation as he crawled on.

Then he sensed an energetic shift and blinked his eyes open. A glimmer of light up ahead helped define the size of the tunnel. It was gradually becoming larger as he moved deeper into it. Soon he was standing up and running toward the light.

Finally, he broke free of the soggy tube and raced into a dimly lit clearing. He stopped, realizing that it felt oddly familiar. Just then a vein of lightning cut through the darkness, throwing purple and blue flashes all around him. In the blaze he could see the skeletons of trees and dried clumps of grass amid what seemed to be a destroyed landscape. A déjà vu began to creep into his consciousness as a tremendous clap of thunder broke the silence.

Frightened, he dropped again to his knees and shielded his head. A huge limb fell within feet of his trembling body. Then came the voice, the booming voice from the sky. It was the voice from his dream the night before.

"Go back and try again. This is what you asked for."

The wind kicked up and a wild rainstorm filled the dreamscape. Vibrant azure liquid swirled him into a bright, white container. A turbulent roar filled his ears as he was thrown in circles, around and around, in the blue water.

The light from the hall flickered in his eyes as he twitched into awareness. Lilith slipped back into bed beside him as he listened to the toilet refill.

She kissed his forehead and caressed his cheek, then swept the hair back from his eyes and kissed him again, gently, on the lips. She pushed him flat on his back and kissed her way down past his chest, to his waist, and on to his hips. A moan escaped his lips. He could not contain his feelings. She had a power over him that he could not fight.

She coaxed him to a full salute and mounted him before he could protest. He gave in for a few minutes, unable—and not wanting—to struggle out of the sensation. In spite of his inability to control his elevation, he found the power to quickly reverse their position and flip her onto her back.

"Let me take the top," she snarled as she licked and then bit his wrist, causing him to pull his arm back.

"No way," he bellowed.

"It is my place!" she insisted.

"No!" he argued.

"Side by side," Lilith bargained. "As equals."

Don weakened in his excitement and complied.

In a tangle of passion, they rolled to their sides and exploded.

Almost immediately the wrestling match began again, and the lovers continued. The tangle of bodies resumed a power struggle, vying for the the top. Intense passion burned out of control.

"It's my place. I'm a man!" Don growled, drawing his last bit of strength in order to dominate.

"No!" Lilith shrieked, feeling her back slam against the bed.

"It is a man's place!" he yelled as he exploded inside her.

"It is mine," she brooded as she wriggled out from underneath him.

Don passed out instantly as Lilith peeled away from his embrace. His astral body traveled back immediately to the desolate landscape of his recent dream. It was as if he had never left.

"I don't want this!" he screamed, shaking his fist at the grey clouds. "I don't want to be less than a man. I want her to obey me! She is so raw and intensely frightening. I need her to do as I command!" he roared, and then, once again, the same powerfully booming voice began to rumble. The vehement sound threw him back on the ground, and Don's dream self was sure that his eardrums had ruptured.

"Only I command!" blasted the voice. "Your task, your duty, is to listen! Prostrate yourself to me, for it is I who create all that is. It is I who gives to all beings. It is I who demands your devotion, your respect, and your surrender!"

"But…" murmured Don as he flew up into the air and slammed face first into the dirt.

"Like that!" disgorged the voice. "I will send her away. She is no longer your concern!" And with that, the scene twisted into a churning of colors and textures.

Queasiness arose in Don as he was swirled back once more into the reality of a South Philadelphia night. He awoke in a sweat of tangled sheets and confusion. It took him a minute to grasp the reality of no longer being in the dream.

Don turned to the left and looked for Lilith. He sat up and squinted into the silent darkness to see if she was in the hall, then patted the bed. She was gone; there was no sign of her. He darted up the stairs to find the drawings missing. He tripped down the stairs to find only silence and emptiness.

He ran to open the front door and looked rapidly up and down the street. There was no sign of her. Leaving the front door open, he ran back to the kitchen, yanked open the refrigerator, and looked for her white bag. It too was gone. He melted to the floor, naked against the cold tiles, and held his face in his hands. Sobs choked him as a glimmer of understanding flickered in the back of his mind. There was nothing of her left behind.

"Please cherish the silence and the aloneness, for that is the time when you have the opportunity to know you are God."

"Who said that?" Don cried, looking up into the glow of the refrigerator light.

"God is the space between your thoughts. When you feel challenged, wrap your monkey mind around it as a gift. When things seem synchronistic, realize everything in this life—in this universe—is happening for a greater purpose. Let go of being the doer."

"Holy crap! I'm losing it!" Don screamed.

"Learn to love yourself through learning to love your seeming aloneness. Begin to realize yourself and know the all, the everything, and that which is Divine Love is already you. Embrace what the ego foolishly tells you is aloneness, and know that you are a part of unity. Love yourself, and in that pure self-love, know that you are loving God. Take the trickery of the mind and that which you perceive as pain, and hold it in your heart. Seize the opportunity! This is growth."

"Who are you?"

"No! The question is: who are you?"

"I have no idea!" responded Don.

"You are the love of God in every set of eyes you gaze into, in the warmth of every stranger's smile, in any laughter or music or color. You are waking up and realizing that you are the oneness, the greater. You are God."

Chapter 40

Aftermath

The outcome of any reaction is that it becomes history.

Lilith pulled the covers off Don and up to her nose as she tossed onto her left side. The change of position inspired her to rapidly slip into a dream of an early experiment with sex. In her mind's eye, she saw a rustic hot tub surrounded by a rough wooden deck. In the dreamscape, she watched her younger self seducing potent teen boys. She pounced on them, consuming them, one after another, like a hungry lioness. The water in the tub began to bubble rapidly, and then out of control. A swarthy hunk rose up from the foaming bubbles, his hair curly and thick and stuck to his tanned forehead. She noticed the chiseling of his muscles and the texture of his smooth skin. Her dream body jumped with reckless abandon into the frothy water.

As she made contact, the fluid changed her into a giant serpent. The endless ophidian body encircled the young man in spiraling rings as he began to transform into a shaggy satyr. Autumn leaves sprouted from his head, forming a crown. Lilith wrapped herself tightly around his bronzed torso and the two wrestled into the hot water, driven by the savage forces of mating. An earthshaking crest caused a colossal tidal wave of foam to flood the landscape.

Then Lilith's serpent body sprouted wings and flew, as a dragon, high into the air. She glided on thermals, ignoring the changing landscape below. The clouds felt moist and cool against her pearly greenish-blue scales. She snapped at them with her dragon mouth, feeling the dampness against her whiskers. The scene changed to night as stars began to twinkle in a moonless sky.

A craggy mountain peak reached high into the air, inviting her dragon-self to perch so she could peruse her new surroundings. Her giant clawed feet reached for the sharp pinnacle rocks as she folded her wings to land.

"This is all a little strange," thought Lilith, slipping back into the surroundings of Don's bed. For a moment she noticed the stillness and silence. She decided to sleep a bit more and flipped the pillow over to feel the coolness against her face. This immediately launched her deeper into the dream.

To her right she saw a strange land with a dark stone castle.

"How lonely," thought her dragon-self.

To her left lay foothills rolling to the base of the great mountain where she perched. Time moved in hyper speed. The sun prepared to rise, and the damp fog of morning clung heavily to the landscape. She spotted a strange building in the forest below.

"What is that?" thought her dream dragon-self.

Almost hidden in the dense foliage of the wood was a most amazing structure. It reminded her of the fairy houses she had built as a child. In her mammoth dragon-state, she could almost reach an iridescent foot out to grab at it.

"Better not!" squawked a rather odd bird from a treetop just below where dragon-Lilith perched.

"What are you?" asked the dragon.

"I am not a what, but rather a who!" retorted the bird.

"Oh! Forgive my rudeness. I am Lilith, though I seem to be dreaming," said the dragon.

"Aren't we all, then?" responded the raven.

"Careful, my beloved, this is tricky territory," warned Deagadh in a silent whisper meant only for the bird's ears.

"What was that?" snapped Lilith the dragon, causing a few sparks to flare from her lips and nostrils.

Some boys in the woods below thought they had seen a shooting star. They were scurrying around preparing for an initiation, a ceremony to honor their births and deaths.

"Should I get in there?" asked Alwyn.

"Can you handle it, boy?" Deagadh inquired sternly.

"I have been training my whole life for this moment, Master!" answered the apprentice enthusiastically.

The wizard reached inside his cloak. He threw a handful of sparkling silver dust over the boy and incanted, "*Verto ut exsisto amicus o extraho.*"

Wind swirled through the laboratory, sweeping books and glassware into the air. The cyclone of energy grabbed Alwyn as it gathered momentum.

"A faint scream came from the center of the funnel cloud.

"Master, help!"

"That may have been a bit much," thought Deagadh, reaching into another pocket.

"*Exsisto somnium! Exsisto à amicus fiducia, fides, credo, ordìnis!*" chanted Deagadh as he threw some green powder fetched from a nearby table at the funneling chaos.

"That should do it," he muttered to himself.

"Is he really going to bury us up to our necks in the dirt?" asked a village boy of the apprentice, who was dusting off his sleeve as he approached.

'Yes. Yes, he is," answered Alwyn.

"Why?" cried another. "I don't want to die!"

"It is not the physical body that will die, little one," assured Alwyn, realizing he was fitting in quite nicely. "It is the ego."

"Did you hear that?" asked the dragon of no one in particular, thinking she was alone and obviously dreaming.

"I did indeed," responded Zahra.

"What the…!" exclaimed the dragon, looking around to see who had spoken. "Who are you?"

"I am no one. Nothing to see here!" squawked the bird.

"But you are speaking to me, so you must indeed be someone."

"Shh," said the bird. "I am here on a mission, and having you as a dragon is sure to screw things up! It is best if you shift."

"Shift?" questioned Lilith the dragon. "Shift into what?"

"This one is on you, boss," Zahra projected telepathically.

"I can hear you!" said Lilith.

"Oh, sweet girl! Don't call me boss!" retorted Deagadh.

"Great! She is tuned in!" the wizard and Zahra said simultaneously, meaning completely opposite aspects of "great."

"Hello!" called Alwyn so loudly that Lilith heard him as well.

"Who was that? Where am I?" asked the dragon. "Who am I?"

On the hillside below, a group of what appeared to be young boys had dug a row of holes and, one by one, had stripped their clothes off and crawled into them. An old man poured dirt around them, burying them up to their necks. He then sat down on a rustic chair made of rough tree boughs and began to rock slowly as the sun made its day-long journey across the sky.

"I'm cold!" complained one boy.

"Ask the Great Mother to warm you!" responded Alder.

"I'm thirsty!" screamed another.

"Pray that the Father Sky sees fit to rain down upon your parched tongue!" the teacher said.

"I have to pee!" squealed a third.

"Let it rip. I just did!" added a fourth. "As a matter of fact, I recommend it. It takes care of the cold feeling."

The boys burst into ringing laughter.

"Master, tell them why we are here," suggested Alwyn. His presence caused Alder's chair to creak to a halt and Deagadh to hold his breath.

"You have come here to die," began Alder, "and—"

"I knew it! I knew he was going to kill us!" screamed the first complainer.

"Calm down, you ninnies!" Alwyn said firmly as he received a nod from the wise one. He ran over to hold his hand over the crying boy. "Quiet! The master has a teaching for all of us."

Alder began to rock once again. The wise teacher's eyes closed and in a soft voice he began, "You have come here on a breath and you will leave on a breath. The breath is the energy you ride upon in this flesh-robe you call a body. Until you experience yourself, really experience what this body is, how can you possibly appreciate what you have here?"

"Mine is cold and growing stiff," whimpered a voice.

"That is how the body will be when you leave it," bellowed the teacher.

"I see one of the king's major mistakes," projected Zahra. "He is not present."

"This is indeed the beginning of his many mistakes," added Alwyn telepathically.

"Maybe it just wasn't in the cards for him," squawked the raven out loud.

"Blasted bird!" growled Alwyn under his breath. "I knew you swiped that card from me this morning!"

"Will you ever release us?" begged a boy.

"The only release is your death. Quiet yourself and experience it!"

In a puff of amber smoke, Lilith's dragon body was suddenly transformed into a very tiny beetle. She found herself crawling on little legs across the mounds of dirt that held the boys in stillness. Her oily, dark, rainbow-colored shell glistened in the light, giving the frightened boys a place to focus their attention. The jabbering quieted and allowed the lesson to continue.

Alder began to sing an ancient story of the Great Mother. The verses described how she gives birth to and sustains all living creatures.

"Mother Divine, we crawl from your womb, we eat of your skin, we howl at your moon. Great giver, sweet nurturer, in your heart, this heart beats true, devoted to you."

The next verse told of how the Divine Masculine opens his arms to give space and support to the Great Mother.

"Great, invisible, eternal, obscure, in your infinite arms cradle Mother, it is she you adore."

The final phrase spoke of the third element, a powerfully potent magnetic energy.

"Drawn irresistibly, as if by an outside force, know that Mother is the continual source."

As the singing went on, the tiny beetle crawled from dirt mound to dirt mound, inspecting every plant, every pebble, and each tiny grain of earth that entombed the boys.

The beetle wondered if she was an important part of this sacred rite of passage. She didn't realize that she was always in the right place at the right time. When a boy was on the edge, struggling with the fear of being buried alive, the beetle managed to offer a necessary diversion. Sounds blurred and disappeared as their gaze drew them into her otherworldly exoskeleton. This saved many, if not all, of them from becoming completely unhinged.

By the end of the day, the ancient science of alchemical shifts had been revealed through the simplicity of Alder's mystical teachings.

One by one, the great sage began to dig the boys out of the ground in a birthing ceremony. At the moment of individual release, each of the boys was renamed and declared a man.

That night a circle of sharing took place around a warm and comforting fire. Alwyn fed the hungry young men from a steaming cauldron of soup he had prepared. The group laughed as they discussed the initiation and philosophized on the topics of birth and death.

"You may now speak your heart, young men," invited Alder. "State your new name in the way I have instructed you. Who will go first?" he asked, holding a beaded staff in the air, offering it to the one who was ready to share.

"Simply reach for the staff and gather your thoughts. We are all ears from the centers of our hearts," said Alder as he patted his chest. "We are listening."

The great teacher handed the stick across the circle to an outreached arm.

"I am William. I no longer feel I am a boy, yet I am still a child of the Great Mother."

"*Verus*, William!" responded the group.

A second arm reached from the same side of the circle, and William passed the staff to the open hand.

"Master, is there a stage of contentment where a person says, 'I can go no further?'" the young man asked, and then waited for an answer. The circle was silent. Realizing his mistake, he began again.

"I am Crewe. There is a place of letting go, of surrender. It is of total release."

"*Verus*, Crewe!" responded the group in acknowledgement. Crewe shed a little tear of knowing. Several arms were now reaching for the talking stick.

"I am Burke," the young man who next received the staff announced. He took time to look into each set of eyes before continuing. "There is

no need to go forward or backward. I am the center!"

"*Verus*, Burke!" the group cheered.

The bejeweled talking stick continued to be passed from young man to young man.

"I am Gladstone. Happiness is in the place of existence."

"*Verus*, Gladstone!"

"I am Saxon. A life lived in stages and on stages is not in this present moment!"

"*Verus*, Saxon!"

One by one, each new man spoke his truth. As they did, the space around them breathed contentment, calmness, and happiness.

"It is as if they have been welcomed into utopia," thought the little beetle, realizing she was still there.

"Shh," was the response out of the darkness, as a slimy shell scooped the insect up.

"Oh God. I'm being eaten!" came a muffled cry from inside the raven's beak.

Help me to calm her until I reach you, thought the raven.

Alwyn disappeared into the dark of the wood. No one in the circle seemed to notice him missing as they continued their sharing into the wee hours of the morning.

"I'm over here, Zahra," a telepathic whisper called from between two large oak trees. The bird landed gently on Alwyn's outstretched arm and ever so carefully opened her beak. A very confused and rather slimy little beetle crawled out into his open hand. Alwyn gently placed the bug on a leaf.

Later, when Lilith returned from the dream, she remembered being a seed in the moist darkness, wet from the slime of creation. She recalled the shapes of trees and a twinkle of stars in a moonless night. Right before she woke up, she saw a white lily growing in a clearing.

"That was a close one," Zahra croaked, trying to swallow.

"Good job, bird!" praised Alwyn. He lifted his wand and swirled the two of them into a phosphorescent cloud of dust. All at once they fell onto the floor of the laboratory.

"Did you learn anything about the king while we were with the boys, boss?" asked Alwyn.

"I did, indeed, young sir!" Deagadh responded, watching his lovely Zahra pick up the Lovers card and then fly over to her perch. She immediately dove into a much-needed drink of water. As she looked up, Alwyn was already there, ready to refill her supply. Coyly, she began to preen her grey wing feathers.

In a ballet of unspoken words, the bird lifted a feathery eyebrow. Alwyn retaliated by withdrawing the pitcher. Zahra fluffed her feathers and reached toward his silver ring to grab it with her beak. He countered with his free hand by snatching up her seed bowl.

"Stop that," scolded Deagadh, "the both of you! Zahra, let go of his ring!" he hissed. "Alwyn, give her the seeds!"

As Alwyn replaced the bowl into its holder on the perch, Zahra smugly went back to preening and munching.

"Not so fast, young lady! Give Alwyn his card back right now!" The bird made a horrendous sound, inspiring a louder bellow from Deagadh as he walked toward her. "Now!"

Alwyn snatched the Lovers card out of the bird's talons.

"Give that to me, boy! We need it right now!" roared Deagadh. Zahra swiped the card and stepped back on her perch.

"I had one eye on the two of you, and at the same time I watched the king's life in fast-forward."

"What did you see?" asked Alwyn, giving up his teasing of the bird. This inspired Zahra to leave her perch and fly over to the cauldron. She landed softly on Deagadh's shoulder and placed the card gently into his outstretched hand. Deagadh reached up and scratched her head, causing her feathers to puff out in contentment.

The three assumed their original positions, watching the smoke and steam reenact the story once again as the wizard explained what he had learned.

"Heron's mother did everything for him as a child. She washed his body and made his sisters tidy up his room. She cooked his food and cut his meat and never let him learn the mundane tasks of living and taking care of himself. As a result, he never learned to serve others." The questioning looks on Alwyn's and the bird's faces let Deagadh know he had to explain the details more clearly, since this lesson was meant for his little kinfolk as well.

"This was indeed a grave mistake," the alchemist continued. "Learning to clean is a devotion of the highest order to the Divine Source of our being. Keeping one's own body clean is our gratitude to the Holy."

"But why is cleaning a house so important?" asked Alwyn.

"When we clean our living space, we are honoring the subtle bodies of our being. A home is a reflection of the many sides of the self. The ground floor is the physical. It is the foundation and strength that holds the rest of the building up. The second floor is the emotional layer. The third floor is the mental, and the fourth, the spiritual."

"What if the home is in one floor or in one room?" Alwyn asked.

"Excellent question, young Alwyn! If the home is all on one floor or less than four, the areas which represent the facets of our beings are distributed to the cardinal directions and their midpoints. To clean and tend to these areas is a reflection of how we feel and treat the Divine."

"And what about cleaning up after another? As I do for this bird every day!"

"To clean for another is service in honor of their being. To do it in the surrender to love is a high devotion."

"So I clean up bird droppings and become enlightened?

"If it is done with great love of the Divine, yes, it is so."

"So Heron didn't clean. So what? He became a king and had a huge staff to do this for him."

Deagadh furrowed his eyebrows and continued, "Heron never had this experience, and so many of the most beautiful facets of his soul became dull and lifeless. They no longer sparkled. Unable to catch the light reflection of the Divine, he withered. As Heron grew, he began to think that mundane tasks were beneath him. The toxic acid of pride ate away at his soul until he spoiled like meat left in the sun. Adding more insult, the doting of his mother ruined any chance of him turning it around.

"Heron was always treated better than the rest. His mother always gave him the thickest wedge of bread with the sweetest slab of butter. He was always served first, even before his father or his siblings. Heron was the golden child, and this made everyone jealous. He was a prize and, as he grew, he was trained to own it. The village clan trusted that he would be the one to bring them great success."

"Success in what?"

"Jaulan had been under siege since the time of Heron's great grandfather. But for Heron, the ways of the old warriors had, sadly, been lost. For many harvest moons prior to his birth, the artful skills that at one time had been mandatory training for a warrior faded away and were soon gone forever.

"There once was a time when a warrior was required to know many arts beyond the skills of combat. He was trained in dance, for it was believed that he should know the joyful, silky movement of his body as well as the forceful. In dance we interact with one another purely for the pleasure of expression. In the physically manifested movements of the music, we touch one another in a silent communication that says, 'I'm okay, you're okay.' While dancing we spin, and in this sacred spiral we face the magnetic point of our origin.

"Dancing as a group, spinning and trading partners, is a way to physically weave a village together. The people hold hands and intertwine as their breath synchronizes with the music. Beautiful geometric patterns are created. Everyone smiles to greet the next partner. There is laughter and joy. After switching partners, when one returns to their favorite, they are able to appreciate them even more.

"Dance was only one of the arts considered important for the training of a man, especially a warrior. Can you tell me what else you think might be of equal value?" asked Deagadh, quizzing his wards.

"Writing?" blurted Alwyn, not completely sure if this was a worthy answer.

"Yes," Deagadh affirmed, very pleased with his protégée. "The ancient ways of a warrior taught writing, indeed! Splendid answer! What type of writing?"

"Poetry," answered Alwyn.

"Why?" asked Deagadh.

"To teach him to create evocative images with words," Alwyn responded, "in order to express his innermost feelings."

"What else?" Deagadh questioned.

"Painting," returned Alwyn, which inspired Deagadh to smile at his pupil. "To have him express his feeling through color, which gives true light to the emotions," Alwyn explained.

"Very good indeed! Ah, I have taught you well, Alwyn. You have become a mighty warrior without a sword!"

A smile cracked Alwyn's pensive face as his teacher continued.

"It is true that a warrior has strength and fierce cunning, but in poetry he can balance the weight of his heart through the expression of its most intimate feelings. The wise ones have loved to write since they learned to etch the symbols of communication into bark and leaves. Before the glyphs of written words, they memorized and passed their stories down around the evening fire."

"What has this got to do with the king and his pain?"

"Heron never got to practice any of this. Now he is trapped, wondering if he can survive another night. If only he could get his deepest feelings out, he would create a great amount of space and free himself from the prison of his mind."

"Space is good!" squawked the parrot as she flapped her wings, causing her to lift just a bit off of the alchemist's shoulder.

"And what do we know of the power of space?"

Alwyn and Zahra were stumped.

"Think!" commanded the teacher.

"How do we know?"

"You witnessed it!"

"Ah! I've got it!" shouted Alwyn. This caused a frustrated scowl to appear on the bird's feathery face and was followed by a plop on the shoulder of Deagadh.

"Zahra! Go and fetch me something to wipe that up with!"

"I've got it, boss," said Alwyn, pulling a moist cloth from the air. He then wiped up the goo. The bird looked suddenly sheepish and began preening her feet and legs.

Alwyn continued, "We witnessed it in the burying of the boys. In stilling them and forcing them to be in their own excrement, they became like they had been when they were in the womb. Only this time, they were placed into the womb of the Divine Mother, buried in her cool, earthy skin. Alder used the time while they were held still to sing the ancient songs and tell the stories of existence to them."

"Exactly!" said Deagadh, placing the oar down and resting it against the side of the cauldron. "The tales of the old ones are the essential medicine of survival. The narratives of those who came before us are the necessary food we need to ingest in order to continue and evolve. And why do you think this is important?" asked the wizard.

Alwyn responded, "I believe it is essential as a foundation stone, to support the young people so they may grow and flourish."

"Ah, you are becoming wise and making me proud, Alwyn."

"Was there a greater teacher?" asked Alwyn. "Did you see anything more that the king missed?"

"I did. I witnessed a most fascinating lesson that he missed. It was believed that the most important art a warrior could be taught was the art of tea," responded Deagadh. "This art came from the Far East, where it was believed that the making of tea essentially explained everything."

"But how did an Eastern view of tea come to the kingdom of Jaulan?"

"Tea was indeed discovered in the East. There lived an ancient ruler who believed that to drink water without boiling it first was poison to one's body. Somehow he had come to understand that water is what we are made of. In turn he perceived that to understand water is to understand life.

"The old ones knew the power of words and placed their most potent prayers into water before they took it into their bodies. Long before there were priests or any sort of organized religion, there existed the earth and air, fire and water, and space. In the study of the elements of nature, the ancient ones received a great many lessons. The element of water spoke to them. Through the art of creating tea, they were able to pass this on."

"This is fascinating. But it is not completely lost, is it?" Alwyn asked and then added, "You love tea, Master."

"Unfortunately, the complexity and great depth of the lesson of tea was lost with the emperor who insisted his water be boiled."

"Did you see it? Can you teach us?"

"I did and I can. What I witnessed is this. One day the ancient emperor was out in the woodland at the edge of his kingdom. He sat on a blanket upon the ground while his attendant boiled his water. Keep in mind that the water is a symbol representing the Divine Feminine.

"The water bubbled and steamed. A stiff breeze began to blow, causing some tiny leaves from a nearby bush to fall into the water. The attendant wanted to spill everything onto the earth and begin again, but the great ruler prohibited this. He recognized the event as a sign."

Alwyn was getting the hang of this teaching session and responded with an answer. "He recognized that the leaves were an icon of the Powerful Masculine, so he let them brew and blend together with the water?"

"Yes," Deagadh replied, then continued. "Being curious, the emperor took a sip of the liquid and found it to be quite flavorful. This was the birth of tea, and it became known as a magical link of transformation. It was believed that to understand how to create tea was to understand the sacred union of a man and a woman."

"The water being of the feminine and the leaves the masculine?" Alwyn reiterated.

"Indeed! And what else do you see here?" asked the wizard.

"To create tea for another is to truly understand how to humble oneself in service. To partake of tea with another is to understand that each encounter with another being is unique and can never be duplicated," answered Alwyn.

"Well done, Alwyn!" praised Deagadh. "This was understood in the swirling patterns of the steam from the tea, which are never the same twice. What else has this characteristic?"

"Believing or expecting to step into the same water of a river twice?"

"Truly."

"But how did this teaching reach Jaulan?"

"The fine art of tea was brought by a caravan of traders who came from the Far East. They possessed a cure for the queen, who was stricken with ill health. When she recovered from a refined daily ritual of tea drinking, the ancient king declared the brew a sacred part of every afternoon. Soon it was believed that the preparation of tea was a gesture of caring for another as well as a way to feed the mind, body, and spirit."

"What became of Alder?" asked Alwyn.

"Alder was the last to teach the old ways. The ritual you witnessed was his final gift. King Heron was never able to reach the great teacher in time."

"Heron truly missed out," said Alwyn sadly.

"Yes, it is most unfortunate that Heron missed out."

"Is there nothing we can do?" asked Alwyn.

"We can only pray that Heron finds space, for in that space, the pain lessens and the mind frees itself. It is not our place to interfere."

"So," said Alwyn, "in spite of Heron's ability to battle, there is nothing he can do to fight this pain?"

"Spot-on! He can only give it a place to be. It is only in his mind that he has this ability."

"Is there nothing we can take to him to ease this suffering?"

"There is no need to travel back there. We can only stay here, at a distance, and bear witness. I am so proud of you both and very grateful to have had the opportunity to be of support on this journey today. I am always here for you as teacher, guide, and—most importantly—a friend. I am here to love you, both softly and with the strong, powerful arm of knowing. In many ways, I am your father. Now, in this moment, you are experiencing a higher vibration where there is no need for any foodstuffs or chemical substance other than the magic of the air we breathe, the light of the sun on our skin, and the passionate fire of love that burns in our hearts."

Zahra's feathers fluffed into a full poof, and Alwyn's face flushed.

"There is just one more thing we must do," said the alchemist, and with that he waved the number VI card of the Lovers in the air. Then, with a flourish, he threw it into the bubbling caldron, which caused a dense cloud of greenish smoke to fill the room.

Chapter 41

Blessings

Gratitude multiplies and inspires more.

The rocking chair had been squeaking a steady beat to the rhythm of Lilith's thoughts. Her eyes eased open, once again soaking in the watery horizon. She turned her gaze and focused on the two winged beings hovering nearby.

"What do Gandharvas and Apsaras eat?" asked Lilith of the two floating angels.

"We don't eat food, if that is what you mean," responded Saruk AUM.

"I realize that," said Lilith, "but there has to be something that you take in for energy and power. I can't imagine that you live off thought alone. If you did, I imagine that your hearts would shrivel and you would die from lack of fulfillment."

"Is that so?" asked Ambo Shanti as she swooped in a little closer in order to look into the eyes of her liege. "And what do you imagine it is?"

"Perhaps," said Lilith, "you are fed by watching the sunset on a rainy day, or by the smell of the ocean. I, on the other hand, feel only loneliness, and it seems to be a double-edged sword."

"Yes, we understand," said Ambo Shanti. "But this is a great gift. Realize this intense emotional level is brought on by your perception of extreme loneliness. It is the only way you are able to have this experience."

"It scars the heart," Lilith claimed, placing her hands on her chest.

"No, it does not. Rather, it scores it—opening the windows, allowing it to breathe."

"On rare days, I long for another to take part in conversation with and to be in someone's—anyone's—company, to untangle the tentacles of sorrow and isolation that are wrapped around my soul."

"This is poetic, indeed," responded Saruk AUM. "But your soul is so light that nothing could ever choke it or wrap it so tightly. Remember that we have taught you the law of extremes."

"Yes, I do remember," answered Lilith.

"And what is this law?"

"In order for me to feel high levels of elation and bliss, I must experience the darkest depths of despair."

"And therefore…?"

"Therefore, if I feel this low," continued Lilith, "There is a great height I will potentially be able to reach. My heart is throbbing in the illusive moments of the unconscious-mess of mind disturbances."

"This will be found and experienced in many ways. Soon you will find a new, delicious taste in the sweetness of water and the textures and blessings of food. May you decorate and worship the physical molecules that make up the temple of the body in which you have the honor to reside. For once the body is worshiped as a miraculous abode, the spirit then has a great platform upon which it is able to stretch upward and higher into the realm of the Gods. May you know your divinity, little one," said Ambo Shanti, beaming love from her heart.

"May you realize you are God!" punctuated Saruk AUM.

They continued in unison, "We send you a thousand blessings, each infused with the love of the many names of God that are carved on the facets of your soul and meant only for you."

"May all of your prayers be answered," said Saruk AUM.

"May all of your dreams come true," added Ambo Shanti.

Lilith looked down at the giant book in her lap and noticed she had left a Tarot card marking a particular page. Letting her finger find the exact spot, she slowly opened the book, read the card, and began to understand.

Chapter 42

Infinity

Space has no edges.

Don felt a chill as he blinked his eyes open. He realized he was in his bed and Lilith was beside him. For a moment, he looked at the way she held the folds of the blanket to her face, and admired the textures and shadows and shapes. Lilith slowly opened her eyes and met his.

"What would it take to get you back into my bed?" he asked. It was his hope to find the sacred key that would open the door which would lead him back to her consecrated temple.

"Into your bed?" she countered with a sigh, thinking, *Silly man, I am in your bed!* Lilith's face screwed into a disappointed expression.

"I think you mean into your heart, don't you?" suggested the Poet.

Yes, that's it, thought Don, and corrected himself. "Into your heart," he said out loud, with great sincerity.

"Ah, into my heart!" exclaimed Lilith with a glistening smile. "For you to do this, an expression of worship must be displayed. It should be told like a story unfolding in the heat of a desert night.

"I want you to gently stroke my hair and look deeply into my eyes. I need to feel you admiring every molecule of my being in the weight of your stare. It is in this observance that you win me. It is in this undivided attention that you are able to draw the energy up from the bottom of your soul and bring it through the wide-open windows of your very existence."

Don's eyes broadened as she continued.

"Next, gently transmit your feelings through your fingertips. Do not imagine jumping on me or pounding me like a pestle squashing the fragrance from dried pods of cardamom. But rather be like sesame oil and drip your love all over me, penetrating every pore, until I alone am the Great Goddess, shimmering in all of my splendor, reflecting the light of your beauty.

"Then and only then are my knees subtle enough to bend into the ground and the velvet petals of my lotus heart ready to fully open and accept your adoration, your affection. Wrapping my m—"

"Wrapping your…?" he grinned, a little saliva at the right corner of his mouth.

"No, ridiculous man!" she squealed, losing her strand of thought for a moment. "Wrap your mind around this," she growled sternly, thinking of leaving once again. "Can you stop the teenage come-ons? Try to absorb the information I am giving to you. Once the blood drains from your brain into your groin, all hopes of the deliciousness of what we women want and need and crave and fantasize that you men will give us is desperately lost."

"Dude, you totally screwed that one up!" laughed the Stoner, coughing out a cloud of smoke. "She's like a rainbow of wisdom, and all you can see is the red of her cape taunting you like a bull."

"Exactly!" added the Guru, floating above the Boardroom table.

"Yes, yes. I am getting this, too!" exclaimed Reason.

"She is full of wisdom," whispered the Guru, opening his third eye and letting a flashing bolt of light fly out from the unfathomable depths of Don's Ajna Chakra.

A gasp glazed the Boardroom, squelching out the last sounds of chatter, and a collective deep breath occurred in unison. This came audibly from Don's mouth in a deep sigh. He closed his eyes and breathed again even more slowly as he felt himself beginning to relax. He took a third long deep breath.

"Know her. See her," hummed the Sun.

"Be in her reflection and become her in a reflection" added the Great Mother, her voice soft as she glistened in a dewdrop on a leaf of grass.

More literary brilliance
from Mythologem Press!

Mythologem Press
Publishing Literary Brilliance

www.ingramcontent.com/pod-product-compliance
Lightning Source LLC
Chambersburg PA
CBHW072318020726
47501CB00002B/560